D1398946

MURDER OF A
SWEET OLD LADY

Also by Denise Swanson
in Large Print:

Murder of a Smalltown Honey

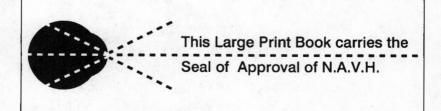

This Large Print Book carries the
Seal of Approval of N.A.V.H.

Murder of a Sweet Old Lady

A Scumble River Mystery

Denise Swanson

WILLIAMSBURG REGIONAL LIBRARY
7770 CROAKER ROAD
WILLIAMSBURG, VIRGINIA 23188

Thorndike Press • Waterville, Maine

DEC - - 2001

Copyright © Denise Swanson Stybr, 2001

All rights reserved.

This is a work of fiction. Names, characters, places, and incidents either are the product of the author's imagination or are used fictitiously, and any resemblance to actual persons, living or dead, events, or locales is entirely coincidental.

Published in 2001 by arrangement with NAL Signet, a division of Penguin Putnam Inc.

Thorndike Press Large Print Mystery Series.

The tree indicium is a trademark of Thorndike Press.

The text of this Large Print edition is unabridged. Other aspects of the book may vary from the original edition.

Set in 16 pt. Plantin by Al Chase.

Printed in the United States on permanent paper.

Library of Congress Cataloging-in-Publication Data
Swanson, Denise.
    Murder of a sweet old lady : a Scumble River mystery / Denise Swanson.
        p.   cm.
    ISBN 0-7862-3674-4 (lg. print : hc : alk. paper)
    1. School psychologists — Fiction.   2. Women psychologists — Fiction.   3. Large type books.   I. Title.
PS3619.W36 M89 2001
    813'.6—dc21
                                        2001053013

To my grandparents,
who all died perfectly natural deaths.
Kathryn Votta 1906–1960
Albert Votta, Sr. 1902–1973
Laura Swanson 1902–1997
William Swanson 1900–1977
and
To Purrcie the Cat,
who inspired the character of Bingo.
1979–1999

Scumble River is not a real town. The characters and events portrayed in these pages are entirely fictional and any resemblance to living persons is pure coincidence.

ACKNOWLEDGMENTS

I would like to thank the following people: Joyce Flaherty for her continuing belief in my talent; Ellen Edwards for extraordinary editorial expertise; my fellow Deadly Divas Susan McBride, Letha Albright, and Sherri Board for their efforts as promo group extraordinaire; Jane Isenberg, Aileen Schumacher, Laura Renken, and Mary Jane Meier, fellow writers who shared the ups and downs; Cindi Baker, Andrea Pantaleone, and Valerie McCaffrey, friends who let me talk endlessly about my ideas and aspirations; the Windy City Chapter of RWA who are always supportive; Marie Swanson and the late Ernie Swanson, who understood my need for time to write; and, finally, my husband, Dave Stybr, who supports me through this new adventure.

ACKNOWLEDGMENTS

I would like to thank the following people who helped bring to fruition this book...

CHAPTER 1

HEY, DIDDLE, DIDDLE,

THE CAT AND THE RIDDLE

Skye Denison warily studied the hostile faces of Gus Yoder's parents. As a school psychologist, she often attended uncomfortable meetings, but this one was murder.

Scumble River High School principal Homer Knapik was seated to her right, and every time she glanced his way, her attention was drawn to the hair growing out of his ears. The long, wiry strands quivered like the curb feelers on a car's wheels. Skye had heard the students call him Mr. Knitpick behind his back, and she was beginning to understand why. The man could not make a decision to save his life . . . or hers.

Across the table Leroy Yoder raged, threatening the school with everything from a lawsuit to an atomic bomb. He and his wife, Charlene, had come in demanding that their son be allowed to graduate with his class, and nothing either the principal or Skye said seemed to penetrate their anger.

Homer and the parents had been posturing and snarling for more than an hour, with no sign that they would stop anytime soon.

Skye watched in hypnotized fascination as a drop of sweat danced on the tip of Leroy's off-center nose. In Illinois, even the first day of June could have temperatures reaching into the nineties. The underarms of her own blouse were soaked and she squirmed uncomfortably in the plastic chair's too-small seat. She thought longingly of her morning swim, the last time she'd been truly cool.

Tucking a loose chestnut-colored curl behind her ear, she narrowed her green eyes and tried once more to intervene, rephrasing what she had been saying over and over again since they had first sat down. "Mr. Yoder, Mr. Knapik and I have told you that whether or not your son graduates is not up to us. It is a matter you must bring up to the school board. Since we have only a week of school left, you need to request a special hearing so you have a decision before graduation night."

Homer glared in Skye's direction and Charlene Yoder hunched farther down in her chair, looking as if she would like to cover her head with her arms.

Leroy Yoder swung his massive head toward Skye and pinned her with his frenetic stare. "I want my son to graduate. Gus passed all his courses. You got no right to keep him from getting his diploma with everyone else."

She felt sorry for these parents. Like many others, they couldn't let themselves believe that their child could do the awful things of which he was accused. "As Mr. Knapik and I have explained, our handbook states that a student who is in the process of an expulsion is not eligible to participate in any school activities, including graduation. This is a school board policy. We have no choice in the matter."

"You people should never've started this whole thing. Gus didn't do nothing wrong," Leroy shouted.

"He tried to rape a girl at knifepoint, and was found with drugs in his possession," Skye stated calmly.

Charlene Yoder started to speak but was interrupted by her husband, who sprang out of his chair and lunged across the table, bringing his face to within inches of Skye's. His breath was like a furnace belching rotting eggs, and she unconsciously moved back.

He grabbed her upper arms and dragged

her halfway across the conference table. "My son didn't touch that girl." Yoder gave Skye a shake as if to emphasize his point. "The boy didn't have no weapon." He shook her again. "And Gus don't use no drugs."

Skye tried desperately to free herself from his grasp. Her breath was coming in shallow gasps and she felt lightheaded. She couldn't get her voice to work.

Homer seemed paralyzed. Nothing moved, including his eyes.

After a final shake, she was abruptly dropped back into her chair as Leroy Yoder continued, "The whole business will be thrown out as soon as we get ourselves a hearing." Ignoring his wife, he stomped out of the room, his words trailing behind him: "Let me make myself clear. Either Gus graduates with the rest of his class or you two don't see another school year."

It was a relief for Skye to return to her office at Scumble River Junior High. She slid down in the chair until she could rest her head on its back. From this angle, all she could see was the stained white ceiling. The odor of ammonia was strong today, brought out by the humidity, but at least she was spared the sight of the battered, mismatched furniture in the claustrophobic six-by-six foot room.

Skye didn't dare complain about the conditions. It had taken a minor miracle to get what she had. In the elementary and high schools, she had to scrounge for any open space each time she needed to work with a student. That meant she had to lug any equipment she needed from school to school like a door-to-door salesman. Still, she counted her blessings. She knew of many psychologists who had it worse.

It was nearly one, but she didn't want lunch. She was still too upset from the morning's events at the high school to consider eating. Skye was accustomed to parents whose walls of denial went up like the force field on the Starship Enterprise, but the Yoders had no clue that their son was hooked on something, and it wasn't phonics.

Even though she'd been gone from Scumble River for many years before her recent return, Skye remembered that the townspeople liked to handle their problems by themselves. Still, she was upset that Homer had refused to call the police on Mr. Yoder, and had forbidden Skye from contacting them. She rubbed her bruised upper arms and shivered. Yoder had clearly assaulted her and threatened them both.

After brooding for a bit, Skye remembered the emergency chocolate bar she had stashed away for just such an occasion. In one smooth motion she snatched her key ring, turned toward the file cabinet, and retrieved the candy.

She was just peeling back the silver wrapper of a Kit Kat when the PA blared. "Ms. Denison, please report to the office. Ms. Denison, please report to the office."

Skye reluctantly rewrapped the bar and tucked it into her skirt pocket. Why did everything always have to happen on a Monday?

The junior high's new principal, Neva Llewellyn, paced outside her door. She had held the job only since September, having been promoted from high school guidance counselor when the previous principal was forced to leave unexpectedly. For some reason, the Scumble River School District had great difficulty holding on to its employees.

"What's up?" Skye asked as she stopped in front of Neva.

"It's Cletus Doozier."

"Junior's brother?"

"Cousin. His father, Hap, and Junior's

father, Earl, are brothers."

"I got to know Earl and Junior pretty well last fall. They really helped me out." She smiled wryly. "That's quite a family."

Neva wrinkled her nose. "Wait until you meet Hap. The cheese slid off his cracker long ago."

"Wonderful. Is that his real name?"

"Far as we know."

Sighing, Skye asked, "So, what's up with Cletus?"

"He's got a black eye and bruises all along the side of his face."

Skye drew a sharp breath and winced. "Did he say what happened?"

Neva put her hand on the knob. "Says his father beat him up."

Skye closed her eyes for a moment and shook her head sadly, then gestured for Neva to open the door. She entered the office and looked at the eleven-year-old sitting at the table coloring. He was small for his age, and his feet dangled above the floor. The left side of his face was entirely black and blue.

She pulled up the other chair. "Hi, Cletus, my name's Ms. Denison. My job is to talk to kids who need help or have something bothering them. Would you tell me what happened to you?"

15

"Dad beat on me again last night." Cletus didn't raise his head from his drawing.

She knew better than to try and touch him. Abused children didn't like to be handled. "Has this happened before?"

"Yeah, usually when he's drunk. But this time I thought he was gonna kill me." Cletus stared at her with dead eyes.

Skye kept her face expressionless with great effort. Pity was the last thing this child would accept. "Cletus, I have to call and report this. Then someone else will want to talk to you. In the meantime, I'm going to get the nurse to look at you. Okay?"

He nodded without emotion and went back to his coloring.

After closing the door, Skye asked Neva to locate the school nurse and fill her in. Then she found Cletus's cumulative folder and sat down to call the Department of Children and Family Services to report the abuse.

She was surprised when DCFS said they would have a caseworker at the school within the hour and would talk to the parent immediately afterward. It was usually the next day before they sent someone. Skye shrugged. They must be under investigation again.

After Skye completed her call, Neva came

16

over and sat on the edge of the desk. "Be prepared. Hap is not going to take this peacefully."

Skye reached into her pocket and retrieved the Kit Kat bar. Its smooth chocolate surface felt soothing under her fingertips. She broke it down the middle and handed Neva half. Both women took bites. The afternoon was shaping up to be as bad as the morning had been.

The three o'clock sun beat down hotly as Skye walked toward the parking lot thinking about buying a new car. She had to make a decision. She'd been borrowing her grandmother's for nine months and that wasn't right, even if Antonia couldn't use it anymore. Skye's Impala had been totaled last fall. Luckily she had walked away without a scratch.

A voice interrupted her thoughts: "Skye! Skye Denison, is that you?"

Skye looked to the left and spotted a woman hurrying across the grassy area that separated the senior from the junior high school. *Oh, no, it's someone else I should remember but don't.* She hated hurting peoples' feelings by admitting she didn't recognize them. It was tough to be back in her hometown after having been gone for twelve years.

17

As the woman got closer, the breeze ruffled her short brown hair from its smooth caplike style and played with the hem of her simple gray knit dress. Everything about her seemed familiar, but it was her expression that finally struck a spark of recognition in Skye. Her open features bore a look of good humor and high spirits.

"Oh my God, Trixie Bensen! What are you doing in Scumble River?" Skye grabbed her old friend and gave her a big hug. Trixie and her family had moved away during the girls' sophomore year.

Hugging Skye back, Trixie said, "My husband bought the old Cherry farm a few months ago. I'm interviewing for a job at the high school." She took both of Skye's hands and stepped back to look at her. "How about you? Don't tell me you live in town. You vowed never to settle down here."

By unspoken agreement the women moved to a concrete bench along the sidewalk.

Skye sat with one leg tucked beneath her and said, "Well, I did manage to escape for quite a while. I went to the University of Illinois, then spent several years in Dominica serving in the Peace Corps. After that I attended graduate school and did my internship in Louisiana, and spent a year working in New Orleans."

"Wow! So how did you get back here?"

"Oh, last year I had a little trouble with my supervisor and ended up breaking up with my fiancé, so I needed a place to recoup. I'll look for another job in a year or so, once I get a good evaluation."

Trixie patted her hand. "I'm so sorry for all the bad stuff." She grinned. "But this is too cool. We're together again."

"Tell me what happened since you moved. Why didn't you write me back?" Skye frowned, remembering how hurt she had been when she never received a reply to her letters.

"When we moved to Rockford, my parents had a misguided idea that I would adjust better if I didn't have any reminders of Scumble River, so they never gave me any mail. They never told me until I was getting ready to move back here."

"Well, that explains a lot."

Trixie screwed up her face and shook her head. "Parents."

"So tell me the rest."

"Okay, it's not very exciting. I finished high school in Rockford. Went to Illinois State for my B.A. and then got my master's in library science from the University of Illinois. I married Owen Frayne right out of

19

college and we've been renting a farm in Sterling until we could save enough to buy our own. And voilà, here we are." Trixie beamed.

"You might be just in time. A lot of farmland is being purchased by developers who are gambling that Scumble River will become the next satellite suburb of Chicago."

"Boy, I'll bet people around here are hot on that subject."

"Lots of fighting going on between neighbors, and even between fathers and sons."

Trixie frowned. "That's a shame. Is your family thinking of selling?"

"No. Grandma Leofanti would rather die than sell an inch of her land."

"That's good. Does she still make those fantastic apple slices?"

A look of sadness crossed Skye's face. "No, I'm afraid not. She's still strong as an ox physically, but her mind's not too good for recent stuff, and she forgets to take care of herself sometimes. Around Christmas the family hired someone to live in and make sure she's okay."

"That's too bad. She was such a fun person. So outspoken. And a real feminist. She always seemed ahead of her time. More modern than your aunts." Trixie was silent

20

for a moment. "Did you have trouble finding someone to take care of her? We sure did when Owen's mother was sick."

Skye nodded. "Yeah, we finally had to hire someone from an agency in Chicago. They supply women fresh off the boat from Poland. Mrs. Jankowski, the one we have now, seems okay, but she speaks very little English and that can't be good for Grandma. Plus, she doesn't drive, so she and Grandma are both stuck on the farm unless someone picks them up."

"It makes you scared to get old. Maybe that's why people stop going to visit the elderly. They see their own future and can't stand it." Trixie shuddered.

"At first I sort of felt that way," Skye admitted. "But then Grandma started telling me the family history. She'd never talk about the past before, so I'm finding out a lot about my family. We're up to her first year of marriage. Grandpa was not her only fiancé. The first guy got killed in an auto accident. Sounds to me like she married Grandpa on the rebound. I stop by almost every day after school. Actually, that's where I'm heading when I leave here."

Trixie jumped up. "You'd better get going then. She'll be looking for you." She rummaged in her purse, finally locating a

21

scrap of paper and stubby pencil. "Here, write your number down."

After Skye complied, Trixie tore the slip in two and wrote her number on the other piece. They hugged and Trixie scurried back the way she had come.

Skye climbed into her borrowed car and turned the air conditioner to max. After pulling her hair into a ponytail, she peeled off her pantyhose, slid on a pair of blue chambray shorts, and removed her skirt.

The fuel gauge showed less than a quarter of a tank. She'd better stop for gas on her way back from seeing Grandma. Her visit with Trixie had put her behind schedule and she didn't want to arrive just as her grandmother was sitting down to eat.

Grandma Leofanti lived halfway between Scumble River and the neighboring town of Brooklyn. Skye's Uncle Dante, her parents, and her Aunt Mona all lived along the same road — separated only by acres of corn and beans. They could all see one another's houses when the crops weren't mature.

Heading north, then turning east, she spotted the remains of the original Leofanti farmhouse, which had been leveled in the tornado of 1921. The only thing left was the building's chimney, which rose out of the field like the stack of a ship sailing on a sea of corn. A few minutes later she passed her relatives' farms. No one was in the front yards and all the garage doors were closed.

As Skye pulled into her grandmother's driveway, she noticed a large group of hawks circling the isolated farmhouse, braiding the breeze with their feathered wings. She frowned. That was weird. She didn't remember ever seeing more than a single hawk at a time before. A shiver ran down her spine and she was glad to emerge from the car's icy interior into the heat of the June afternoon.

The white clapboard house was situated about a quarter of a mile back from the road, surrounded on three sides by fields. It was small by today's standards and Skye often wondered how her mother, two younger sisters, and a brother had managed to live there without killing each other.

She had parked in her usual spot beside the garage, and as she crossed the concrete apron, her grandmother's cat, Bingo, paced anxiously near the front door of the house. He was solid black with a tiny patch of white on his chest. Antonia had told Skye she named the cat Bingo because it was the only way she'd ever get to call out the word, since she never won the game when she played.

Skye bent and scooped him into her arms.

"What are you doing here? You know you aren't allowed outside. Did you get away from Mrs. Jankowski?"

Bingo blinked his golden eyes and yawned. Hoisting the cat up to her shoulder with her left hand, Skye grabbed the knob and pulled with her right, only to stumble backward when the door wouldn't open. That was odd. First Bingo was outside, and now the door was locked. Grandma hadn't locked her doors since she'd stopped leaving the house.

The key was kept on a nail hanging on a nearby window frame. Skye used it to open the door and replaced it before going inside. The entryway was painted a dark green, with worn gray linoleum. Its dankness reminded Skye of a cave. Straight ahead, five stairs going up led to the rest of the house.

She called out as she climbed the steps into the kitchen, "Mrs. Jankowski, it's Skye."

There was no answer. The kitchen light was off and the stove empty. She set Bingo down. He immediately ran to his water bowl and hunched down for a long drink.

What in the heck was going on? Her grandmother liked to eat at four and it was already ten to. And where was Mrs. Jankowski?

The dining room was empty and the door to the bathroom was open, so she could see that no one was inside. Skye peeked into Mrs. Jankowski's room. The bed was made and the dresser top was clear.

"Yoo-hoo, anyone here?" Skye's voice quavered. Had something happened to her grandmother? The only reason she left the house was to go to the doctor. Where was Mrs. Jankowski?

The living room was empty. Grandma's chair was placed against the wall, squared with the empty eye of the television set. Beside it, her knitting bag was partially open with needles sticking out the top. Pink, blue, and yellow yarn seeped out the edges, indicating that Grandma was working on another baby afghan.

Taking a deep breath, Skye forced herself to walk toward her grandmother's bed-room. Other than the screened front porch, it was the only place she hadn't looked.

The door was closed. She knocked. "Grandma, are you okay? It's Skye."

No answer. The knob turned easily under her hand but the door squeaked loudly as she pushed it open. At first she couldn't see because the blinds were drawn and the room was completely dark. Skye fumbled for the light switch.

Grandma Leofanti lay unmoving in the bed, the white chenille spread pulled over her face. The only thing visible was a cloud of snow-white curls. At five feet tall and ninety pounds, she didn't take up much space on the double bed.

"Grandma!" Frightened, Skye stepped closer and pulled the counterpane down to her grandmother's chest. Who had put the cover over her head? Antonia Leofanti was claustrophobic and couldn't abide anything covering her face. She wouldn't even wear a dress that had to be put on over her head.

Skye's sense of fear grew. Putting her hand on the old woman's shoulder, she gently shook her.

Antonia was unresponsive. Skye felt for a pulse, and when she couldn't feel one, laid her head on her grandmother's chest, searching for a heartbeat. Nothing. Throwing the bedclothes all the way back she started CPR, ignoring the fact that her grandmother's body felt cold and stiff.

Oh, please, Grandma, it's not your time. You haven't told me the rest of your story yet.

She paused. The CPR wasn't having any effect, but she bent to try again. *The doctor just told us that there was nothing wrong with you physically, that you could live to a hundred. Come on, he gave you twenty more years.*

There still was no response, and drawing a ragged breath, Skye conceded defeat. She sat on the floor, laid her head on the bed, and sobbed.

CHAPTER 2

HUB-A-DUB-DUB, TWO MEN,

THAT'S THE RUB

Bingo stood at the open bedroom door, tail and ears flattened, fur ruffled. The sound of his mournful yowls finally penetrated Skye's prayers.

She rose unsteadily and picked up the cat. "What do I do now, Bingo? Everything feels like it's out of control. I can't think."

The cat twitched his ears and nudged Skye's chin with his head.

"I need to call someone. Who? The emergency squad? Father Burns?"

Wiggling out of her arms, Bingo landed on his feet and ran from the room.

Skye followed him into the kitchen. She couldn't call for the police or the ambulance. Skye's mother, May, worked for the Scumble River Police Department as a dispatcher. She also handled the phones for the fire and emergency departments. Her mom might be working. It wouldn't be right to have her find out that way.

The cat jumped onto the counter and peered out the window over the sink.

"I should call Father Burns."

Bingo put his paws on the sill and pressed his nose to the window.

"Maybe I could call Simon. He would know what to do. After all, what's the use in dating a guy who's the coroner and owns the funeral home if he can't take over in a situation like this?"

But instead of picking up the receiver, Skye sat on one of the chairs drawn up to the table. She listened to the roar of the window air conditioner, studied the smell of long-ago cooked meals, and talked to God.

Skye looked at the phone. She hated to make the call, knowing that by doing so she was admitting her grandmother was dead. Sighing, she picked up the handset and punched in the number.

He answered on the first ring. "Reid's Funeral Home. May I help you?"

"Simon? It's Skye."

"What a pleasant surprise. You don't usually call me at work." The warmth in his voice washed over her.

"I, ah, don't like to bother you there, but I need your help."

"Sure, what's wrong?" His tone changed to one of concern.

"I'm at my Grandma Leofanti's and . . ." Skye took a deep breath and forced back tears. "She's dead."

"I'm so sorry. Are you alone?"

"Yes."

"Have you called anyone else?"

"No." Skye swallowed. "The thing is I'm not sure, I mean it could be a natural death, but, ah, Mrs. J is missing."

"Sit tight. I'll be right there."

The click of the phone being hung up made Skye feel cut off from the rest of the world. Her gaze wandered over the kitchen and she noticed Bingo's dish was empty. She searched the cupboards, but couldn't find the cat food. Then she remembered. Grandma believed freshly prepared chicken and fish were better for the feline's health and kept only a few emergency cans of food in the pantry.

Finally she located the Friskies on a back shelf and emptied the contents of the can into Bingo's bowl. Skye took the cat from the counter and set him in front of his dish. He sniffed suspiciously, but eventually gave the food a nibble.

Gnawing on her lip, she thought, *I hope that wasn't a "girl" thing to do, turning everything over to Simon to solve my problems.*

The sound of tires crunching over gravel

captured Skye's attention, and her glance flew to the window Bingo had been guarding. The garage door was ajar. She was sure it had been closed when she pulled in. Why would anyone go in there? She was driving Grandma's car and there wasn't anything else in there but junk.

Maybe it was someone from that survivalist camp a couple of miles down the road. Their property shared a fence with the Leofanti's back forty and all spring Antonia had complained about them trespassing and hunting on her land.

Skye grabbed a flashlight from a drawer on her way out. She crossed the grassy area between the house and garage at a good clip, but slowed as she neared the door. This was really idiotic. When she read about some heroine doing this in a book, she always called her stupid.

The door swung fully open at her touch. The overhead fixture didn't come on when she flipped the switch so she thumbed on the flashlight. Staying on the threshold, Skye swept the small interior with the beam. Everything seemed to be the way she remembered it from last September when she'd backed out her Grandma's old green Buick.

The garage was just big enough for one

car, a few boxes, and a couple pieces of discarded furniture. There was no place for anyone to hide and nothing looked disturbed.

Shrugging, Skye backed away and closed the door, making sure it was firmly latched. She circled the house and sat on the front steps. Within seconds Bingo stood at the screen door and yowled until she let him join her.

Questions were starting to intrude upon her grief when she heard the first siren. She stood up for a better look, disturbing Bingo, who had been twining between her ankles. He meowed sharply and disappeared under the porch.

A procession of official vehicles led by a Scumble River police cruiser, followed by an ambulance, with the Reid Funeral Home hearse bringing up the rear, roared down the gravel road.

A man leapt out of the cruiser and another out of the hearse. Both raced toward Skye. Walter Boyd, the chief of police, got there first and put his arm around her shoulder. He was a handsome man in his late thirties whose warm brown eyes held a look of concern. Running his other hand through his thick black curls, he hugged her wordlessly. His hair was just beginning to show threads of gray, but both his tan and muscular build declared him to be a man of action.

While the two paramedics plunged indoors, Simon stopped at Skye's other side and took her free hand, narrowing his eyes at the chief. In appearance, Simon was the antithesis of Chief Boyd, tall and lean, with elegant auburn hair and golden-hazel eyes.

The chief spoke first. "Your mom wasn't on duty, so I sent Officer Quirk to find her."

Skye nodded. "Thanks, Wally."

It had taken her a year to feel comfortable calling him by his first name. When Wally had first come to Scumble River as a twenty-three-year-old patrolman, Skye, then a teen, had been convinced she was in love with him. She'd followed him around, turning up wherever he took a break or stopped for a meal. He was always a perfect gentleman, never mocking her or taking advantage of the situation. Nevertheless, when she first returned to town she was embarrassed to remember how lovesick she had acted, and she had found it difficult to look him in the eye, let alone call him anything but Chief Boyd.

"I called Vince when no one answered at your folks'," Simon added, squeezing her hand.

Vince, her brother, owned and operated a

hair styling salon called Great Expectations. He was usually the easiest one in the family to locate because he worked there fourteen hours a day.

"Thanks. I'm a wreck. I keep thinking about the stupidest things."

Before Skye could elaborate, one of the paramedics poked his head out the door and called for Simon. He kissed her cheek and hurried inside.

Well, that settles it. Grandma is really dead. They don't call for the coroner otherwise. This thought brought a fresh bout of tears.

Wally held her while she cried on his shoulder. When Skye felt herself melting in his embrace, she made herself stop sobbing and pulled away, reminding herself for perhaps the hundredth time that he was a married man and she was dating Simon.

Using the handkerchief Wally provided, she wiped her face and blew her nose.

"So what 'stupid things' are you thinking about?" Wally asked after she had collected herself.

"Where's the housekeeper?" Skye blurted. "Why were the covers pulled up over Grandma's face? What was Bingo doing outside? The doctor just said she was fine. Why is she dead?"

Wally patted her shoulder. "Now, Skye

34

honey, there could be lots of reasons for those things. The housekeeper's a foreigner, right?" Skye nodded. "Well, she could've gotten scared when your grandmother died and called for someone to pick her up. The cat probably got out when she left. And she, no doubt out of respect, covered your grandma's face."

Wally's answers made sense, but Skye still felt troubled. Something just didn't add up.

After a few minutes, Skye sighed and made a move to stand up. "I've got to call my aunts and uncle. She's their mother too."

"Sure, but why don't you give Quirk a little while longer to find May so you can tell her first? Isn't she the oldest?" Wally kept hold of her hand.

"The oldest of the three girls, but my Uncle Dante is the oldest. He's sixty."

Before she could break away from Wally, the paramedics poured from the house, yelling, "Gotta go. Another call," as they rushed by. They piled into the ambulance and squealed out of the driveway, sounding the siren.

They almost crashed into an old Cadillac that came barreling into the drive, throwing up gravel and blowing its horn. It shuddered to a stop and the door was flung open. The six-foot-tall, three-hundred-pound man who emerged from the front seat charged over to Skye.

He grabbed her in a bear hug, lifting her off the ground. "Baby, are you okay? I heard the call about your grandma on my scanner. Sorry it took me so long. I had someone checking in at the motel and I had to get them settled."

"I'm fine, Uncle Charlie. Everything is under control." Skye managed a tremulous smile.

Charlie Patukas was actually her god-father, not her uncle, but he was closer to her family than most of their blood relations. Charlie owned the Up a Lazy River Motor Court, and had a hand in most of the town's business. He had always been protective of Skye and Vince, but since she'd moved back to town last fall and gotten involved in solving a murder, his concern had often led him into the realm of paranoia.

The chief watched them for a moment, then shrugged. "I'll go take a look at the housekeeper's room."

Skye related to Charlie the events leading up to her call to Simon, then spent the rest of the time in silence.

Quite a while later Simon joined them on the front steps. He spoke softly. "I've done what had to be done before we could move her."

Simon stepped back inside to talk to Wally, but Skye could hear their conversation. Simon's voice was low, but clear. "Since she died unattended, we'll have to keep her until we can determine the cause of death."

Wally's deeper tone was a little harder to discern. "Fine, I'll call Doc Zello and have him meet you at the funeral home. He recognizes death by old age when he sees it."

Skye frowned. Wally was still treating her like she was fifteen and dismissing her concerns.

Simon had already left with her grandmother's body when May's white Oldsmobile careened into the driveway. The chief was looking around inside the house and Charlie was with him, supervising.

May flung the door open and ran to Skye. "Are you okay, honey?"

Skye saw the tears running down her mother's cheeks. "I'm fine. How about you?"

"It's such a shock. Doc Zello saw her just a few days ago, and said she was in excellent health." May sat down on the front porch beside Skye.

May was only five feet two, with short salt-and-pepper hair and eyes the same green as her daughter's. Skye got her height from the Denison side of the family.

"I was out back planting flowers when Quirk came over. Thought for a minute they needed me at work." May dabbed her eyes with a tissue. "Vince will be here in a little bit. He's looking for Dad in the field."

"How about Aunt Mona, Aunt Minnie, and Uncle Dante?" Skye asked.

"I tried all their houses before I left. No answer anywhere." May shook her head. "Hope we can find them before the grapevine does."

That was odd. None of the women worked outside their homes. It was a Monday and almost five, supper time for most farm families. They all should be in their kitchens cooking. Where could they be?

Skye was sitting on the sofa talking softly to May and Charlie when her brother, Vince, arrived. He was an extremely handsome man of thirty-five. Although Vince had the Leofanti green eyes, his hair was a rich butterscotch-blond. They never could figure out to what ancestor he owed its color.

After greeting everyone, Vince took a seat next to his mother and patted her hand. "Dad's on his way."

"Thanks, hon."

A few minutes later, Skye's father entered the room. He snatched a John Deere cap off his head, revealing a steel-gray crew cut and faded brown eyes. His tanned face crinkled like a leather handbag when he frowned.

Jed nodded to everybody and lowered himself into a side chair. "I'm sorry, May. Antonia was a good woman."

They all agreed, and then sat silently, Skye getting up to let Bingo back in when he meowed at the door.

Chief Boyd coughed politely, standing at the archway between the dining and living rooms. When they became aware of his presence, he entered.

As soon as he was settled on the edge of an overstuffed chair the chief spoke. "Looks like that housekeeper of yours hightailed it out of here. The closet and drawers in her room are empty, and there's no sign of any personal possessions. Do you have a way to reach her?"

"The only thing we have is the number of the agency we hired her through. We send our check to them, and they pay her from that," May said.

"Well, I'll need that address and number as soon as possible." Wally shifted in his chair.

"I'll get it to you first thing tomorrow." May turned to Jed. "Don't let me forget."

Jed mumbled something that seemed to satisfy May.

The chief made a motion as if to get up, but May asked, "Why did Simon take her away before we got here?"

He looked down at his immaculately polished shoes and reached down to rub out an imaginary scuff mark. "Well, if a person dies alone, not in a hospital or with a doctor attending, then it's considered suspicious until we get someone to sign off on the cause of death." He stopped, obviously choosing his next words carefully. "So Simon had to take certain precautions in case things were ever needed for evidence."

"I see. I guess I knew that from work." May's face screwed up, but she didn't cry. "When can we make the arrangements?"

"Real soon, I expect. Doc Zello is good about taking care of things like this." The chief stood and edged toward the door. "I'm going to get going now, unless I can do something for you folks." He looked at May. "I'm sorry for your loss. Take as much time off work as you need."

May nodded her thanks.

Skye finally remembered to call Father Burns. After that, she and her mother took turns on the phone trying to reach May's sisters and brother.

Vince was sent to check the various fields that the different families owned, rented, and/or farmed; Jed went back to their place to take care of the equipment; and Charlie finally agreed to go home.

It was nearly seven and they had still failed to get in touch with any of the siblings. Skye and May sat at the kitchen table drinking from cans of soda. There was an untouched plate of saltine crackers and cheese in front of them.

May subtly nudged the food nearer to Skye. "Where in the heck could everyone be? I know the guys are probably staying late in the fields. Those heavy spring rains really put everyone's planting behind schedule. But Minnie, Mona, and Olive should be home."

Skye absentmindedly took a wedge of cheddar. "Should we try their kids' numbers?"

"Soon, but I wanted to tell my sisters and brother about Mom before we told their kids." May took a cracker but didn't put it in her mouth. "When Vince gets back, we'll have him take a ride by the cousins' houses and see if their parents' cars or trucks are there."

"I could do that right now." Skye put the cheese down.

Minnie's twin daughters, Ginger and Gillian, lived next door to each other in town. Dante's son, Hugo, lived in Clay Center, only fifteen minutes away.

"No, honey, stay with me. Okay?" May squeezed Skye's knee.

"Sure, Mom. As long as you want."

Vince got back about an hour later. Some of the farmland was as far away as Streator. He flung himself into a chair and grabbed a piece of cheese. "I found Uncle Emmett. He was over near Gardner. Says Aunt Minnie is at Carle Clinic and he'll call her."

May paled. "What's wrong with Minnie? Why'd she go all the way down to the hospital in Urbana by herself?"

Vince shrugged and took a cracker, which he carefully layered with Swiss. "Uncle Emmett didn't say. I was in a hurry to find the others so I didn't stick around and ask. Sorry."

"That's okay, sweetheart. You did a good job. Did you find anyone else?" May got up and took the bread from its box.

"Nope. No one was at home or in any of their fields."

May put out sliced roast beef and chips. "I'm going to call Hugo. Maybe he knows where his parents are. I don't know what to do about Mona and Neal, since they don't have any children." She nodded toward the food on the table. "Make yourself a sandwich, kids. This is stacking up to be a long night."

About eight-thirty Jed returned and sat down at the table. May immediately filled a plate for him and he started to eat without a word. Lines of exhaustion creased his forehead and radiated from his eyes. During spring planting, farmers often worked from dawn until they could no longer see by using their tractor's lights.

She spoke while he chewed. "Minnie's down at Carle Clinic. God knows why. I sure hope she doesn't have one of her spells when we tell her about Mom." She paused to put more food on Jed's dish. "Emmett and the twins should be here soon. Hugo says his parents left for an auction about five, and were going to stop for dinner afterward. Still nothing on Mona and Neal."

Jed nodded.

May sat back down and buried her head in her arms. "I can't stand it. Mom's dead, Minnie's sick with who-knows-what, and Mona's missing. What's going on?"

Skye patted her mom's hand. "Maybe Minnie is finally getting some help for those spells she gets." For a long time Skye had thought Minnie's spells were probably a form of a depressive disorder such as dysthymia. Not that the family had listened to her gentle hints that Minnie should see a psychiatrist for an evaluation.

"How about Mona and Dante?"

Skye rubbed May's back. "I'm sure they're all fine."

Hearing her own words, she frowned. *Where have I heard that before?*

CHAPTER 3

A DILLER, A DOLLAR,

SEE HOW THEY HOLLER

Skye was in the bathroom talking to Simon on the phone. She had stretched the cord as far as it would go in order to talk in private. "Simon, you can't call it natural causes. Grandma may have been old but she wasn't sick. What did Doc Zello say?"

"Doc Zello isn't happy with that cause of death either, but he can't give me an alternative, and considering her age and your family's reputation in the community, he'll sign off."

Sitting on the closed lid of the toilet, Skye gripped the receiver. "No, it isn't right. If Doc has doubts and I have doubts, then we should have an autopsy done."

"But why? Surely you don't suspect that someone murdered your grandma."

"I don't want to think so, but I do want to know for sure what happened." Skye paused and petted Bingo, who had insisted on following her into the bathroom.

45

"Simon, there's a lot that doesn't feel right. I told Wally earlier all the things that were weird about the situation."

"What do you mean? Wally didn't mention anything."

Skye took a deep breath. She knew Wally had ignored what she said. "First, the cat was outside. He is never, ever allowed outdoors because he is declawed and has no way to defend himself. Second, the housekeeper is missing. No note, nothing. Third, when I found Grandma she was all tucked into bed. The covers were pulled over her face. She wouldn't have done that herself. She was claustrophobic. And, I know this last one is lame, but between the time I pulled in and the time I called you, someone was in the garage and left the door ajar."

When she finished, the only sound from Simon's side of the line was static. Finally he said, "Okay, I'll talk to Chief Boyd and Doc Zello, but don't let your imagination run wild. I'll come out to your grandmother's after I finish up tonight."

Minnie's husband, Emmett Overby, and their identical twin daughters arrived around nine. Ginger Allen and Gillian Tubb were twenty-nine, with big blue eyes and baby-fine blond hair. Emmett, at fifty-two, looked like the farmer from Grant Wood's famous painting, *American Gothic.*

Sinking into the remaining kitchen chair, Emmett took off his cap and ran his fingers through his graying hair. "I couldn't get ahold of Minnie. The motel she's at says she's not in her room."

May glanced sideways at Ginger and Gillian. "Why is she down there, Emmett? What's wrong with her?"

He looked at his hands dangling between his legs. "Woman trouble."

"Oh? Why'd she go all by herself?" May swept cracker crumbs into a pile.

Tugging at the neck of his T-shirt, Emmett refused to look up. "Says it's private."

"What do you girls know about this?" May turned to the twins.

Both answered, "Nothing, Aunt May."

May narrowed her eyes until Ginger continued, "Mom's been having some problems with the change." She turned red as she caught Vince's eye.

Gillian claimed a stool next to the wall near the telephone. This left Ginger to drag a chair in from the dining room.

Gillian eyed the food spread across the tabletop. "I see you all have been making yourselves at home." She turned to Skye. "Next thing we know you'll be clearing out

47

the closets. I hope you realize this is not a case of first come, first served. My mom has just as much claim on Grandma's property as yours does."

Skye had been silent, mulling over the inconsistencies leading to her grandmother's death, but Ginger's comment penetrated her fog. "Ginger, let me ask you a question. When the Lion King was killed trying to save his son, did you find that a sad moment . . . at all?"

Vince let out a bark of laughter, but bit it off before it could grow. Jed's lip curled slightly. May shot Skye a mother-look that silenced her, at least temporarily.

Expressions of confusion were replaced with those of rage as Ginger and Gillian began to understand what Skye had said.

Gillian spoke up. "That was entirely uncalled for. How could you be so cruel? After all, we're still reeling from Grandma's passing." A sob broke her voice. "Unlike your family, we just found out about it a little while ago." She paused for breath. "Speaking of that, why did it take you so long to let us know?"

May got up and started to put the food away. "We were trying to reach the aunts and uncles, so they could tell their own children."

"But, of course, Vince and Skye were an exception," Gillian said flatly, her tears miraculously disappearing.

"Look, it's hardly a privilege to be the one who finds poor Grandma dead. And if you can't see why I would contact my family before yours, then I don't have any way of explaining it." Skye got up to help her mother clear the table.

"You always have an answer, don't you? But the true story is you've always been jealous of Ginger and me. We're prettier, we were co–prom queens, and we're married. You just can't stand that." Gillian crossed her arms and sneered at Skye.

"Why, you little —"

"Skye!" May said sharply.

Sitting back, Gillian smiled nastily. "I know when I've said enough."

"Obviously not," Skye muttered. She shouldn't have said that. Why did she let the twins push her buttons? Maybe she was a little jealous, which was silly. They weren't six years old anymore and they hadn't just been given a better doll than she had for Christmas.

Gillian opened her mouth, but Vince was quicker. "Uncle Emmett, when do you expect Aunt Minnie home?"

Emmett scratched his head. "She was

supposed to have some more tests in the morning, then drive home. Planned on being back by supper time."

"Did you leave her a message at the motel?" May asked from the sink.

"Told her to call here, no matter what time she got back."

May shut off the faucet and stuck the first glass in the soapy water. "I had Vince put a note on Mona and Neal's door, saying pretty much the same thing. Hugo's going to bring his folks over here soon as they get home. Guess we're stuck here for a while. Let's try not to fight anymore."

No one had said anything for the last fifteen minutes. Both Jed and Emmett were dozing in their chairs, but the noise of the back door slamming woke them.

Dante Leofanti rushed up the steps, trailed by his wife, Olive, and son, Hugo. Skye watched her uncle push his way into the center of attention. He was less than five-six with all his weight in his chest and stomach. When she was a little girl, she'd loved to listen to his stories. But as she grew older, she and her uncle had grown apart. It was sad that now they seemed to have nothing in common, couldn't sustain a conversation past the topics of health and weather.

He reached for May and enveloped her in a hug. "You poor thing. Having to handle this all by yourself."

Skye glanced at the room full of people and wondered, *What are we, weeds in his cornfield?*

He smoothed back his thick gray hair and spotted Skye. "You poor angel. How sad to be the one to find your grandma like that. Too bad it couldn't have been one of the boys. You know Hugo stopped by almost every day."

Skye stifled a grimace. Uncle Dante was already rewriting history. Hugo only visited his grandmother on holidays and birthdays, and then for such short periods of time he rarely sat down. But she didn't say anything. Maybe this was the only way Dante could handle his grief.

Hugo had been fortunate. He carried his forty years well, and had gotten the better physical traits of both his parents. His mother's side allowed him to be of average height, five-ten, and his father had provided thick black hair. He had the Leofanti green eyes but something was missing in his. Maybe it was openness. He was good at keeping his thoughts to himself, an advantage in his job as a car salesman.

After getting chairs for his mother and

father, he stood behind Olive with his hands on her shoulders. It was hard to tell whether the gesture was one of comfort or control.

Olive always seemed uneasy among the Leofantis. She was from Chicago, and although she and Dante had been married for thirty-nine years, she still acted like someone who was just visiting from the city.

Skye noticed that she was pleating the hem of her pink floral dress. She seemed to feel Skye's glance and reached up to pat her short blond hair, though every strand was already in place.

Skye smiled at Olive. "Pretty dress."

Olive seemed flustered. "Thanks. I've had it for years."

"Hugo told us what happened, but I'm confused about a few things." Dante looked from May to Skye.

"Oh?" May had been handling her brother's chauvinistic manner for years.

When it was clear May wasn't going to go on, Dante elaborated. "Why did Skye call the coroner?"

Skye couldn't tell which of her cousins, either Ginger or Gillian, whispered, "She probably just wanted an excuse to call her boyfriend. I hear he hasn't been coming around lately."

Tamping down her irritation, Skye faced

her uncle. "Who would you suggest I should have called instead?"

"Your mother, your aunts, me." Dante's smile didn't reach his eyes.

Crossing her arms, Skye leaned back. "I didn't want to tell Mom over the phone that her mother was dead."

"How about me or your aunts?" Dante leaned his chair back on two legs.

Skye considered her answer briefly. The truth was she didn't want to deal with her aunts and uncle, but she couldn't say that so she resorted to the near truth. "I didn't think about it."

Dante thumped his chair onto the floor. "Well, young lady, I don't believe that for a minute. What's the real reason?"

May gripped Skye's arm and Vince shook his head wildly. Skye smiled. "Uncle Dante, you really, really don't want to go down that road. Let's just say the family and I usually think in opposite ways."

"Fine, we'll let that go for now. But I still don't understand what's going on. Where is Mom right now?" Dante looked around as if he thought they had hidden the corpse in one of the cupboards.

Skye answered. "Because she died alone and without any documented health problems, they have to treat it as a suspicious death. They're waiting for Doc Zello to rule on the cause."

"Well, why haven't we heard anything yet?" Dante asked.

"I talked to Simon a little bit ago. He said he'd come out as soon as Doc Zello makes a determination," Skye answered, trying hard to keep her voice even and not reveal the true contents of her conversation with Simon. "And I believe there was a wake tonight from seven to nine." Before anyone could ask who, she added, "I think it was for old Mrs. Doratto."

Gillian piped up, "Well, I hope Simon doesn't think we're going to use the Reid Funeral Home for Grandma's funeral just because he already has the body."

Vince shook his head. "Gillian, you are just like a politician raising taxes. You don't know when to stop and you always go too far."

It was a little past ten when Mona and Neal O'Brian finally arrived. They had been at a dinner at the Knights of Columbus. The KC prided themselves on being defenders of their faith. As Grand Knight, Neal was the head of the local council.

Mona, dressed in an expensive beige pantsuit, carried a quilted Chanel handbag.

She was the youngest of Antonia's children, only forty-eight, and looked nothing like her sisters or brother. Every ash-blond hair was sprayed into a chignon that did not move even in high winds.

Tall and physically fit, the O'Brians had an air of money and elegance. Skye always imagined them in tennis whites on the court at the country club.

Mona scanned the crowded kitchen with her pale blue eyes, stopping on May, who was talking on the phone. May covered the receiver and mouthed, "Minnie."

Mona nodded, then looked pointedly at Vince.

Vince leapt up and offered her his chair. She sat carefully, smoothing her trousers and making sure the creases were not undone.

Neal raised an eyebrow at Mona. "Where am I suppose to sit?"

A look of uneasiness crossed her face. She popped up from her seat and hurried to the dining room, returning with another chair that she wedged next to hers. Neal sat, his bright red hair a contrast to all the blonds and brunettes gathered at the table.

Vince remained standing. He leaned against the counter and crossed his arms.

They were all silent, listening to May say

into the phone, "Okay, okay, don't cry. I still don't understand why you went down there alone." She started to sob. "Yes, I would too have taken off work to go with you or one of the twins could have found a baby-sitter." She paused. "Well, Mona doesn't even have a job or kids."

All eyes turned to Mona, whose frozen expression did not change.

May continued to weep. "I've got to go, Mona just got here. What time will you be back tomorrow? Okay, see you then. Bye."

Looking around the table, May explained, "Minnie felt guilty that she didn't stop over to see Mom today before leaving for Urbana." May blew her nose on the tissue Skye handed her, and continued almost to herself, "Minnie checked in every morning. She must have really been upset not to stop today."

Mona dabbed at her eyes and stole a peek at Neal. "I missed coming over today, too."

Shaking her head, May made her way back to her chair. "I'm sure Mom understood." After she was seated, she asked, "Where were you this afternoon? I thought for a minute you had gone back to Maui."

"I had a dentist appointment in Joliet, so I decided to go early and do some shopping. When Neal finished in the field, a friend dropped him at the Knights of Columbus hall." Mona inspected a perfectly manicured nail. "You know, not to criticize, but a note on your front door saying your mother died is not the best way to hear the news."

"They stopped poor Daddy in the field and told him by the side of the road," Gillian said.

"I guess it's a good thing it wasn't *his* mother then," Mona replied.

Skye felt a guilty pleasure in her aunt's response to her cousin, although she experienced a twinge of unease, reminding her that she had been on the wrong side of Mona's tongue many times herself.

Ginger whispered into Gillian's ear but neither twin spoke to the group.

Folding her hands on the table, Mona looked toward May. "So, tell me all about it."

May started, "Well, Skye has been stopping by every day after school. Mom's been telling her the family history, but today . . ."

As May finished retelling the events of the day, Mona wiped away a teardrop, sat back, and stared at Skye. "We really can't trust you to do anything right, can we?"

"What?" Skye frowned.

"Most people find their eighty-year-old

grandmother dead, say a prayer of thanks that she's out of her misery, and call the family doctor. But not Miss Big Shot. Like Neal says, it's not healthy the way you always have your nose in a book. You want to live like they do inside the pages of your latest novel. So you involve the police and the coroner and God knows who else. Now instead of a quiet funeral, we've got a situation. You're just never happy unless it's your way. And look what you've gotten us into." Mona finished without raising her voice. "I'll bet you didn't even call Father Burns. It's a good thing I had him out here Sunday to give Mom and the housekeeper confession and communion."

The silence around the table was broken only by the scraping back of Skye's chair as she stood. She walked to the sink and ran cold water as she took a glass from the cabinet. Bingo wandered in and sat at her feet.

After her drink, she turned to the room full of staring faces. "Well, it sure is enlightening to hear what you truly think of me, Mona. I'd share my insights about you, but it would upset my mother and she's already been through enough today. But, be warned, if you ever speak to me like that again I won't restrain myself. Understand?"

Vince came over and stood beside Skye.

58

Mona's features stiffened and she opened her mouth.

Before she could speak Neal said, "Drop it, Mona."

"But, Neal." Her voice sounded whiny and a drop of sweat ran down her temple. "It's pretty bad when a person is threatened by her own niece on the day her mother dies."

Neal put his hand on her wrist, his fingers digging into the soft skin. "I said, drop it."

Skye looked at the people around the table and saw no sympathy for her aunt.

Mona's tone changed. "Darling, this has all been too much for me. I'm feeling faint. Could I have a drink?"

Neal got up and went to the sink. He filled a glass of water and put it in front of Mona. When Mona didn't immediately reach for it, he asked, "What's wrong, sweetheart? Not the kind of drink you had in mind?"

Conversation died after Mona's outburst, lethargy seeming to take over. The sound of a car door slamming made them all look up. Knocking on the door startled them. No one ever knocked at Grandma's.

When everyone remained seated, Skye shrugged and went down the steps to see who was there. It was a little after ten-thirty

59

at night, not a time many people in Scumble River came calling.

Simon was standing on the concrete apron, dressed in a black suit and white shirt. His expression was grim. "May I come in?"

"You might want to reconsider that request. The situation hasn't brought out the best in the family."

"Then they're really not going to like what I have to say. Let's get it over with."

Skye tried to question him, but he insisted on speaking to everyone at once. They walked into the kitchen together, but Simon stayed at the door and Skye rejoined Vince by the sink.

Simon cleared his throat. His gaze swept the room. "First, let me say I'm sorry for your loss. I was fortunate to get to know Antonia when Skye brought me out to visit, and she was a special lady who will be missed by everyone. Sadly, it is my conclusion, as coroner consulting with Doctor Zello, her personal physician, that she did not die of natural causes."

As Simon spoke, the twins started to cry, a twitch appeared near Dante's eye, and Hugo blew his nose. But upon hearing Simon's last sentence, everyone froze.

Finally, Dante pushed his way over to

Simon. Thumping his index finger into Simon's chest, he shouted, "What are you talking about? If this is some sick joke . . ."

Simon pushed Dante's finger aside and went on as if he hadn't been interrupted. "We found some irregularities when we examined her. This means we will have to perform an autopsy. I will take care of that as soon as possible and let you know when you can make funeral arrangements."

A stunned silence followed until May asked, "By not dying of natural causes, do you mean . . . ?"

Simon nodded. "We suspect she was murdered."

CHAPTER 4

ONE, TWO,

WHAT SHOULD WE DO?

Suddenly voices bounced off the walls and filled the small room. Dante's was the loudest: "What is the meaning of this? You can't go cutting up someone just to prove you're a big shot to your girlfriend." He flung a look at Skye. "Skye, tell him you don't want your grandmother to have to go through this."

Skye considered her response. Simon would understand if she didn't admit that it was her idea in the first place. And Wally and Doc Zello would never tell. But she believed an autopsy was necessary, and it would be spineless not to say so.

Everyone was looking at her, waiting. Vince moved closer.

"I'm sorry, Uncle Dante. I can't ask Simon not to do an autopsy because I'm the one who talked him into it."

The roar of voices was deafening, and this time May's rose above the rest. "Oh, Skye, why?"

Looking at her mother's face, which seemed to have aged ten years since that morning, Skye was torn. Maybe she should have just let things be. Why did she always seem to be the one stirring the pot?

She had taken too long to answer and now others were shouting questions.

Skye pushed off from the sink and stood straight. "Because when I got here —"

Simon broke in. "Skye, I don't think you should discuss what you saw. I'm sure the chief would not want that information disseminated."

The room began to buzz again. Skye heard various bits but couldn't tell who said them.

"What do you think she saw?"

"Anyone know where Mrs. J is?"

"She's probably making this whole thing up."

Most of the babbling stopped at the sound of the door slamming. The appearance of Chief Boyd at the top of the stairs silenced the rest. He looked at Simon, who nodded.

"You all have my sympathies for your loss. I'm sorry that circumstances aren't different, but I'm sure you all want to know if Antonia was murdered, and if so by whom. The only one who would gain by the termination of this investigation would be the killer."

When Chief Boyd finished speaking, Skye noticed that the atmosphere in the room began to change. Now her aunts, uncles, and cousins were eyeing each other, perhaps wondering who had been loudest in their objections. Chairs shifted slightly and they appeared to withdraw into themselves.

Chief Boyd allowed them to digest what he had said a little longer, then went on. "We have put an all points bulletin out on the housekeeper. Now, you can all understand when I ask you to leave this house immediately. We will need to keep it secured until we know if it is a crime scene or not, so please do not return without my permission. Also, anyone who went into any room besides the kitchen tonight, please stay behind for a few minutes."

Some grumbled, but everyone started to gather their belongings and move toward the door. As they formed a natural line, Wally stopped each one of them and asked them to come into the police station the next day to make a statement.

Mona, Ginger, and Hugo admitted to taking a chair from the dining room, but stated they'd gone no farther into the house.

Everyone else had left by the time the

Denisons reached the front of the line. Jed, Vince, and May had been through the entire house except the bedrooms. Skye, of course, had been everywhere.

When he heard this, Chief Boyd shook his head. "Okay, well, Skye, I guess that means first thing tomorrow we fingerprint you."

"Great. When's first thing to you guys?"

"How about eight?" He didn't look up from the notes he was taking.

"How about nine?" Skye wasn't a morning person, and since she'd be taking a personal day due to her grandmother's death, it would be nice to sleep in a little. She felt tired to the bone.

"Eight. Don't push it." He slapped the notebook shut. "Come on, folks, it's time to leave." He shepherded them all down the stairs.

After they all shuffled outside, May fetched the hidden key and handed it to the chief, who turned it in the lock. He then went to his car and took a roll of barricade tape out of the trunk. Tearing off a couple of strips, he put them in an X across the front and back doors.

They walked toward their vehicles, everyone having driven separately. Simon accompanied Skye to her car, which was parked in a dark corner beside the garage. As they reached it she noticed that something didn't look right.

Simon put his hand on her elbow. "I'm surprised your grandmother didn't have a yard light. Almost everyone in the country does."

"She does." Frowning, Skye looked up and pointed. "It must be burnt out."

"Can you see to unlock your door?"

"It's not locked. I never lock my door when I'm on the farm."

"Why? Don't you think criminals can drive on a gravel road?"

"No, smarty. It's a habit. On a farm, machinery is always being moved in and out and they have to be able to move the cars to get around."

"So, you leave the keys in too?"

"Yeah, most of the time."

"That is really dumb in this day and age."

"Look, things are different on a farm. I know it doesn't seem like it now, but usually . . . It's hard to explain to a city boy. Can we do this a different time? Say anytime except right after my grandmother's been murdered." Skye felt tears pushing to overflow but forced them back.

"Fine."

Her eyes had adjusted to the dark as they

stood talking, and what she saw made her gasp.

Simon grabbed her arm. "What's wrong?"

"Oh my God. My tires." Skye pointed to the four flats on her car.

"Shit." Simon walked around the vehicle.

"They couldn't all go flat at the same time." Skye moved closer, trying to get a better look.

"No, they couldn't. Someone slashed them on purpose."

Skye leaned her head on the leather seat back of Simon's Lexus. The chief had told Skye he would dust the Buick for prints immediately, but she could wait and fill out a vandalism report when she came in to the police station the following morning. Jed had insisted he would get the tires fixed first thing the next day. Skye hadn't been able to convince her father that she was capable of arranging for her tires to be replaced herself. And she was too tired to argue for long.

The country roads were dark and Skye almost dozed until Simon stopped for the traffic signal at Maryland and Basin Streets. She shook her head; the only stoplight in town and she always managed to find it on red.

Basin Street, Scumble River's main thoroughfare, consisted of a six-block area that housed most of the town's smaller businesses, including the bank and the dry cleaner. Larger establishments, such as the supermarket and hardware store, had moved to the outskirts about ten years earlier in search of parking.

As the Lexus turned onto Stebler, the streetlights became fewer and fewer until they disappeared completely by the time Simon pulled into Skye's street. She rented a small river cottage from a divorced couple who couldn't decide who should get ownership. The cottage was ideal for Skye, and she hoped the couple wouldn't settle their differences until she was able to save some money, find another job, and make her escape from Scumble River.

Simon parked in her driveway and turned to Skye. "Would you like me to come in?"

She frowned, misunderstanding his intent. "I'm really tired and just want to go to sleep."

He raised an eyebrow. "That's fine, but wouldn't you feel better, after all that's happened, if I made sure the place is safe?"

Skye began to slide out of the car. "Oh, well thanks, but I can take care of myself."

Simon followed her, watching as she tried

unsuccessfully to fit the key in the lock. "Look, your tires were slashed and you're the one ruffling everyone's feathers about your grandmother's death. Don't you think there might be a connection?"

"Okay, you're probably right. I'm too tired to think straight."

The door finally opened and Skye trudged wearily inside. On her way into the great room that acted as her living and dining areas, she threw her purse on a table.

She watched Simon scan the room. It was half of the large octagon shape that made up the cottage. The outer arc was comprised of windows and sliding glass doors that faced the river. He made sure they were all locked, with bars across their tracks, before moving on. Skye trailed behind him.

The bedroom was a quarter of the octagon and also had a set of sliding glass doors with windows on either side looking over the water. He secured these and checked out the closet and bathroom.

The only remaining space was the small kitchen/utility area that looked out on the driveway, and the half bath off the foyer. Both were empty.

Skye, following Simon, bumped into him when he stopped in the foyer. "Sorry."

He put his arms around her. "Make sure

you turn the dead bolt and put on the chain when I leave."

Skye nodded mutely, having trouble keeping her eyelids open.

Simon kissed her softly on the lips. "I'll call you tomorrow after you've been to the police station." He turned and spoke over his shoulder as he went through the door. "Don't forget you're supposed to be there at eight."

Skye locked up behind him, turned, and made her way into the master bathroom. *I should take a shower.* She stripped off her clothes and stuffed them into the hamper. *At least, I should wash my face.* Grabbing her nightgown off the hook behind the door, she slipped it over her head. *It would take only a second to put on some Fruition lotion.* She sank into her pillows. *Esteé Lauder would be so disappointed in me . . .*

Her alarm buzzed at six, its usual time. Skye reached out and slapped it off. A few seconds later she forced herself out of bed and grabbed the telephone. After letting the schools know she wouldn't be in due to a death in the family, she crawled back between the sheets.

The next time she awoke, the numbers on her clock radio glowed seven-thirty. She leaped out of bed and into the shower, stripping off her nightgown on the way. The hot water revived her and she soaped, shampooed, and rinsed quickly.

After toweling her body and hair, she threw on underclothes then stood at her closet, stymied. What should she wear to be fingerprinted, taking into account it was the day after her grandmother died and it was going to be hotter than heck out?

As she contemplated her inadequate wardrobe, her glance fell on the clock. Damn, she was going to be late and she still hadn't done her hair or put on any makeup.

Skye dialed the nonemergency number for the police. She had it memorized since she often called her mother when May was working at the station.

Thea Jones, another of Scumble River's dispatchers, answered. At the sound of Skye's voice she said, "Oh, honey, I'm so sorry for your family. You know, we all love May. She's gonna take it real hard. She was real close to her mama."

"Thanks, Thea. Could you let Chief Boyd know I'm going to be a little late? He wanted me there at eight, but it doesn't look like I'm going to make it until eight-thirty or quarter to nine." Skye stretched the cord and grabbed a black-and-white gingham skort outfit from her closet.

"Sure, honey. You take your time. That man ain't got nothin' else to do anyways."

The doorbell rang as Skye hung up the phone. She grabbed her robe and fought her way into it as she ran to the foyer. May's face was framed in the side window.

Skye released all the locks and ushered her mother inside. "Hi, what are you doing here so early?" As soon as the words passed her lips, she knew it was the wrong thing to say.

"Early? You call five to eight early? We've got to do something about those slovenly habits you picked up in New Orleans."

Skye edged back toward her bedroom. "Okay, okay. What's up?"

"I came to drive you to the police station. Your dad's still working on the tires." May followed closely on Skye's heels. "What are you wearing?" May was dressed impeccably in navy cotton slacks and a white blouse.

Skye held up the ensemble she had picked out.

May puckered her mouth. "You know, honey, since you've gained weight, do you really think you should wear things that are sleeveless and above the knee?"

Skye frowned. About eighteen months ago she had decided to exit from the diet roller coaster. At first she had gained quite a bit of weight, but then she'd reached her setpoint. She exercised regularly and now felt comfortable with who she was.

Ignoring her mother, Skye took the outfit and walked into the bathroom. When she emerged twenty minutes later, she was wearing her original choice, had styled her hair in a French braid, and wore her usual makeup.

May didn't comment.

Thea grabbed May in a hug as soon as Skye and her mother entered the police station, then drew May behind the counter, sat her down, and began to converse in low tones. Skye was left to find Chief Boyd on her own.

Obviously, Tuesdays were slow days for criminal activity in Scumble River. The building seemed deserted and so quiet that Skye could hear the rustle of paper as she approached the chief's office.

He looked up as she entered. "Glad you could finally find time in your busy schedule for us."

Sighing, Skye sat on one of the visitor chairs. "Sorry. I'm sure you don't want to hear the litany of excuses any more than I want to go through them."

Chief Boyd made a note in a file and stuck it in a drawer. "You're right. I'm in a bad mood today and didn't mean to take it out on you. Let's start over."

She wiggled, trying to get comfortable in the cracked leather seat. "Thanks. How come you're in a bad mood? I hope it's not because I insisted on an autopsy for my grandmother."

"No, personal problems." His face closed and he lost all expression.

Skye knew he and his wife, Darleen, had been having difficulties with their marriage for the last year or so, but she thought things had gotten better. "I know how tough that can be. Maybe you both should talk to a counselor."

"Are you volunteering your services as a psychologist?" He raised an eyebrow.

Blushing, Skye shook her head. "No. I'm only qualified to work with children and their parents. But I could give you a name of a very good therapist who specializes in couples."

He moved around the desk and sat on the edge. His knees were a fraction of an inch from hers. "I thought maybe you couldn't take the case because you were too close to the people involved."

Turning a deeper shade of red, Skye tried

to find the words to answer him. "Well, ah, that too. After all, I've known you since I was a teenager and I work with Darleen."

She felt herself getting lost in the depth of his brown eyes. It felt as if something were sitting on her chest. Of all the men she knew, why did this one have to be married?

The sound of a throat being cleared in the doorway stopped her before she could speak.

Skye's eyes darted in that direction, and she met her mother's worried gaze. She stood up and turned to May. "Mom, we were, ah, filling out the report about my tires."

May smiled thinly. "Fine. I'll help."

Chief Boyd went back behind his desk and pulled out a partially completed form. "So, Skye, give me a list of all the people you've recently infuriated."

CHAPTER 5

THERE WAS A CROOKED MAN

The phone was ringing as Skye unlocked the door to her cottage later that morning.

She hesitated, figuring it was either more bad news or one of her relatives calling to yell at her about last night.

Tugging Skye's arm, May pulled them both into the kitchen. "You'd better hurry and answer the phone before they hang up."

She sighed, and lifted the receiver. After a few minutes of conversation she said goodbye and turned to her mother. "Great. Just what I needed."

May held up the dishcloth she had been using to wipe out the sink. "What's up?"

"I have to go into school."

"Why? Surely you're entitled to a personal day off." May looked around and attacked a spot she noticed on the counter.

"They're sorry for my loss, but they've got an irate parent coming in at one, and Neva Llewellyn wants me there."

"Couldn't you say no?" May unplugged the toaster and shook it over the trash can in the corner.

"I suppose so, but after what happened at my last job I need to get sterling references from this one or I can kiss my career good-bye."

May finished emptying the crumbs from the toaster's trap and started polishing the chrome. "But what happened in your last school was not your fault. You did the right thing."

Shrugging, Skye pulled out a chair and sat down. "You know I was right, and I know I was right, but if anyone calls that school system, all they're going to be told is that I was fired for insubordination."

Both women were silent as May finished with the toaster and plugged it back in. She finally spoke. "It's only a little after eleven-thirty now. How about if I take you to lunch and then drop you off at school? Dad and I will bring Grandma's car there as soon as he finishes with it."

"That sounds good. I'm sorry you guys have to chauffeur me around. As soon as I get my insurance check, I'll buy a car." It was tempting just to give in and let her parents take care of her, but there was no way Skye could stay in Scumble River if she didn't keep fighting to remain independent.

May stopped cleaning. "Skye, you know we want to make your life easier. We wouldn't offer if we didn't enjoy it. We do the same for Vince."

Skye nodded. It was a fine line between accepting help she needed and insisting on doing things for herself. "Are you going to call Dad?"

"No, he won't be near a phone. He'll either be fixing the Buick or in the fields." May walked into the tiny bathroom across the foyer from the kitchen.

Skye raised her voice to be heard above the running water. "You guys really need to get a cell phone and an answering machine."

"We've been just fine for thirty-five years without any fancy gadgets. Next thing you know you'll be wanting us to get a computer like Hugo talked Dante into." May snorted. "To keep updated farm records, my eye. He just wants to play around on that Sinnernet. I heard down at the police station that pictures of naked women just pop up when you turn the machine on."

Knowing when to end a conversation was an art Skye had picked up early in dealing with her mother. She wasn't about to begin to explain the Internet to May, let alone pornographic Web sites. "Okay then, let me freshen up and get my briefcase. Where do you want to go to lunch?"

May and Skye slid into a mauve-colored booth. The Feedbag had recently been redecorated, and was now only ten years behind the times.

They picked up the plastic-coated menus and silently studied the multiple pages. After a few minutes Skye closed hers, but May continued to contemplate the choices.

"What are you having, Mom?"

"I don't know. There's too much to pick from." May flipped the pages frantically and tears started trickling down her cheeks.

Skye plucked the menu from her mom's hands. "You've had a lot to deal with in the last twenty-four hours. You don't have to carry on as if nothing has happened."

Her mother's quiet weeping turned into sobs.

"It's okay to cry." Skye scooted around the booth to sit beside May. She put her arms around her mother. "You and Grandma were very close and her death is a shock to all of us."

After a few minutes, May straightened and took the tissue Skye offered. "I loved her so much. We weren't just mother and daughter, we were friends." May wiped away a lingering tear. "It was funny. She was always in total control of everything in the house until Dad came home from work, and then suddenly she turned into a meek little lady. When he was gone she was a tiger — we'd play music real loud and sing, but when he was there we had to be quiet and make sure we didn't disturb him." May's voice faltered. "It was almost as if Mom was afraid of him."

"I really don't remember Grandpa," Skye said. "My earliest memories of Grandma are going to her house to help her bake and hearing about her childhood. She never wanted to talk about her adult past, so I was really surprised when she decided to tell me the family history."

"When we hired Mrs. J, Mom finally realized she wasn't immortal. She didn't want those stories to die with her."

"But they did. It was too late." This was a side of May Skye rarely saw and she wanted to keep the conversation going. "You seem to have had a different relationship with Grandma than your siblings did."

"Ever since Dad died, Dante's treated Mom like a child. And he's always whining about having to sell off *his* land because the housekeeper was so expensive. He wanted us sisters to take eight-hour shifts and get rid of Mrs. J."

"You're kidding!" Skye was surprised by the extent of her uncle's self-centeredness.

"No." May smiled ruefully. "And Mona and Minnie were always afraid of her." May smiled sadly. "She wasn't one to mince words and they don't like to hear the truth." She paused and patted Skye's hand. "You remind me of her. Not afraid to tell it like it is."

"I thought you didn't like me to do that."

May touched Skye's face. "It's just that I'm afraid for you. You have such a strong sense of right and wrong that you make a lot of people uncomfortable. And you never know what a nervous person will do."

Skye glanced at her watch as she hurried into Scumble River Junior High School. It was five after one and she was late.

Just as she was about to knock on the principal's closed door, Skye remembered. Simon was supposed to come over to her house that afternoon. He'd be ticked if she wasn't there. She'd better call and hope she caught him before he left.

She turned back to the secretary's unoccupied desk, snatched up the phone, and dialed Simon's number. She got his answering machine at his house, his assistant at the funeral home, and his pager; she left messages everywhere.

It was now quarter after and Skye knew Neva would be seething. At first she frowned when no one answered her knock on the principal's door; then she smiled and sat down. No secretary, no principal, she could easily have been waiting fifteen minutes for someone to tell her where the meeting was.

Ursula Nelson, the school secretary, rushed around the corner and came to a halt when she spotted Skye. "Why aren't you with Mrs. Llewellyn and Mr. Doozier?"

"Where are they? I've been waiting here for quite a while."

"They're using the art room. The art teacher is sick today so it's available."

"Why aren't we using Neva's office?" Skye nodded toward the closed door.

"Mrs. Llewellyn felt it would be unwise to meet with Mr. Doozier in such a confined, windowless space," Ursula said.

"I guess she really is afraid of him." Skye picked up her briefcase.

As she headed down the hall, Ursula called out, "I was only gone a few minutes. You couldn't have been waiting long."

★ ★ ★

The small art room smelled of turpentine and glue. Scraps of construction paper were scattered on the faded blue linoleum. The windows were open, but there was no breeze to ruffle the paintings thumbtacked to the bulletin board.

Neva and Hap Doozier sat facing each other across a long table. Neither was speaking. Skye would have recognized Mr. Doozier without Ursula's warning. He was short and skinny like his brother Earl, although not as densely tattooed.

Skye assessed his mood by his clothing. He appeared to be dressed for a Saturday night date, in tight blue jeans, a belt with a huge silver buckle, and a shiny western-style shirt. As she stepped near the table, the stench of his cologne mixed with the alcohol on his breath was overwhelming.

She extended her hand. "Hello, I'm Ms. Denison, the school psychologist. Sorry I was late, but I didn't know where this meeting was being held."

Mr. Doozier looked at her outstretched hand and gingerly gave the three middle fingers a hurried squeeze, releasing them as if they were infectious. "Hap Doozier. My kid's Cletus."

Neva started to speak as Skye eased into

the molded plastic chair. "Mr. Doozier has been telling me that Cletus is a liar, and we are not to believe any further stories he tells us."

"Oh?" Skye raised an eyebrow. "I spoke with his teachers yesterday afternoon, and they all felt him to be too impulsive to make a very good liar."

Frowning, Mr. Doozier leaned forward. "It ain't no one's business in this school to go talkin' about my boy. Not to his teachers, or to no caseworker from the government."

Skye forced her hands to remain still and looked Mr. Doozier in the eye. "I'm sorry you feel that way. I know you care for your son and want the best for him. That's what we want too."

He pounded his fist on the table. "I give the boy everything he needs. He ain't got no mama or brothers or sisters. It's just him and me. No one has got a right to tell me how to raise my own kid."

Speaking in a neutral voice, Skye said in a low tone, "I'm sure you do what you think is best, but maybe we could help you find ways that might work better."

Mr. Doozier's face turned red and veins popped out alongside of his neck. "No one tells me how to punish my own flesh and blood. If I think he needs to be whupped,

I'll whup him, and no DCFS bitch is goin' make me stop."

Skye glanced nervously at Neva, who sat with her mouth partly open and her expression trancelike. "Mr. Doozier," Skye said, "I hear you saying that you don't like people to interfere in your business, right?"

He nodded grudgingly.

"Well, if you continue to hit Cletus, we have no choice but to keep calling the Department of Children and Family Services. They then have no choice but to send a caseworker. If this continues, DCFS will ultimately have no choice but to take Cletus away from you. Is that what you want?"

For a brief moment, Skye was sure she had succeeded in talking some sense into Mr. Doozier, but within seconds he lunged out of his seat, making the chair fly backward. Leaning on the table with both fists, his face a dark shade of crimson, he sputtered, "Ain't no one doin' no such thing. Y'all think you're so smart in your fancy clothes, with your fancy degrees, but Cletus and I can disappear with the snap of my fingers. Then what you and DCFS goin' do?"

When neither woman answered he seemed to become more enraged. He grabbed one of the chairs and flung it at the window. The glass shattered into a spider web of cracks. "But I ain't goin' nowhere, because all you old maid busybodies are goin' quit stickin' your noses in my business, or you're goin' get hurt worse'n that window."

Neva and Skye sat in stunned silence for long minutes after Hap Doozier stomped out of the room.

Finally Skye shook her head. "Forget about registering guns, register six-packs. Each can of beer takes you closer to shooting yourself in the foot."

Neva stood up and smoothed her skirt. "That guy fell out of the stupid tree and hit every branch on the way down."

They walked down the hall, glancing around nervously as they proceeded through the empty corridor. Both breathed a sigh of relief when they reached Neva's office.

Neva settled behind her desk and gestured for Skye to take a seat. "Now what?"

"I'm not sure. I think he threatened Cletus so that means another call to DCFS." Skye dug out a tissue from her briefcase and dabbed at her face. She wasn't sure if she was sweating because of the heat or the adrenaline. "The tires on my car were slashed last night. I wonder if Mr. Doozier had anything to do with it."

"Well, there is no question he threatened us. I'm calling the police." Neva reached for the phone.

Grandma's Buick was waiting for Skye in the parking lot when she finished talking to Officer Quirk about Hap Doozier. The broken classroom window was a misdemeanor, Quirk had explained, but there was little the police could do about Hap's threats.

This was not reassuring to Skye as she got into the unlocked car. The keys fell from behind the visor as she pulled it down. Jed's hiding places were very predictable.

Skye didn't bother with the radio or airconditioning, since the drive home would take less than five minutes. When she arrived, Simon was pacing in front of her door. From the look on his face, Skye guessed he had not received any of her messages.

She reluctantly got out of the car. They'd been fighting a lot lately. Her head was pounding and she was soaked in sweat. "Gee, looks like you didn't get my messages. Sorry. I hope you didn't have to wait too long."

Simon, a thunderous expression on his face, stood between her and the house.

"That's it? Everything is supposed to be all right just because you say you're sorry? Where have you been all afternoon?"

"To hell. Care to join me next time?" Skye brushed past him, unlocked the door, and slipped through, letting it swing shut in his face.

He caught it before it closed and followed her inside.

She stopped on the threshold of her bedroom, turned, and crossed her arms. "Do you mind? I'm going to take a shower."

Frowning, Simon took a step back and Skye shut the door.

She stood under the showerhead, letting the hot water knead her tense muscles. When her fingers started to wrinkle, she reluctantly turned off the spray and toweled dry. She sat at the bathroom's built-in dressing table and worked a wide-toothed comb through her tangled curls. *I shouldn't have been so short with Simon.* She smoothed lotion over her face and throat. *He was just concerned. It was my fault for not getting in touch with him earlier.*

After putting on a pair of denim shorts and a plain white T-shirt, Skye hesitantly opened the bedroom door. Simon was gone. She felt a heaviness in her chest. Why had she treated him so badly? Why weren't they getting along anymore?

Angry at herself, and upset from the last twenty-four hours, Skye put a Pam Tillis CD on the player and lay on the sofa. She fell asleep to the beginning strains of "Mi Vida Loca."

The doorbell's persistent ringing woke Skye. She wasn't sure of the time but it was dark outside.

A shiver ran up her spine. What if it was Hap Doozier or Gus Yoder's father?

She grabbed her baseball bat and went to the door. Looking through the peephole, all she could see was flowers.

"Who is it?" She raised her voice to be heard through the wood.

"It's me. Simon."

Skye unlocked the door and held it open. Simon handed her a vase filled with roses. Their scent was intoxicating and she buried her face in the velvety petals.

While she was appreciating the flowers, Simon had returned to his car. Now he was back, carrying brown bags and a bottle of wine.

He set the packages on the kitchen table, took the vase from Skye's arms, and placed it on the counter. "I'm sorry I was so abrupt today." He held her hands and looked into her eyes. "Your relatives have been giving me a hard time about your grandmother's autopsy. And then after your tires were slashed, when you weren't here I was worried."

Skye snuggled into his arms and laid her head on his chest. "It was my fault. Lately I've been mean to everyone. I'm sorry. I did try to reach you."

He stopped her with a finger on her lips. "I know. I finally checked my messages. I had quit listening to them this morning after the fourth time your Uncle Dante beeped me."

She nodded sympathetically. "When I think about dying, one of the things that really scares me is that I'll be surrounded by my family in heaven. I'll be trapped in eternity with people I don't even want to spend Thanksgiving with."

Simon smiled and hugged her. "You have a really twisted sense of humor."

Skye ignored his comment and went on with her train of thought. "My day was horrible, but I shouldn't have taken it out on you. Can you believe I had to go into school the day after my grandmother died?" She traced his jaw with her finger.

Simon turned his face and captured her finger with his lips.

Skye's pulse quickened. *If I don't stop now,*

I may not be able to later, and I'm not ready for this. "Simon, it's been wonderful dating you these past nine months, and I'm very attracted to you, but I'm just not ready for an intimate relationship." She paused and looked into his hurt-filled eyes. "It makes things too complicated."

Simon held her loosely and stroked her hair. "I'm not going to push you. I know after what your ex-fiancé did, you don't trust men."

"I really, really want to keep dating you, but I also want to be fair." Skye could feel a tear etch its way down her cheek.

"Okay, I really, really want to keep dating you, too. But maybe it would be better not to make it an exclusive thing." Simon wiped her tear away with his finger.

Who was he planning to ask out? Skye pasted a smile in place. "I'm sure that would be for the best. We just won't take each other's time for granted anymore."

"Good."

With one last hug, she forced herself to slip out of his arms. Her smile was shaky as she pointed to the table. "What's all this?"

"Chinese takeout. I know how much you like it."

"But there aren't any Chinese restaurants in Scumble River."

"I drove to Kankakee and got it from your favorite place." Simon smiled.

"Imperial Dragon?" When he nodded, she went over to the bags and sniffed. "Let me guess what you got. Empress chicken, hot and sour soup, crab rangoon, and shrimp fried rice?"

"And a bottle of plum wine."

"I'll get the plates and glasses. Then you can tell me what my awful relatives have been doing to you today, and I'll tell you what the awful citizens of Scumble River have been doing to me."

CHAPTER 6

PUSSY CAT, PUSSY CAT,

WHAT HAVE YOU SEEN?

Bingo! She had forgotten all about Bingo. Skye slammed down her cup of Earl Grey tea. Her grandmother's cat had been locked up alone with no fresh food or water since Monday night, and here it was already Wednesday morning.

She grabbed the phone and dialed her mother, who answered on the first ring. "Mom, did anyone take Bingo home with them?"

"Good morning to you too. And, no, I don't think anyone took the cat. Why?" May was not an animal lover, and had made it clear throughout Skye's life that four-legged creatures belonged in the barn or pasture, not in the house.

Gritting her teeth, Skye asked, "Did anyone go over yesterday to feed him and clean his litter box?" She had a difficult time accepting her mother's attitude toward pets.

"I doubt it. The police have the house sealed, remember?"

"Well, we can't leave him in there to die of thirst or starvation. I'll call Wally and see if I can pick up Bingo this morning." Skye put her mug in the sink and rinsed it out.

"You're not going to keep that animal, are you? He'll shed on everything."

"Technically, he's property of the estate. Do you know what Grandma's will says?" Taking the dishcloth, Skye wiped up the table.

"Everything is in a Bypass Trust, so she really didn't have a will."

Skye grabbed a pad of paper and a pen from a kitchen drawer. "What's a Bypass Trust?"

"Grandpa put everything into a trust, so Grandma wouldn't have to pay inheritance tax when he died. After his death, all income from the estate was paid to Grandma, but the property itself is jointly owned by me, my sisters, and brother."

Skye sat down and made a note of that on her tablet. "Okay, so you're saying that Grandma didn't own the estate anymore, but she received the profits from the farm."

"Right."

"But although you guys own the property, it wasn't worth much to you as long as

Grandma was alive."

"Right."

Skye tapped the pen on the table. "Then who is the trustee?"

"Your Uncle Dante."

"Shit."

"Watch your language, young lady."

Standing up, Skye moved toward the wall phone. "Could you call Uncle Dante and see if it's okay for me to pick up Bingo? If not, find out who's taking care of him and when they're going to do it. I'll call Wally and clear things on that end."

Dante awarded Skye "temporary" custody of the cat, pending a valuation by an expert. He didn't seem aware that a used cat was a liability, not an asset. Wally had agreed to meet her at her grandmother's at eight to supervise the removal of the feline and his equipment.

Before leaving for her grandmother's, Skye called the school to tell them she'd be late. She was scheduled to be at the elementary school in the morning, but had no appointments, so she left a message for the principal that she'd be there around ten.

It felt strange pulling into her grandmother's driveway after Monday's events. She steered the car as close to the back door as the concrete apron allowed. Her usual parking spot up by the garage now gave her the creeps. The dilapidated wooden building seemed to exude animosity.

Although it was hot sitting in the closed car, Skye was reluctant to get out or even roll down the windows.

Come on, it must be eighty degrees already, either open the windows or get out. It's silly to sit in this oven just because you're scared. Her thoughts were interrupted by Chief Boyd's squad car pulling up next to hers.

Skye hopped out of the Buick and smoothed the skirt of her denim dress. "Thanks for coming out here, Wally. Sorry to bother you."

"Glad to be of service. I was going to come out here today anyway. I like to take a look-see before anyone else starts in on a crime scene."

"You mean no one has even searched the house yet?" Skye tilted her head up and stared at him. "It's been over thirty-six hours since I found her."

"We borrow the crime-scene technician from the sheriff's department and unfortunately, Stanley County has had several serious crimes in the past few days. The First National Bank in Laurel was robbed Monday night and Judge Fitzwater shot his wife on Tuesday. So since we are not absolutely certain your grandmother was murdered, we received a low priority. The tech should finally be over this morning."

"I see." Skye's brows drew together. "It's not so much whether my grandmother was murdered or not, it's who's got the most clout in the area."

Wally shrugged. "The bank needed to be able to reopen for business and no one wanted to mess up a case involving a judge. That's how the world works."

"I know; I just don't like it."

"The other thing is, since the body was removed and you and your family wandered all over the house, the scene's already been compromised. There's not much hope in finding much in the way of evidence at this point." Wally took her hand. "Not that we won't try, but a few hours' delay just isn't that important."

Skye freed her hand and turned away. "Right." So her grandmother's murder was low priority. She'd have to do something about that.

Chief Boyd took her elbow as they walked toward the door. He swept away the yellow tape and unlocked the door. "We'll have to be careful not to disturb anything more."

Before either of them could react, Bingo

rocketed past them and took off across the yard.

The chief started after the cat but Skye stopped him. "Never mind. You'll never catch him. He'll come back when he's ready. In the meantime, let's get his stuff."

He led the way as they climbed the steps from the entry-way into the kitchen. "Let me gather everything on the table and you take it from there. Probably any evidence that was in the kitchen was destroyed Monday night when your whole family was here, but I'd like to be cautious anyway."

"Okay, I'll need his bowls, which are there on the floor. And his food is in the pantry."

Chief Boyd scooped up the things she pointed out and deposited them on the table. "What else?"

"His litter box is in the bathroom." Skye fought a grin. "It might be a little smelly after three days, so you'd better dump it outside."

When the chief returned from that task Skye continued, "Bingo's carry case is in the closet in the next room."

Chief Boyd went into the dining room. His face was grim when he returned with the Pet Taxi. "Come with me. Put your hands in your pockets and don't touch anything."

Skye frowned. "Why? What's going on?"

He didn't answer, just led the way.

Every room had been trashed. Drawers had been pulled out and emptied in the middle of the floor. The contents of the closets had been treated similarly. Even the cushions had been unzipped and the foam removed.

Chief Boyd stopped in the living room, which allowed them to see into almost all the rest of the house. "Was it like this the last time you were here?"

"No. You were here, too. You saw what it looked like when Simon took Grandma's body away."

"I just wanted to make sure."

"Fine, but remember Mom handed you the key and we all left."

"So how did the intruder get in?" Wally murmured, almost to himself.

Skye ran the layout of the house through her mind. "The basement. There's a window down there that pops off."

Wally looked at her questioningly. "What?"

"My grandfather's family house was destroyed by a tornado when he was a young man. They hid in their basement and fortunately no one was killed. The unlucky thing was that they were trapped for days because all the basement windows were too small and they couldn't get out." Skye glanced at Wally to see if he was following her. "So, when they built this house they put in a special safety window. You press on two little tabs on the top and it comes right out. Originally it could only be opened from the inside, but years of wear and tear have made it easy to push in from the outside too."

He led her back to the kitchen. "Stay here. I'll check out the basement."

She heard his footsteps as they ran down the stairs.

A few thuds, a couple of muffled curses, and he was back. "Looks like you were right. There're some fresh marks in the dust by that window. I'll make sure it's examined for prints." Wally looked around the kitchen. "I wonder why this room wasn't searched."

Skye grabbed on to that thought. "So, you think this was a search rather than vandalism. That would prove that Grandma didn't just die in her sleep, wouldn't it?"

"Probably. I think the autopsy will confirm it."

"We'd better get this stuff in the car and find Bingo. I promised I'd be at work at ten."

After dumping the cat supplies in the

trunk of the Buick, they set out to find the feline. He could be hiding almost anywhere. The yard was more than two acres, with the right half planted in rows of fruit trees.

There was a small front lawn, a long grassy side area, and an untended expanse in the back of the house. The chief took the right part and started searching among the trees. Skye first checked the front and side sections on the left. When there was no sign of Bingo, she unwillingly headed toward the back.

Here, the terrain was uneven and covered with tall weeds. She grimaced at her new cream-colored canvas sandals. There went thirty-eight dollars.

Calling, "Here Bingo, here kitty, kitty," Skye trekked through the prairie grass, feeling it cut her bare ankles and calves.

Finally, she heard a yowl and spotted the cat just a few yards ahead of her. He was sitting by a round concrete slab with a cast-iron ring embedded in the middle. The cover, which was supposed to be flush to the ground, was slightly ajar.

As Skye approached, an odor stopped her. It was sickeningly sweet and smelled a little like the time her refrigerator broke down when she was gone for the weekend. She forced herself closer and grabbed

Bingo, who protested the abrupt treatment by squirming and yowling.

Turning, she ran toward the orchard. "Wally, Wally! Come quick."

Skye stopped at the Buick and retrieved the cat carrier from the trunk. She shoved Bingo inside and secured the door then continued toward the trees, calling for the chief.

He burst out of the grove with his hand on his gun. "Skye, are you all right?"

She stopped to catch her breath. "I'm fine." Panting, she explained about the stench.

They retraced her path until they were a few feet from the concrete slab.

"Do you know what this is?" Chief Boyd asked.

"It may be the old well. We were never allowed to play back here because Grandma was always afraid we'd fall into it. I think they covered it when the great-grandchildren were born."

Nodding, he tried to move the cover with his foot. It wouldn't budge. "It would probably be easy to move using the metal handle, but until it's been dusted for fingerprints I don't want to touch it. Let me see what I've got in the squad car that I can lift it with."

Skye trailed him back to his car, and while the chief got some tools and a big flashlight from the trunk, she fed Bingo. They returned to the well.

The chief inserted a jack handle into the opening. Skye watched the veins pop in his arms as he strained to move the lid. The muscles of his chest rippled under the khaki uniform shirt and his broad shoulders strained against the fabric. Without warning the concrete moved with a loud screech.

Immediately, the odor intensified and Skye backed away. Chief Boyd covered his mouth with a handkerchief and aimed the flashlight beam down the well. "It looks like a body is stuck about nine or ten feet down." He turned to Skye. "Can you stand to look? Maybe you know who it is."

She screwed up her face and shook her head, but finally moved closer. Putting her hand over her mouth and nose, she leaned forward and followed the stream of light with her eyes.

Stumbling back, Skye said, "I think it's Mrs. Jankowski, the missing housekeeper."

Chief Boyd had told Skye she could leave, but cautioned her not to tell anyone about their discovery. One part of her wanted to stay and see what the evidence people turned up, but mostly she was thankful she wouldn't have to view the body as it was dragged from the well.

She stopped at her cottage to drop off Bingo and set up his equipment. When she opened his case in the foyer, he poked out a delicate pink nose and sniffed. Satisfied, he stepped all the way into the room and proceeded to investigate his new surroundings.

Meanwhile, Skye filled his food and water bowls, leaving them for him to discover when he reached the kitchen. She tucked his litter box under the sink in the small bathroom off the foyer, and immediately showed him its location.

Bingo instantly used the facilities.

"That's what I forgot, Bingo, a litter scoop. I better make a list and get to the grocery store sometime today." Skye walked to the kitchen and took a small pad of paper.

Glancing at her watch, she knew she'd never make it to school by ten and decided to take the rest of the day off since they would dock her for a full day anyway. This time when she called she asked to speak to the principal directly.

"Mrs. Greer, this is Skye Denison. Did you hear my grandmother died on Monday?"

"Yes, dear, I was very sorry. Antonia was a wonderful woman. I used to love sitting in her kitchen and watching her bake. We'd talk about gardening. She always had the best tips and grew the biggest peonies."

"Oh, I didn't realize you knew my grandmother." Skye let her tone rise at the end of the sentence, hoping for an explanation.

"Well, it was over forty years ago, but I dated your Uncle Dante for a time when we were in high school together. He was so handsome and had such a wonderful sense of humor. All the girls were crazy about him."

Skye didn't know what to say to that. This was a side of her uncle she hadn't pictured. What had happened to change him? It had been years since she'd thought of Dante as fun. As the silence lengthened, she knew she needed to say something. "Wow. Small world. I guess I shouldn't be surprised. Anyway, I was planning on coming in today, but some things have come up so I was wondering if it would be all right to take a personal day?"

Mrs. Greer didn't answer right away. "I'm sorry, Skye, but I booked an appointment with the parents of Perry Underwood for us this afternoon. Is there any way you can make it? These aren't easy people to deal with, and they would take it as a personal insult if we canceled."

Careful to keep the sigh out of her voice,

Skye said, "What time are they coming in?"

"One-thirty."

"Okay, I'll be in around one."

"Great, I'll brief you then." Mrs. Greer sounded relieved.

After hanging up the phone, Skye went out on her deck and sat on a lounge chair. She watched the river go by with Bingo curled up on her lap, purring as she stroked him. Two more days of school and she'd be free.

Her big plans for this summer included lots of reading and lying on the beach.

She couldn't afford to go anywhere on vacation, but one of the local abandoned strip mining areas had been turned into a recreational club with swimming and boating. It cost five hundred dollars to join and a hundred a year in dues, but her godfather, Charlie Patukas, had given her a membership for her birthday.

Normally, she wouldn't have accepted such an expensive gift from anyone, but Charlie rarely took no for an answer — especially since he'd inherited a large sum of money last year. He had bought Vince an electric golf cart, May new carpeting, and Jed a satellite dish. He got such a kick out of surprising his "family" with gifts and playing the big shot that he made them feel like ingrates when they tried to turn down his presents.

Skye smiled fondly. Charlie was one of a kind. The soothing motion of the river lulled her and she wasn't aware of time passing until she was roused by the ringing phone.

Dumping Bingo unceremoniously inside the door, she ran for the kitchen. "Hello?"

"What in the hell is going on at Ma's now?" It was Uncle Dante.

Skye counted to ten before answering. "Hello, Uncle Dante. Thanks for asking, I'm doing fine."

"I said you could pick up the damn cat, not tear up the backyard."

"Uncle Dante, in case you haven't noticed, I'm talking to you so I can't be the one tearing up the yard." She knew logic was a waste of time with him but she always tried it anyway.

"Then I repeat: What is going on?" Dante's voice was now so loud that Bingo was cowering in the space between the washer and dryer.

"I'm sorry. I've been asked not to discuss that with anyone. You need to talk to Chief Boyd." Her eyes fell on the microwave clock and she was startled to see it was already twelve-forty-five.

"You tell me right now, Missy. I'm trustee of the estate and have a legal right to know what's going on." His voice cracked. "What are you doing to my mother now?"

She heard the pain in his voice, but didn't have an answer. "I truly am sorry. This is not hurting Grandma, honest. She'd want us to find out the truth."

He jumped on her words. "What have you found?"

"I'm really, really sorry, Uncle Dante, but Chief Boyd ordered me not to talk about it. I don't want to get in trouble with the police over this. Please call Wally and ask him to explain."

She let him yell for a moment, then cut back in. "I have to go now. Sorry. The chief will explain. Bye."

CHAPTER 7

THREE, FOUR,

THE COUSINS ARE SORE

Skye pushed open the door of Scumble River Elementary School. The principal, Mrs. Greer, was waiting in the hallway. She was a tiny woman with a puff of white hair, dressed in a soft pink suit. They walked to the office without speaking and closed the door. Mrs. Greer sat in a royal-blue wing chair and indicated that Skye should take its companion.

It was obvious to Skye that Mrs. Greer had spent her own money fixing up her office. The Queen Anne–style desk was mahogany and the cream-colored walls were hung with quality reproductions.

Picking up a file, Mrs. Greer said, "Perry Underwood is a first grader who receives assistance from the special education teacher and the speech therapist. He began receiving services when he was three and attended a special education preschool until this year. He transferred to Scumble River Elementary last fall."

Skye nodded. "Yes, I've observed him in Mrs. Hopkins' room. He has a language disorder that makes it difficult for him to process what is said to him and almost impossible for him to communicate complex thoughts."

"Exactly. Have you met his parents?"

"No, the special ed coordinator from the co-op held the intake staffing without me. All I've done is review his file and take a look at him in class."

"Well, supposedly Perry was involved in a dreadful fight yesterday in the hallway on the way to lunch. I had the school nurse look at him, and Abby says there's not a mark on him."

Before Skye could reply, there was a knock and Fern Otte, the school secretary, peeked around the door. "The Underwoods are here."

"Send them in." Mrs. Greer stood and ushered the couple inside, seating them on the blue-and-cream brocade sofa facing the chairs. "Would you like some coffee, tea, or a soft drink?"

They refused. While Mrs. Greer made introductions, Skye sized up the couple across from her. Mr. Underwood was dressed in fatigues and his brown hair was cut in a military-style crew cut. His wife wore cargo pants tucked into commando boots and an olive drab T-shirt. Both sat at attention.

Mrs. Greer settled back into her chair and tilted her head toward Mr. Underwood. "You asked to see us regarding your son, Perry."

"Yes," Mr. Underwood said. "I've taught my son to take care of himself, but he was ambushed yesterday by three boys. He managed to defeat them and give them a good thrashing, but I'm concerned about the security in your hallways."

"I spoke to his teacher. She says the boys weren't in the hall long enough to have the type of fight you describe. Could Perry be exaggerating?" Mrs. Greer smiled kindly at both parents.

"No." Mr. Underwood clenched his cap in his hand. "My boy doesn't lie. Your teacher doesn't want to admit she's at fault."

Fixing him with a steady gaze, Mrs. Greer said, "My teachers don't lie either." She let silence prevail before continuing. "Setting that aside for a moment, your son doesn't have a scratch on him."

"I told you he's been taught to take care of himself. It's the other kids who got hurt, not Perry." Mr. Underwood puffed out his chest.

"There are no injured students in any of the first-grade classrooms. And none of the children recall anything happening yesterday beyond the regular hallway pushing and shoving." Mrs. Greer did not yield eye contact.

"Kids stick together."

"None of the teachers in the surrounding classrooms heard any commotion in the hall."

"They want to keep their jobs," Mr. Underwood said. "I know my boy."

Skye leaned toward the parents. "We're not saying that Perry lied. Everyone's perception of reality is slightly different and your son has a severe problem with the usage and comprehension of language, which makes his understanding even more dissimilar than those around him. Maybe this is no more than a misunderstanding."

"What?" Mr. Underwood frowned.

"Can you recall the exact words Perry used when he told you about the fight?" Skye asked.

The Underwoods looked at each other and shook their heads.

"Think back now. What was his manner like? Excited? Scared?"

Mrs. Underwood spoke for the first time. "At first, I thought he seemed happy."

"So, could it have been that the three boys included him in their group and the play was a little rough?" Skye held her breath.

Mrs. Underwood started to nod, but her husband shot her a censorious look and she turned it into a cough.

Skye directed her next remark to the woman. "I'm wondering if maybe the speech pathologist, Mrs. Whitney, might be able to help you understand what Perry is saying a little better."

Mr. Underwood's face closed. "We don't need an outsider interpreting for us. We understand Perry good enough."

"But —" Skye was cut off as the Underwoods rose to their feet.

"I told you it was a conspiracy," Mr. Underwood hissed into his wife's ear. "They've got the whole incident buried deeper than the real identity of Kennedy's assassin."

When the door closed behind them, Skye let out a big sigh. "That felt like an episode of the *Twilight Zone*."

Nodding, Mrs. Greer leaned back in her chair. "This is a good example of why you should have all your ducks in a row before meeting with parents. They're so sure of themselves they can almost convince you that you're mistaken."

"You were great. I think handling the parents is the hardest part of the job. It's so difficult for them to admit that their children could ever be in the wrong."

"We make a good team. I take them down with facts, and you give them something to go home and think about."

Reflecting upon the meeting, Skye asked, "Are Mr. and Mrs. Underwood in the military?"

"No. They're a part of that survivalist group that bought some of that land from the mining company and moved in all the trailers and mobile homes."

"Oh, the ones up against the back forty of my grandmother's land." Skye narrowed her eyes. "She had a lot of trouble with those people — trespassing and hunting near the house. Maybe I should go visit the Underwoods. I'm concerned that they have such a bad opinion of the school."

Skye was almost safely to her car when her cousins struck. Ginger and Gillian surrounded her and started haranguing her before she could speak.

Ginger was first. "We're tired of you causing trouble in the family."

"You always have to be the center of attention, but you've gone too far this time."

Gillian poked Skye in the chest with her index finger.

"What are you two talking about?" Skye edged closer to the Buick.

"Oh, no you don't." Each twin took an arm and forced Skye to walk with them.

Although Skye had several pounds on each of them, combined they were a force to be reckoned with. Skye's thoughts were mixed. She didn't want to create a scene in the school parking lot. All she needed was for it to get around that she was punching it out with her cousins. But this was getting a little scary.

"Where are you taking me?" They didn't answer. "Look, this isn't funny."

When the trio reached Ginger's van, they shoved Skye into the open back door and Gillian climbed in beside her. After Gillian slammed the sliding panel shut, Ginger walked around to the other side, climbed into the driver's seat, and started the motor.

Skye tried again. "What's going on? This is just silly."

Ginger put the TranSport in gear and squealed out of the parking lot.

"I'm sure we can work this out like civilized human beings." Skye was losing her initial feeling of annoyance and beginning to get alarmed.

"Relax," Gillian said. "We just want to talk to you, alone and uninterrupted."

They drove out of Scumble River, passed Skye's parents' place, and seemed to be headed for their grandmother's farm when Ginger slowed and pulled into a driveway obscured with weeds. It was the old Leofanti homestead that had been destroyed by the tornado.

The twins climbed out of the van and Skye followed, after checking the ignition to see if Ginger had left the keys. She hadn't.

"Now what?" Skye asked.

"We want to know what's going on with Grandma," Gillian said, settling on a concrete block. The foundation and chimney of the old farmhouse were the only reminders that there had ever been a building in that spot.

"The last I heard, Simon ordered an autopsy," Skye answered. "That takes a few days. After they determine a cause of death they'll release the body. Then we'll have the wake and funeral as usual."

"Grandma died of old age. She was eighty, for heaven's sake. You're just making it harder on all of us by refusing to admit that, and making us go through all this mumbo jumbo with the police," Ginger said.

"You would have never gotten your own way on this if you weren't dating the coroner. Which, by the way, is pretty pathetic in itself." Gillian stood and crossed her arms.

"Whether you two like it or not, Grandma was murdered. I'm sorry if it isn't convenient for you." Skye turned on Gillian. "And it would be a real good idea to leave my relationship with Simon out of this, or I might be forced to examine your marriage a little closer."

"What's that supposed to mean?" Gillian screeched and started toward Skye.

"Let's just say I've heard things about Irvin that make me think he's a real prince — only spelled differently." Skye refused to back down.

Gillian raised her hand and swung at Skye, who grabbed her by the wrist and twisted it to the right. Gillian howled in pain.

"Try not to forget that I've had training in takedowns for uncontrollable kids." Skye stepped back.

Ginger joined her twin. "This isn't getting us anywhere. Skye, this whole murder investigation not only gets everyone in town talking about us, but it also holds up getting the estate divided."

"Yeah," Gillian added, "just because you already have the Leofanti emerald ring doesn't mean the rest of us wouldn't like our share. I still think it's a bunch of crap that the ring goes to the oldest female. We're only ten months younger than you and we have children to pass it down to." Gillian's face was red and her lank blond hair hung in clumps.

"Interesting. Do you both agree that the emerald shouldn't go to the oldest female?" Skye looked between the twins, then focused on Ginger. "Or does Gillian just think that because her daughter is a few months younger than your daughter?"

Ginger gave her twin a speculative look, but before she could speak Gillian said, "Never mind. Leave Kristin and Iris out of this. The real money is in the land itself. And now because of your interfering, getting everything settled will take forever."

"So? What's the rush? The grandchildren won't get anything anyway. Mom says everything's in a trust." Skye looked puzzled.

"Well, maybe your folks don't need the money, but ours do." Ginger walked over and leaned on the van.

"Shut up!" Gillian yelled. "Are you stupid? Don't tell her anything."

Ginger scowled. "Then we're back to

square one. Why are you so sure Grandma was murdered?"

"I can't tell you that," Skye said. "Chief Boyd has asked me not to discuss it."

"Fine, then on your long walk home you just think about where your loyalties should lie." Gillian hopped into the front seat of the TranSport.

Ginger climbed into the driver's seat. Skye hurried to the side panel and was just in time to hear the lock click into place. The vehicle pulled out in a cloud of dust, leaving Skye with her hand still reaching for the handle.

Sighing, she glanced at her canvas sandals. They were already stained from the morning's excursion through the wilds of Grandma's backyard and their two-inch wedge heels were not made for hiking.

Skye peered inside her purse for anything that might be helpful, but since she was carrying only a small shoulder bag there was nothing useful. Her gaze swept the fields. Not a soul in sight. She was going to have to walk.

At the end of the driveway she turned onto the main road. Sweat poured from her face as she concentrated on putting one foot in front of the other. *Boy, I thought I was in better shape than this. This is pathetic. I bet I haven't even walked a mile in half an hour.*

Her breathing was so loud she didn't hear the car until it pulled up beside her. The black Mustang convertible gleamed in the sunlight. Trixie Frayne sat in the driver's seat. "What happened? Need a ride?"

"You're a lifesaver. I don't think I could have taken another step." Skye slid gingerly into the passenger side.

As Skye sagged against the seat, she explained to Trixie about her grandmother's death and what had happened with the twins.

Trixie whistled. "Those cousins of yours are wild. Remember how they used to trade clothes and try to trick your grandmother when she babysat for them?"

"Yes, they tried that on their teachers too, but Grandma fixed their wagon. After they traded identities one too many times, she grabbed them both and put a big red Magic Marker dot on Gillian's forehead and a matching black circle on Ginger." Skye smirked. "It took a week for those marks to wear off. Everybody and his uncle asked them what had happened. By the end, even I felt kind of sorry for them."

Trixie giggled. "With the way they used to torment you whenever your mothers made the three of you play together, I'm surprised you'd feel any sympathy toward those two."

"One of my many character flaws," Skye joked.

"What are you going to do about them kidnapping you?"

"Nothing. What can I do, tell their mommy?" Skye looked disgusted.

"Yeah, I guess you're right. But maybe sometime, someplace you'll get a chance to get even, and I'd love to be there." Trixie's grin was wicked. "Anyway, where can I take you? Home?"

"No, my car's at school. I hope I'm not keeping you from anything." Skye examined the blister on her heel.

"Nothing. I was just taking a ride." Trixie put the Mustang in gear.

"This is a beautiful vehicle. I can see why you'd like driving around." Skye ran an admiring hand over the upholstery.

"I bought it for my thirtieth birthday. Owen wanted me to get a minivan."

Both women looked at each other and said, "Men."

The twins' little detour had cost Skye a lot of time. It was nearly six o'clock when she turned off the Buick's ignition and exited the car in front of her cottage. She immediately noticed something was wrong.

Broken glass littered the area around the

house. The foyer and kitchen windows were shattered. Circling the house, Skye saw there was not one intact pane left on the building. She started inside, but stopped before crossing the threshold. Seizing Bingo, who had come to the door to greet her, she backed toward her car, checked the backseat for intruders, and slid inside.

After locking the doors, she sat for a moment to catch her breath. Skye was surprised to find herself shaking. Suddenly, the privacy she valued in her home's secluded location seemed like a threatening isolation. She backed the Buick onto the road and headed toward the police station.

Skye knew her mother wasn't working and she figured that Chief Boyd would have already left for the day, so she wasn't sure if she'd know anyone on duty.

The dispatcher was a stranger to her. Skye couldn't believe the woman was above the twenty-one years of age required for the job. Her name tag read "Crystal."

Taking a deep breath and smoothing her hair, Skye spoke across the counter. "Hello, my name is Skye Denison and I need to report some vandalism to my home."

Crystal wrinkled her forehead. "Like, okay, ma'am, but the, uhm, officer is out patrolling."

"Could you radio for him to come in? I'll wait." Skye frowned. *Ma'am? Do I look like a ma'am? How old does she think I am? I'll never go to bed without putting on my face lotion again.*

"Uhm, well, okay, but it could be a while." Crystal sat down in front of her console and grimaced.

Skye took a seat in the cracked vinyl bench provided for those who had business with the police.

Only a few minutes had gone by and she was rummaging in her purse for something to eat, having missed lunch and not yet had dinner, when the door was flung open.

Officer Quirk marched past her and leaned across the counter. "Crystal, how many times have you been told not to mention names on the radio?"

Crystal chewed on a nail. "Sorry, I forgot." Her face darkened. "Like, there are too many rules and things to remember. This is way harder than my last job."

Quirk seemed to see Skye for the first time. "Her last job was of the fast-food variety," he said. "She told us it was too much pressure."

Skye followed Quirk to the back of the station into a room with a table and chairs. "So why did she get hired here? She's obviously a few fries short of a Happy Meal."

Quirk grabbed a pen and a clipboard with a pad of forms attached, then sat at the table. "Did you catch her full name?"

Sitting across from him, Skye pursed her lips. "No. What is it?"

"Clapp, Crystal Clapp."

"That's awful. So she was hired out of pity?" Skye arched a brow.

"No, she was hired out of self-preservation. Eldon Clapp, our beloved mayor, is her father." Quirk sat back, his leather utility belt squeaking. "Now what can I do for you, Ms. Denison?"

Skye explained about the windows and reminded him that earlier in the week her tires had been slashed.

"Sounds like you've got an enemy. Can you think of anyone who would want to harass you?" Quirk didn't look up from the form he was filling out.

Her mind flew to the Yoders, Hap Doozier, and the Underwoods before flitting briefly to the twins and her Uncle Dante. She took a deep breath. "Would you like the list alphabetically or divided by family versus workplace?"

CHAPTER 8

LADYBUG, LADYBUG,

FLY AWAY HOME

After finishing with Quirk, Skye called her insurance agent, a cousin on her father's side. "Kevin, this is Skye. How're you doing?"

"Fine, fine. Sorry to hear about your grandma."

"Thanks." Skye took a deep, calming breath. It was difficult to talk about her. "I'll really miss her."

"Yeah, I remember you were close to Antonia. When you were gone for so many years it seemed like, besides your parents and Vince, she was the only one you kept in contact with. I think our mutual grandma was a little jealous."

"I sent Grandma Denison a postcard every week I was away." Skye felt guilty she hadn't been to see that grandmother in a while. "Anyway, the reason I called is business rather than family. The cottage I'm renting was vandalized."

125

Kevin's tone became serious. "Are you all right?"

"I'm fine. I wasn't home at the time. On first glance it looks like they broke all the windows, but I didn't go inside."

"Did you report this to the police?" Kevin sounded concerned.

"I'm calling from the station. Officer Quirk is filing the necessary papers and has headed out to investigate. Can you believe he ordered me not to go with him?" Skye frowned at the memory.

"Yes, I can believe it. Especially after your adventure in investigation last fall. Let the police do the job they're paid to do." He paused, as if reluctant to ask the next question. "Did you ever get the check for your car?"

"Not yet, and I need it so I can give Grandma's Buick back to the estate. Isn't there anything you can do? The company did finally admit my car was totaled."

"There was some hang-up because technically the damage didn't occur due to an accident. Still, I thought they had resolved that issue. I'll check on it tomorrow." Kevin paused again. "Did I hear that your tires were slashed a couple days ago?"

"Yes." She answered cautiously, wondering what his question was leading up to.

"Are you going to make a claim?" he asked.

"Shouldn't I?"

"I wouldn't recommend it. Your premium has already been raised because of the other incidents. And you'd barely get anything after the deductible. You really need to be more careful."

"Yeah, right. Like I go around trying to get my property destroyed." Skye abruptly changed the subject. "So, what's the drill for my windows?"

Kevin sighed. "Get two estimates. Have the cheapest do the work. Send us the bill and the police report. If everything is in order, we'll cut you a check."

"That's it? Where am I supposed to live while all this is done?"

"You opted for the cheap policy, remember? It doesn't provide for motel stays or rental cars."

"Oh, yeah, that's right." Skye chewed her lip. "I just didn't have the extra hundred at the time and I didn't want to ask my parents for money." Skye clutched the receiver. "So, that's it, then. Anyone you can recommend to do the job?"

"We aren't allowed to make suggestions. All we do is pay the bill. Provided you follow directions." Kevin sounded uncomfortable.

"I see. So I'm covered with you guys as long as I don't actually need anything." Skye hung up the phone.

She looked around the police station. Its walls were painted a gray semigloss. Probably so they would wash down easily. The table where she sat was rectangular with a peeling wood-grained plastic top. Not exactly fancy, but imparting a certain comfort.

Skye was reluctant to make the next call, but she knew it would be better to break the news herself than let the grapevine get first crack at it.

Finally, she raised the receiver and punched in the seven digits that were as familiar as her Social Security number. "Hi, Mom, it's Skye."

May was quiet when Skye told her about the windows, distressed when she heard that the farmhouse had been searched, and sobbing when she was told about Mrs. Jankowski. She ordered Skye home immediately.

"But, Mom, I've got to go back to the cottage to pick up some clothes and toiletries." She hesitated. "And, you do realize, I'll have to bring Bingo with me."

"Can't you leave the cat there? It'll be okay overnight." The distaste sounded thick in May's throat.

128

"There's glass all over. He could cut himself. It's either both of us or neither. Maybe it'd be better if I got a cabin at Uncle Charlie's motor court."

May sighed. "No. No. I guess you can bring that animal here. Your dad will meet you at your place in fifteen minutes."

"Dad doesn't need to come. Quirk is checking it out."

May went on as if she hadn't heard Skye. "Don't go in without him."

"Look, it's silly to bother Dad. I'll be at your house in twenty minutes, tops."

"Are you trying to give me a heart attack?" May's voice thickened with tears. "Wait for your father. Just this once, do it my way."

"Yes, Mom."

When Skye got back to her car, she found Bingo standing with his front paws on the window ledge, peering into the darkness. Gently moving him over so she could slide in, Skye felt his sides vibrating in happy purrs. As soon as she was settled, he tried to climb onto her lap.

Shifting him to the passenger seat, Skye put the car in gear and drove off. When they arrived at the cottage, Quirk was gone and Jed hadn't yet shown up.

Skye stroked the cat's lush black fur and let her thoughts tumble through her mind like clothes in a dryer. She had forgotten to telephone Simon again. When he heard everything that had happened he was going to be ticked that she hadn't called him for help.

Maybe she could go inside and call him right then, before her father arrived. Skye looked at the door. It was nearly eight and shadows were forming everywhere.

Before she could get out of the car, her father braked his old blue pickup next to her and walked toward the entrance cradling a shotgun. "Stay in back of me." Jed was not one for idle chitchat.

Skye trailed a few steps behind her dad, feeling like a child. She shouldn't have waited for him. The police had checked out the house and it was safe. She should be doing this by herself.

Jed held out his hand for the keys. Skye rummaged through the inside zippered section of her purse for the spare set since she had given Officer Quirk the ones she normally carried on her ring. Jed tapped his foot impatiently.

After he opened the door, Jed whispered, "Wait here until I check things out."

"Officer Quirk was already through the

place once," Skye whispered back. "Let's just go in, I'll pack, and we can get out of here."

"After I take a look." He gave her a stern look. "Stay."

Skye was leaning against the railing, thinking that if he spoke to his dog, Chocolate, the way he had just spoken to her, maybe he could finally train the animal. Then she heard gunshots.

Without thinking she rocketed through the door, slamming into her father in the foyer as he charged out of the living room. Both of them stumbled back. Jed sat abruptly on the hall bench and Skye fell sprawled to the wooden floor. Without speaking, Jed struggled to his feet, grabbed Skye by the back of the collar, and dragged her out the door. She felt like a crab walking backwards.

Outside, he continued to pull her behind him, not stopping until they were in his truck with the doors locked.

Skye gasped for breath. "What happened?"

"Saw someone in your front room. Came toward me and I shot 'em." Jed snatched the mike from his CB and put in a call to the police.

"But I heard more shots. Did they shoot

131

back?" Skye looked anxiously at her father.

"Yup. That's when I hightailed it out of there." Jed took a red hanky from his pocket and wiped the sweat off his face.

Only a minute or two passed before Quirk's squad car squealed into the driveway, lights flashing and siren screaming.

Quirk and a man dressed as a sheriff's deputy jumped out of the cruiser, conferred briefly with Jed, then approached the cottage. Skye watched them split up, the deputy going toward the back. Quirk peeked into windows and crept around corners.

He finally entered the house after shouting, "Police!"

Moments later, Quirk and the deputy emerged holding something that glinted in the headlights.

"Mr. Denison, I believe this is what you saw." Quirk motioned to the deputy and they held the object up between them.

It had once been a bouquet of giant Mylar balloons. The brightly colored spheres now dangled, deflated and full of holes, from the small sack of sand designed to keep them from floating to the ceiling.

Skye's brows met over her nose. "How did that get inside my house?"

Quirk looked uncomfortable. "It was delivered when I was here looking at your window damage. I let the guy put it in the living room. He set the arrangement on the floor since it was so big. The balloons floated about five feet from the ground."

"The sound of the balloons popping when Dad shot them must have been what we thought was someone returning fire," Skye offered. The men nodded. "What he thought was a person coming at him was probably the balloons swaying forward in a breeze from the broken windows."

The deputy rocked on his heels. "Yup. It could have happened that way."

They stood in silence until Skye said, "I wonder who the balloons were from. Was there a card?"

Shrugging, Quirk rested his hand on his gun. "I didn't see one."

"I'll check with Simon. They were probably from him." Skye turned to Quirk. "Is it okay to go in now? I need to pack a few things. I'm going to stay with my parents until the windows are fixed."

The men communed silently. Finally, Quirk spoke. "I think the chief would be less likely to chew my butt off if I escorted you. Try to make it quick, all right?"

Skye readjusted the strap of her canvas

briefcase over her shoulder as she climbed the steep steps to the high school's front entrance. Her head ached from lack of sleep after having stared at the ceiling all night, trying to figure out who hated her enough to slash her tires and break her windows.

She fought waves of nausea and a headache caused by a breakfast too large, a morning too hot, and a firing squad waiting for her behind the glass doors.

May had insisted Skye eat every bite of the many dishes she had prepared. Being accustomed to only tea and toast in the morning, Skye felt as force-fed as a calf about to become veal.

Once again Skye had tried to take a day off by using a personal day, but this time she'd been told the superintendent wanted to see her at nine sharp. A parent had made a complaint against her.

Nervously clearing her throat, Skye made eye contact with the superintendent's secretary, a tall, voluptuous woman in her late forties with wavy red hair floating over her shoulders. Everyone insisted that she was having an affair with her boss, but no one could prove it.

Skye tried smiling. "Hi, Karolyn. I understand Dr. Wraige wants to see me."

Karolyn arched a perfectly plucked eyebrow and made a show of flipping the pages in her appointment book. "Yes, I see you're down for nine." She looked up at the clock and tsked. "You're a few minutes early and he's on the phone."

Having not been offered a seat, Skye stood off to one side watching the minutes tick by. The outer office was old-fashioned, with dark wood paneling and matching furnishings. The computer terminal on the back wall looked out of place.

She was about to ask to use the adjoining rest room when the phone buzzed and Karolyn rose from her desk. She unlatched the waist-high gate and allowed Skye into the inner office. Knocking once, Karolyn opened the door slightly and stood back.

As soon as Skye squeezed her way through, the door was pulled shut. The superintendent sat in a huge leather chair behind a massive walnut desk. Matching onyx in-box, pencil cup, and blotter were the only items on its smudgeless glass top.

He gestured for Skye to take a seat in one of the wing chairs facing him.

Dr. Wraige laced his fingers across his chest and stared through watery blue eyes. His gray hair, swept back in a pompadour, was the exact shade of his suit and skin. After a few moments of intimidating silence, he spoke. "Miss Denison, we seem to have a little problem."

"Oh?" Skye knew how to play the waiting game, even if she didn't enjoy it.

He drummed his fingers on his stomach. "It seems that one of your recent decisions has caused an upset for some parents."

Her mind raced. *Which ones? The Yoders, Mr. Doozier, the Underwoods? I can't let on there is more than one.* "I see. What exactly is the problem?"

"Don't play coy with me. It's Mayor Clapp's son." The superintendent leaned forward. "He was not happy with the results of your evaluation."

"Why?" Skye was truly confused.

This had been a strange case all along. Cray Clapp was a senior with good grades and a top five-percent ranking in his class. When Skye had first received the referral, she had turned it down since the boy did not seem to have any characteristics that would suggest a learning disability. His IQ and achievement seemed to match, and if he had any processing problems, they weren't interfering with his learning.

The high school principal, Homer Knapik, had ordered her to do the assessment regardless. So, she had wasted three hours of her time and the student's. And as she'd suspected, he'd shown no sign of having a learning disability.

Dr. Wraige squirmed. "Perhaps you're not aware of Cray's score on the ACT."

"No, I can't say that I am." Skye looked puzzled. "That's not the type of testing I do."

"I'm cognizant of that." He scowled. "But you do know that to gain admittance to a top university one has to have the grades, the class rank, and a top ACT score."

"Yes. Last time I checked, a school such as the University of Illinois required anywhere from a twenty-seven to twenty-nine to be accepted by their various colleges."

"Correct. Cray scored a twenty-four." Dr. Wraige's eyes bored into hers.

Skye frowned. "I'm sorry to be so dense, but what does that have to do with me?"

He sat back in his chair and spoke slowly, as if to someone who was not very bright. "If Cray is certified as having a handicapping condition, such as a learning disability, he is allowed certain modifications when taking the ACT. These can include more time, calculators, dictionaries . . . Need I go on?"

"No. I understand." She sagged. "You want me to lie so the mayor's son can get a score he doesn't deserve."

Dr. Wraige scowled. "That statement was impertinent."

She didn't speak.

"Look, you and I both know that psychological testing is not always as precise as we would like to think." He oozed sincerity. "Isn't it possible that you could have overlooked something in your evaluation of Cray Clapp?"

Reluctantly, she nodded. "It's not like a blood test. There is a lot that affects the assessment."

"Exactly. All I'm asking is that you take another look at your results and see if there's anything you might have missed." He opened his drawer and withdrew a sheaf of papers, which he handed to her. "I called Springfield and got this information on students who have both a gifted-level IQ and a learning disability. Maybe they'll point you in a different direction."

"How did you get the state to respond so quickly? It takes them months when I request information." Skye flipped through the pages in her lap.

"Friends in the right places." He smiled insincerely. "You know. You do me a favor, then I owe you one. It's how the big boys play."

CHAPTER 9

LITTLE BOY BLUE,

GO BLOW YOUR HORN

Skye had worked the rest of the day at the elementary school finishing up odds and ends. Now she sat in her borrowed Buick and considered her life. She couldn't go to her cottage. She had called around and the fastest anyone would agree to come and fix the windows was in two weeks.

She still hadn't gotten the insurance check so she couldn't afford to buy a car. And now it looked like she might lose her job.

The superintendent's wanting her to change her test results was so similar to the situation that had gotten her fired from her last school that she wondered if she had missed the day in graduate school when the professor told the class it was okay to falsify records if it meant keeping your job. In both cases her superior wanted her to lie in order to appease someone with power and money.

In New Orleans, the coordinator of special education had ordered her to withdraw her allegation of child abuse. Skye had refused to retract her report, even after the little girl was pressured into saying she had made the whole event up.

Could she go through that again? If she got fired this time, she'd never find another job as a school psychologist. Skye's thoughts grew darker and she sank farther down in the seat, her chin resting on her chest. All those years of education would go down the tubes and she'd be left with nothing but her student loans to repay.

Squealing brakes and a slamming car door roused her from her rumination. Her heart started pounding faster when she heard the slap of leather soles on asphalt. Was someone else coming to harass her? Straightening from her slumped position, she was just in time to see Simon appear outside her windshield. He crossed his arms and looked down at her.

Skye opened the passenger door and motioned him inside.

"Have you been avoiding me?" Simon raised an eyebrow.

"No. My life just sort of got out of hand."

"That seems to happen to you a lot." His voice was steely.

She twitched, feeling that their relationship was another aspect of her life that was slipping out of her control. "Shoot. I've been meaning to call you." It was good to see him, although he was clearly irritated with her. Even angry, he always seemed so calm, so together. She had always been attracted to sophisticated men. "Sorry."

While Skye told him about being kidnapped by her cousins, the new set of crazy parents, and her broken windows, Simon put his arm around her and hugged her wordlessly. She deliberately left out the superintendent's ultimatum, afraid to hear Simon's advice.

"You've had a tough week."

"Yes, I have. Before I forget, I wanted to thank you for the balloon bouquet."

"I didn't send you balloons. What are talking about?"

She shrugged and explained, concluding with, "I wonder who sent them." *I'll have to call around and find out.*

Simon's eyes hardened, but he remained silent.

After a few seconds of wallowing in the comfort of his arms, Skye pulled away. Simon was such a take-charge kind of guy that she feared he would take over and "fix" her life if she showed the slightest indication of allowing that to happen. "Everything's fine now. I was just a little shaken. Sorry to worry you."

He took her face in his hands and leaned forward until their lips were touching. "When all this is settled, we need to have a serious talk." He kissed her lightly and sat back.

Skye tried to keep her expression non-committal as her thoughts raced. *I can't think about that right now.*

Simon glanced at his Rolex and reached for the door handle. "Sorry to run off on you, but I've got a wake at four, and it takes at least half an hour to get everything set."

"Sure, I understand. By the way, I'm staying with my parents until my windows are fixed, so call me there. I do plan on being at work tomorrow, since it's the last day and I hate to miss the awards assembly. One of the kids I see for counseling won the essay contest." Skye craned her neck to look up at him.

"I forgot to tell you why I was looking for you in the first place." Simon squatted beside the open doorway, took her hands, and lowered his voice. "We got the results of your grandmother's autopsy. She was poisoned." He offered her the snowy white handkerchief from the breast pocket of his gray suit.

Skye waved it off. She wasn't going to cry, even though she felt a catch in her throat and was saddened that someone had shortened a life that was already starting to wane. After a few moments of silence, she took a deep breath and asked, "How about Grandma's housekeeper? It was her in the well, right?"

"Yes, it was her. We don't have results of her autopsy back yet, probably tomorrow."

"Do you anticipate any other cause of death?"

"No, it was probably the same poison that killed your grandmother." A line formed between Simon's brows. "The chief told me to share this information with you, but I can't say I approve. It's his investigation; still I don't think he should be spreading evidence around. It's hard enough to keep a secret in Scumble River."

"Maybe the chief realizes that I can help in finding out what happened to my grandmother." Skye shook off Simon's hands, remembering how she disliked his arrogance, his belief that he was always right. "And since ninety-nine percent of my job requires confidentiality, Wally probably trusts me enough to know I'll keep my mouth shut."

Simon raised an eyebrow. "There was a pan of brownies wedged in the well alongside Mrs. Jankowski. That's apparently how the poison was administered. And the stomach contents of your grandmother contained brownies."

"What kind of poison was it?" Skye asked.

"We don't know yet."

"I guess it doesn't matter. Dead is dead."

May and Jed were sitting on lawn chairs in front of the open garage when Skye drove down the gravel lane. Their house, a red brick ranch, was situated on an acre of lawn that looked like the plush fur of a green stuffed animal. Flowers lined the sidewalks and edged the buildings. Perfectly trimmed evergreens protected three sides of their lot.

A family of plaster deer stood guard near the edge of the drive, and a concrete goose dressed in a graduation cap and gown graced the back steps. Skye shook her head, wishing she could persuade her mother to get rid of the goose, or at least stop dressing it up.

Skye yelled a greeting to her parents as she slid out of the car and headed inside. She showered and changed into blue denim shorts and an orange University of Illinois T-shirt. A quick check showed Bingo asleep on Skye's bed. Full food and water bowls were on the floor and his litter box was clean. Her mother might not like indoor animals, but she was sure taking good care of this one.

Skye grabbed a can of Diet Coke from the fridge and slid her feet into sandals, then joined her parents outside.

Not surprisingly, May spoke first. "So what was so important that you had to go into work?"

Skye contemplated the issue of confidentiality before speaking. "I'm not sure how much I can tell you. There's a youngster I evaluated and did not find learning disabled. If he had been diagnosed with an LD handicap he would get certain help in taking the college entrance exams, which would probably raise his scores. His father is pressuring the superintendent to make me change my mind and call him LD."

"And if you don't?" May asked.

"Dr. Wraige never said, but I had a feeling I would be fired." Skye slumped against the side of the garage. Just saying the word made her feel weak.

"I think I'll invite Charlie to dinner tonight." May hopped up from her chair.

"That wouldn't be because he's president of the school board, would it?"

May shrugged. "Of course not. It's just been a while since he's been over and since you're here, I thought it would be nice for him to get a chance to visit with his god-daughter."

"Thanks, Mom, but Uncle Charlie has done enough by helping me get this job in the first place. I'll work this one out on my own." Skye leaned down to scratch a mosquito bite.

"Okay, but call him if things get rough." May continued into the house, talking over her shoulder. "I've got to check on dinner."

Jed took a swallow from his can of beer and stared off at the fields. "I hired Warner Post to fix your windows. He said they'll have it done by Sunday."

"But I already called around. Everyone told me it would be two weeks before they could even start. I hired someone else."

Jed crossed his arms. "They'll be fixed before those other guys get around to it."

"Dad, you don't have to do stuff like this. I can take care of it myself."

"It's better to hire people we know."

Skye took her mother's vacant seat, leaned back, and contemplated the clouds. Finally she said, "Thanks. But from now on let me handle stuff like this myself. I'll ask for help if I need to."

Jed adjusted his cap. "I'll go out to-morrow and make sure they're working."

She counted to ten, all the while reminding herself how much her parents loved her. "Thanks, Dad. I've got to go into school tomorrow since it's the last day." Skye sipped her soda. "I'd better go give Mom a hand with dinner." Skye headed toward the door.

May was peering into the oven when Skye entered the kitchen. The smell of roasting beef made her mouth water, and reminded her that she had eaten only a few crackers and cheese for lunch.

She leaned against the counter. "Mom, have you spoken to Chief Boyd lately?"

"I'm working midnights this week so he talked to me this morning when he came in at seven. I know Grandma was poisoned."

"Did he tell you about the pan of brownies?" Skye reached to get plates from the cabinet.

"Yes. He's going to have everyone in the family back in for questioning." May's expression didn't give away her feelings. "He also said I could go in and clean up the mess from the search."

"Want me to help?"

"No, I'll do it tomorrow morning when you're at school."

They were silent as Skye set the table and May stirred a pot on the stove.

Skye finally said, "I'm sorry. I didn't want to be right."

May put down the wooden spoon and wrapped her arms around Skye. "It's okay. Bad as it may be, I want to know who murdered my mother." She held Skye away from her and looked into her eyes. "But the others probably won't feel that way."

"Especially the one who killed her."

"Maybe it wasn't one of the family." May turned back to her cooking.

"Maybe. Do you know anything about those survivalists who were bugging Grandma?" Skye drummed her fingers on the countertop.

"Not really. We've had a lot of complaints about them at the police station, but we haven't been able to catch them in the act or get any evidence against them." May narrowed her eyes. "Why? Do you think they may have had something to do with Mom's death?"

"I don't know, but I'm going to talk to the chief after school tomorrow and make sure he investigates them."

"I could talk to Wally."

"No, I need to ask him about other stuff too." Skye didn't want to admit that she wanted to find out who in the family had an alibi and who didn't.

"Just remember he's a married man," May muttered.

"For crying out loud. I was fifteen when I had that crush on him. It's been sixteen years. Give it a rest."

"I don't like the way you two look at each other." May shook her head. "Tell Dad to come in. Supper's almost ready."

Skye was more than willing to change the subject. "What are we having?"

"Stuffed round steak, green bean casserole, salad, and corn muffins." Steam billowed out of the oven door as May removed the roasting pan.

When Skye got back from calling her father, May was ready to slice the meat. She had placed it on a wooden cutting board and held a huge carving knife. Golden stuffing oozed from each portion as she set it aside and went on to the next. The smell of sage mixed with the aroma of roast beef.

While Jed washed up in the half bath off the utility room, Skye set various bowls and platters on the table. May poured iced tea for Skye and herself. Jed brought his can of Miller Lite with him.

After the food was passed to everyone and they had started to eat, Jed said, "Have you been out by the old Leofanti farm lately?"

Skye wondered if Jed had heard about the

twins kidnapping her. "Yes, I took a ride out there yesterday. Why?"

"How about you, Ma?" Jed helped himself to another muffin.

"No. Can't say as I have. Why?" May reached for her glass.

"The Barillos sold ninety acres to a housing developer." When the women didn't respond, he elaborated: "It shares an eastern boundary with the Leofanti land."

"Shit." Skye set her fork down.

May gave her a stern look. "I won't have language like that in here, young lady."

"Sorry, Mom." Skye took a sip of tea. "Does that mean that whole area has been zoned for housing now?"

"Probably only the Barillo farm, but it makes it a whole lot easier now to get the zoning changed on the neighboring land too." Jed finished his meal and laid his silverware across his empty plate.

May dashed from the table and returned with a lemon meringue pie. She sliced it and slid the wedges onto dessert plates. Adding forks, she passed them to Jed and Skye.

Skye forced herself to take a few bites of the pie, not wanting to hurt May's feelings, but her appetite was ruined. Ninety acres to a housing developer, at nearly one house per acre, meant more people trying to use roads that weren't designed for such numbers, more kids in an already crowded school system, and worst of all, less land being used for farming.

After he had eaten his pie, Jed stood and headed toward the back door. He and May had their usual argument as to what part of the leftovers Chocolate, their Labrador retriever, was entitled to consume; then Jed said, "Can you believe a hundred new families moving in almost next door?"

"The last day of school." Skye felt the magic in those words as she repeated them to herself.

Ten weeks of summer vacation stretched ahead of her without deadlines, meetings, or alarm clocks. Refreshed from her morning swim, she whistled as she sat in her office at the junior high, cleaning out her file cabinet.

The satisfying act of shredding paper was interrupted by the PA. "Ms. Denison, please report to the office, Ms. Denison."

Sighing, Skye stopped what she was doing and made her way to the front of the building.

Ursula motioned Skye into the principal's office.

Skye's heart raced when she found her

Aunt Mona sitting across from Neva Llewellyn. "Aunt Mona, did something happen to Mom?"

"No. I'm here on school business." Her impersonal blue eyes raked Skye.

"Oh." Skye felt such relief she was almost giddy. She sat next to her aunt and faced the principal. "What's up?"

Neva shook her head slightly and gestured for Mona to answer.

Mona turned to Skye. "It's about the ceremony this morning. I'm chairwoman of the awards committee and I've just been going over the list of winning students with my delegation. One of the mothers recognized the name of the author of the prize-winning essay, and told me this boy has barely made it through junior high. So I had Ursula run off a copy of his discipline record. There were so many detentions it took the computer ten minutes to print them all up."

"I see." Skye searched Neva's face for a clue as to why she was being involved. Actually, the secretary should not have given her aunt that information without a signed release of records from the child's parents.

Neva started to answer, "It turns out this boy is someone you see for counseling and we —"

152

Mona interrupted. "So we've decided to go with the second-place entry instead. It is written by a lovely girl who has never caused a moment's trouble."

Neva refused to meet Skye's eyes. "Since the boy was already notified, we thought it might be better if you told him he won't be getting the award after all. We're sure you can put it to him gently and make him see it's for the best."

"Who are we talking about?" Skye stalled.

"Justin Boward." Mona's lips twisted as if she tasted something putrid.

"The eighth-grade English teacher was most impressed with his writing," Neva added. "Although his topic was somewhat controversial."

"Exactly. Neal would be appalled if I allowed a pro-choice essay to win a prize. After all, he is the head of the Knights of Columbus." Mona straightened a pleat in her white silk skirt. "It is inappropriate for someone like this boy to triumph. People would think that we approved of his type of good-for-nothing behavior."

Skye picked her words carefully, fully intending to maintain the confidentiality of her sessions with Justin. "I've worked with Justin all year. He's a youngster who, although very smart, refuses to put any effort into doing well at school. As you know, he is passing eighth grade by the thinnest of margins."

"Exactly." Mona smiled meanly.

"There are a lot of interpersonal and emotional reasons for his behavior, which I can't share with you, but I've made some progress with him. I discovered that he loves to read, as long as it isn't a class assignment, and that he has a talent for writing. With my encouragement he was motivated to enter the contest."

Mona said, "A prize like this should go to a serious student who has put forth effort all year. Not someone who rattles off a paper at the last minute."

"If you take this prize away from him after you've already told him he won, you will be reinforcing every negative thing he already believes about authority figures." Skye looked from her aunt to the principal. "You will undo an entire year's worth of therapy."

Mona shrugged and patted Skye on the knee. "Quite frankly, Skye, I don't much believe that mumbo jumbo. Neal says it's more like the work of the devil than of Jesus."

"How can he say that? Even the church offers counseling." Skye squared her shoulders and clenched the arms of her chair.

"Well, that's completely different." Mona crossed her arms and sat back.

"I'll take care of this from here, Mona," Neva said. "Perhaps you'd give us a few minutes alone?"

Mona picked up her purse and walked toward the door. "Then I'll see you in the gym."

As soon as Mona left, Skye shot out of her chair and leaned on Neva's desk. "Why do people who know the least know it the loudest? And why are you letting her get away with this?"

Neva stood. "That was getting us nowhere. Skye, the decision has been made. Justin Boward is not getting the award." When Skye tried to interrupt, Neva raised her hand, palm out. "There are too many people in Scumble River who feel as your aunt does, and the school district is planning a referendum in the near future. We can't afford to offend such a vocal part of our voters."

"I won't be the one to tell him."

"That's fine with me. I have no problem telling Justin. But is your refusal to tell him in his best interest or because you're in a snit?" Neva asked quietly.

Skye's reason fought with her emotions. "Okay, I'll tell him, but nothing I can say is going to make up to him for this betrayal."

Before leaving the office, Skye asked that Justin be paged and told to report to Ms. Denison. They met at her doorway. She noted that instead of his usual T-shirt and baggy shorts, he wore a white shirt and tie, with black dress pants.

His mood was different too. He stood tall and looked her in the eye, speaking without being prompted to do so. "What's up, Ms. Denison? I can't stay long today. The awards ceremony starts in a few minutes. Can you come and watch me get my trophy?"

Skye closed her eyes briefly and wondered what she was going to say. They hadn't covered a situation like this in graduate school.

"Ah, Ms. Denison, are you okay?"

How could she destroy this kid just because some committee felt he wasn't "good enough"? He had come so far. When she had first started to see him they had gone whole forty-minute sessions exchanging fewer than ten words apiece. He never made eye contact and was failing all his classes.

She knew now that whatever she said and however she said it, her words were going to destroy Justin's emerging faith in adults. Skye wished she had more experience. She had no idea how to minimize this kind of damage.

Finally, she took a deep breath and spoke. "You really like *Star Trek*, don't you? You watch all the reruns, right?"

He nodded, looking confused.

"Do you always think that the captain does the right thing, makes the right decision?"

Justin looked at her strangely. "No, not always, but usually."

"If you were a member of the *Star Trek* crew, would you go against the captain when he or she gave an order you thought was wrong?"

After a long pause, he shook his head. "No, that would be mutiny. But I would enter a protest into my log."

"Well, I'm sort of in that position now. Mrs. Llewellyn has ordered me to tell you something I don't agree with, and I don't think she agrees with it either, but her boss has ordered her to do it." Skye leaned forward and put her hand over his as it lay on the table. "Justin, I'm sorry to have to say that you won't be getting the award for best essay after all."

Justin jerked his hand away and scrunched up his face. "Why? What happened?"

"They decided to give the prize to the second-place winner. They thought, even though you're a great writer, hers was better when all things were considered." Skye didn't want to tell him he was considered unworthy, but she was also trying not to lie.

His shoulders slumped and he turned to leave. "It figures. The whole thing was bogus anyway. I knew I wasn't good enough to win."

Skye got up and joined him at the door. "That's not true, Justin. You are a great writer and I can't explain this. But just remember, even the captains on *Star Trek* occasionally make mistakes. And this is one of those times."

"Can I go now?" He refused to look at her.

"Are you okay?"

He nodded, once.

"I'm really sorry. Don't let this ruin your summer."

Justin shrugged. He was back in nonverbal mode. All those months of therapy had been lost.

"I'll see you next year in high school."

Another shrug and he was gone.

Skye sat down at her desk and reached for the phone. She needed to notify Justin's parents, so they'd be prepared when he arrived home. When she got their answering machine it dawned on her that they were probably already at the school for the awards ceremony.

Great. She'd have to find them before the program began. How could Neva and Mona do this to a family? Her hand clenched around the ceramic jar she had been fingering. It had the word MIRACLES printed across the front. She had purchased it when she finished college. Suddenly she snatched it off her desk and hurled it at the wall. As she watched the jar explode into tiny fragments she smiled grimly. There were no miracles in this job.

CHAPTER 10

DIDDLE, DIDDLE DUMPLING,

MY SON GUS

After finding the Bowards, explaining what had happened, and directing them to Neva to lodge their grievance, Skye left the school. It was only one o'clock, but there was no way she was sitting through that particular awards ceremony. It would feel too hypocritical. She would return that evening to help chaperon the graduation.

She pulled into the police department's parking lot. Only two vehicles occupied slots — Thea's old Chevy and her brother's Jeep. What was Vince doing there? Surely he wasn't a suspect this time. It had been a nightmare last fall when he had been accused of murdering a Chicago TV star. Skye hurried across the asphalt and thrust the glass door open.

Thea, the dispatcher, greeted her. "Skye, honey, don't you look cute as a bunny in that pink outfit."

"Thanks, Thea. Is my brother here?"

"Yep, he and the chief are talking." Thea reached for the phone, but let it slide back into the cradle. "They been talking long enough. You go up there and see what's going on."

"Thanks." Skye flashed the dispatcher a smile and ran up the steps. Thea had been one of Vince's staunchest supporters when the police had tried to pin last September's murder on him.

She could hear the two men's voices as she rushed down the hall. Their tones sounded calm. As she pushed open the half-closed door, both men turned toward her.

Wally spoke first. "Skye, I didn't expect to see you here today."

"There were a couple things about Grandma's death I wanted to talk over with you. Simon told me about the poison."

"Good. Vince and I are about done. You might as well pull up a chair."

"Thanks."

The chief picked up a piece of paper and gestured toward Vince. "So, this is a list of customers you had the day your grandmother died?"

Vince nodded. "Yes. I started at seven that morning and didn't leave the shop until Simon called me around five."

"Is there anyone who can vouch for you

before seven?" Wally asked.

"Yes, ah, I was with someone from about eight o'clock the night before." Vince glanced at Skye and his ears turned red. He scribbled something on a slip of paper and slid it over to the chief. "That's her name. I'd appreciate it if you kept this quiet."

"I'll check it out personally. No one else will have to know."

Skye stared at Vince. Who had he spent the night with? He was supposed to be going out with Abby Fleming, the school nurse.

The chief stood and walked around his desk. "Sounds like you're in good shape."

The men shook hands.

Vince turned to Skye before leaving. "Stop by the shop tomorrow if you get a chance, will you?"

"Sure." *And you can tell me who your new girlfriend is.* "I'll be over sometime in the afternoon." Skye closed her eyes and smiled. "Tomorrow is the first day of summer vacation. I'm sleeping until noon."

"At Mom and Dad's?" Vince smirked. "Dream on."

After Vince's departure, Wally took the chair next to Skye. She wished he'd go back behind his desk. Distance was a good thing where she and the chief were concerned.

"So, what's up?" Wally smiled warmly.

162

"Well, one thing I wanted to mention to you was that those survivalists out by the farm had been annoying my grandmother for months, and I was wondering if you'd checked them out."

"I talked to some of them. They probably did trespass and hunt out of season, but I can't really see a motive for them killing her."

"Maybe she saw something she shouldn't have. She liked to sit with binoculars and watch the birds."

"If she was shot, maybe, but I can't see them baking poison brownies. Or her eating them if they were a gift from those people."

Skye was unconvinced, but she didn't have anything solid to offer the chief. She'd have to check them out herself. "I see from Vince you're examining alibis. How is everyone checking out?"

"This is strictly between you and me." Wally turned and grabbed a file. "I don't think the police commissioners would be happy to find out I was discussing this case with a civilian, but I'm sorry for not taking more seriously what you said the day you found your grandmother."

She pushed her hair back over her shoulder. "Thanks. I promise to be discreet. All I want is to help you figure out what happened. Being a member of the family, I have access to facts you don't, but unless I know what you already have I may not realize what info is important and what isn't."

Wally nodded. "That's my thinking too. And I'm convinced it wasn't you or Vince. And your parents were together until about four that day. They had gone out to breakfast at seven, then to Kankakee to Farm and Fleet and a few other stores. Both the waitress and clerks remember them. So, I'm comfortable with this arrangement." He sat back and crossed his legs. All the good old boy humor left his face. "Just don't let me down. I've never been able to forgive a betrayal."

This was one of the things that made Wally so attractive to her. He was straightforward and could admit when he was wrong. She leaned toward him, their knees almost touching. "I'd never do anything to damage your trust in me."

He smiled and brushed her cheek with a knuckle. "I'm counting on that." He turned and picked up a different folder. "Even though the pan of brownies could have been dropped off anytime, we figure Mrs. J was put into the well sometime between noon and three."

"Mrs. J wasn't real big, but I don't think I

could get her down the stairs and all the way to the well." Skye tapped her chin with her finger.

"It'd be easy to shove her down the stairs and then it's flat ground from then on," Wally said. "We found a child's wagon in the garage that matches the tire tracks in the grass. Whoever did it used the wagon to haul Mrs. J from the house to the well and once they were there they just tipped her in."

"Any fingerprints?"

"Nope, everything was wiped clean." Wally threw the manila file on his desk.

"Do you suppose it was the murderer I heard in the garage that day?"

"Seems a good possibility."

Skye shivered. It really had been stupid to go out to that garage. "You didn't say anything about alibis for my aunts, uncles, and cousins."

Wally shrugged. "It's hard to pin the rest of them down. Ginger and Gillian were at work most of the day, but both left to do errands on their lunch hour. Minnie was supposedly in Urbana, but she had no appointments during that time period so she could have driven back and forth."

Skye scratched her head. "And let me guess. Dante, Emmett, and Neal were in their fields, alone."

"Right. Mona was alone too, at her house. Then she went to Joliet to the dentist and shopping. But her appointment wasn't until three. Olive was alone until Dante came home about four and they went to the auction around five. And Hugo was at work at the car lot, but it was a slow day and there were long stretches of time when he was without a customer."

"So any one of them could have done it."

"Afraid so."

Skye looked around the Scumble River High School gym. The bleachers were extended to their fullest length and folding chairs filled the floor. All the lights were blazing from protective cages in the ceiling. The scents of flowers and perfume competed with the long-entrenched effluvium of sweat and the unique hormonal odor of teenagers.

A scattering of people had already claimed seats in the front rows. They chatted with each other, read the program, and otherwise amused themselves while waiting for the ceremony to begin. Three or four small children raced up and down the aisles, looking sweaty and uncomfortable in their dress clothes.

Leaning against the entrance, Skye remembered her own graduation thirteen years ago. She had stood on that very stage as the valedictorian of her class. Back then she thought she knew everything. She was sure Scumble River had nothing to offer her, and life would be perfect if she could just get away from her hometown. She had yearned for bright lights and sophistication without understanding the cost involved in acquiring those wishes.

She had thought everyone else was dumb, but she had been the stupid one. The chance to make a speech to the whole town had gone to her head like cheap wine. And as with too much cheap wine, when she finally woke up, years later, she had a terrible hangover and faced the consequences of her actions.

Skye stared at the podium and saw herself giving the infamous valedictory speech in which she had told the whole town how little she thought of it and its residents. Now she had been back for ten months and people had stopped reminding her of that shameful oration, but she was sure someone would mention it again tonight.

Suddenly the PA cut into her thoughts. "Ms. Denison, please report to the band room."

Hurrying down the corridor, Skye won-

167

dered what was up. They were using the band room as a staging area for the senior girls. Long before she walked through the door, she heard high-pitched shrieks and screams.

From the hall she could just make out two figures rolling on the floor. Both wore pastel nylon frocks that looked more like slips than dresses. As Skye skidded into the room, a crimson-tipped hand snaked out of the melee, grabbed its opponent's fragile shoulder strap, and tore downward.

Homer Knapik, the principal, stood on one side of the writhing mass and his secretary, Opal Hill, on the other. Neither seemed to have a clue about how to stop the fight.

Skye scanned the area, looking for a way to separate the girls without resorting to physical force. She dropped her purse and grabbed a pair of cymbals lying next to a music stand. Wading through the onlookers, she got as close to the combatants as possible and banged the brass discs together with all the strength she could muster.

The brawlers stopped to cover their ears. Skye ignored the pain in her own ears, replaced the cymbals, grabbed the nearest girl by the upper arms, and dragged her out the door.

Homer nabbed the other warrior. He shouted instructions to Opal as he hurried down the hall after Skye. "Keep everyone else here."

After shoving her captive into the health room, with an order to stay put, Skye closed the door and leaned against the wall. She was just in time to see Homer put the other prisoner into his office.

Homer and Skye met at the counter. "What was that all about?" Skye asked.

"The girl in the pink is Gus Yoder's girlfriend. She was shooting her mouth off about how unfair it was that he wasn't graduating tonight with his class. The one in the yellow is the girl he attacked in the rest room." Homer took out a handkerchief and wiped his face.

"Did Miss Pink go after the other one or was it mutual?" Skye tried to get her breathing back to normal.

"From what the onlookers were saying, it sounds as if the girlfriend threw the first punch, but the one in yellow hit back." Homer wrung his hands.

"So neither can graduate?" Skye drummed her fingers on the Formica.

Homer looked at his watch. "We've got less than half an hour to decide. What do you think?"

"If Opal can get me three of the most sensible witnesses, I'll talk to them individually and see what the story is. In the meantime, I suggest you locate Miss Pink's and Miss Yellow's parents."

Skye slipped into a seat in the back of the gym. She had retrieved her purse, and taking out her compact and lipstick, she tried to fix her face, glad she had worn her chestnut curls in a French braid.

It was too bad she and Homer had been forced to remove Gus's girlfriend from participating in the graduation ceremony, but the girl had clearly been in the wrong and they couldn't afford to let her get away with breaking the rules. What kind of message would that send to the other students?

As the music started, the audience stood and faced the entrance, all eyes straining for a glimpse of the graduates. Skye noted that this was Scumble River at its most interesting. Many of the assembly were dressed in their finest T-shirts and jeans. The man in front of her wore his black-and-gray hair straggling down his back, with a grapefruit-sized bald spot in the middle of his crown.

But the real show was the graduates themselves. This class had voted against the traditional caps and gowns, so the entire fashion spectrum was visible. The first girl in line wore a long black skirt with a matching crop top. A gold hoop adorned her exposed navel. Crew socks and heavy oxfords completed the look.

Colonel Sanders came next. This boy wore a red string tie, white suit, and a full beard. One of the last in line was a girl who had mistaken graduation for the prom. She had on a floor-length satin evening gown.

When the graduating class was seated, Homer stepped up to begin his welcoming speech.

Tuning him out, Skye looked over the seniors and mused, *Well, no one can say there aren't individual thinkers in this group. At least they didn't all march out dressed exactly the same like my class did. We looked liked Barbie and Ken goes to graduation.*

She studied them more closely. Looking past the strange hair, body piercing, and odd clothing, she saw the future farmers, scientists, and teachers that these kids would eventually become, and felt an unexpected lump in her throat. Suddenly, her attention was caught by a young man who sat directly behind the graduation candidates. He slipped to the floor and then popped up in an empty chair in the seniors' row. Obviously he had crawled between the legs of the chairs.

Skye half rose from her seat. *I wonder what that's all about? Should I do something about it?* Her thoughts were detoured when the superintendent stood to pass out the diplomas and she sank back down in her chair.

The majority of names were met with polite applause, but there were a few whose families seemed so surprised that their progeny had actually completed high school that the announcement of their names was met with uncontrollable screams of joy. Most of these latter students wore the embarrassed expression teens acquire whenever their relatives show too much enthusiasm for anything.

Skye consulted her program to see how many more students still had to come up to the stage. She needed to duck out a few minutes before the end and help the kids start to form a receiving line. The last of the W's were being called, only four Z's left.

Her head jerked up as the superintendent's voice rang out, "Gustave Yoder."

The young man whom Skye had earlier observed surreptitiously changing seats rose and sauntered forward. From the stage, Homer caught her eye. She shrugged. They had been outmaneuvered.

Her composure was tested when abruptly

Gus moved to center stage and opened his mouth. Only the valedictorian was supposed to speak. Blessedly, a train chose that instant to blow its whistle and they were not forced to listen to whatever comment Gus was making. Skye could see his lips moving, but she couldn't hear a word he said.

An hour later, after everyone had finally cleared out of the gym and foyer, Homer found Skye. They walked together toward his office.

Once they were behind closed doors he asked, "What in the hell happened?"

"No doubt Yoder's girlfriend deliberately started the fight so the office would be left empty and a diploma for Gus could be snuck into the pile on the counter," Skye explained.

"But how did he get a diploma in the first place?"

"Who knows? Maybe he bribed someone at the printers, or a friend stole one from the secretary's drawer while she was in the process of typing in the names. It doesn't really matter; his transcript will still state he didn't really graduate. The diploma is just a piece of paper."

"Well, I don't like it."

"Neither do I. As usual, the woman ended up sacrificing herself for her man.

What a lesson for these girls to learn. Gus got to go through the graduation ceremony, but his girlfriend certainly did not." Skye frowned. "I'm just glad we let the other girl graduate. At least we made the right decision in that case."

Homer nodded.

"On a brighter note, maybe this will get Gus's father off our backs." Skye squared her shoulders. "And if Mr. Yoder is behind all the vandalism I've been experiencing, it better stop now. No more Ms. Nice Psychologist."

Saturday morning started much earlier than Skye wanted it to. The phone at her parents' house began ringing at six and the doorbell at eight. She and Bingo finally gave up trying to sleep and emerged from her bedroom just as her Uncle Dante was leaving.

Skye caught his parting words. "Be there at one, before the police change their minds again."

May turned the fire up under the kettle, put a cup in front of Skye, and pointed to a spot near Skye's feet. "I told you that cat stays in your room."

"But, Mom."

"Don't 'but Mom' me. Put it back now."

May held the bowl of Sweet 'N Low just out of Skye's reach.

"Sorry, baby. I'll take you with me when I run my errands today," Skye apologized to the feline as she thrust Bingo into the bedroom and hurriedly closed the door.

Her tea and toast were ready when she got back to the table. "Why was Uncle Dante here?"

May sat down with her coffee mug. "Since they've finally released Grandma's body and taken the tape off her house, he wants to get together this afternoon and have a family meeting to decide things."

"That doesn't sound like Uncle Dante. He doesn't usually ask for anyone else's opinion."

"He doesn't have any choice. Grandma's intentions are pretty clear on that point." May smiled slightly.

Skye took her things to the sink and spoke over her shoulder. "I didn't think Grandma had a will, since she had the trust and everything."

"The trust takes care of the major part of the estate, so she wrote a letter for the odds and ends. She gave it to me about six months ago, after we insisted she have Mrs. Jankowski live with her." A look of sadness crossed May's features.

"You never mentioned it."

"Grandma asked me not to." May joined Skye at the sink and turned on the water.

Skye frowned. It seemed that Grandma had kept a lot of things secret. "Do I have to be at this meeting?"

"Yes, all the children and grandchildren." May wiped a plate and set it in the drainer.

Skye dried a glass and sighed. "Won't that be jolly, now that everyone hates me?"

"Well, honey, you stirred up the stew, now you're going to have to eat it."

Vince's hair salon, Great Expectations, was located in a stand-alone building on one of Scumble River's busier corners. At twelve-thirty in the afternoon both the streets and the parking lot were empty. Skye grabbed the sack and paper cups from the passenger seat of the Buick, wiggled out of the car, and kicked the door closed with her foot.

As she approached the screen door at the front of the shop she yelled, "Vince, let me in. My hands are full."

Her brother appeared, clad only in a swimming suit. He held the door open for her and took the drinks from her hands.

"Thanks." Skye held out the sack to

Vince. "Hope you haven't eaten yet. I brought subs."

"Nope, I was taking advantage of a lull in the action and doing some tanning."

"That explains the trunks." Skye headed toward the back room and Vince followed. "I was afraid they were the new uniform for your salon."

Vince snorted. "Yeah? Well, how come your hair's like that?"

The sun had dried her hair into a mass of curls. "I just came from swimming at the recreation club."

"Oh. I'll fix it for you before you leave."

"Thanks."

They each took a chair next to the shampoo bowls and spread napkins in their laps before opening the sandwiches. They chewed companionably for a while.

"So, who were you with the night before Grandma died?" Skye asked.

Vince choked and gasped for air. After taking a drink from his cup, he finally said, "Damn it, Skye. Isn't a psychologist supposed to be a little more subtle than that?"

She shrugged. "Probably, but this is the first day of vacation and I'm officially off duty."

"You might want to go back on duty if you expect to get anything out of our relatives about Grandma's murder."

Skye thought for a moment. "You're right, but that still doesn't answer my question. Who was she? And does Abby know?"

Vince finished his sub and got up to throw away the debris. He answered with his back to Skye. "Abby and I aren't seeing each other anymore. She wanted to get married and I wasn't ready."

Skye could certainly sympathize with that. "So who's your alibi?"

"Just someone I met at the gym. It was a one-night thing. I have no plans to see her again." He looked at Skye and added before she could open her mouth, "And yes, I did use protection."

Skye stood looking out the window at the vehicles filling Grandma Leofanti's driveway. She wondered how true it was that you could tell a lot about people by what they drove.

She and her parents had come together in their white Oldsmobile, a middle-of-the-road type of car. Her brother Vince's Jeep was parked next to Aunt Mona's Lincoln. Those automobiles were so obvious they needed no interpretation.

The twins drove matching TranSport

minivans. Again, that selection didn't take a psychologist to figure out. Their parents, Minnie and Emmett, had come by truck, as had Uncle Dante. But while the Overbys' pickup was old and showed years of hard work, Dante's looked as if it had been driven off the showroom floor that morning. Skye wondered how he managed that on the income from a working farm.

Last, just pulling in, was Dante's son, Hugo. His pearl-colored Infiniti gleamed as he parked it carefully away from the other vehicles and in the shade of the house. Skye felt lust in her heart, knowing she could never afford the thirty-five thousand dollar car her cousin drove so proudly.

The living room was crowded, and being the last to arrive, Hugo squeezed in beside his parents on the sofa. Minnie and Emmett had chosen the matching armchairs, a twin sitting on the floor at each of their feet. Mona and her husband, Neal, were on the love seat, looking too elegant for the surroundings.

Skye managed to avoid speaking to Mona and kept her distance from the couple. She was still too angry about the essay contest to be civil.

Jed, Skye, and Vince sat on chairs they had brought in from the dining room.

May was ensconced in Grandma Leofanti's La-Z-Boy.

Everyone stared at one another. No one seemed to know how to start.

Finally Skye said, "How about if we each take a moment and tell how Grandma was special to us?"

A murmur went through the crowd, but no one responded.

"I'd be glad to go first," Skye continued.

Ginger leaned forward. "Yes, you always are, glad to be first, I mean."

Gillian snickered.

"Fine, feel free to go ahead then." Skye sat back and crossed her arms.

Before Ginger could respond, Dante interjected, "Don't be asinine, Skye. Let's just get this over with." He turned to May. "So, what did Ma want us to do?"

May put on her glasses and leafed through a sheaf of papers. "Well, I'm not even sure if it's legal or not, but since most of the estate is tied up in the trust, she just wrote me a letter about the other stuff."

Hugo looked at his father. "Maybe we should talk to our lawyer and see what he says."

"I thought of that," May said quickly, "but he costs so much and this is really just about her burial and the disposal of the knickknacks. I guess it depends if we can agree."

Dante narrowed his eyes. "Go ahead then and tell us what she wanted."

"First, it seems that she already picked out her casket and prepaid for the funeral at Reid's. Here's the contract." May passed a document to Dante. "She also talked to Father Burns and picked out the readings and such."

"Well, I wonder why he's never discussed that with me or Neal?" Mona said. "I am head of the Altar and Rosary Society and Neal is the Grand Knight of the KC."

"So, it seems the arrangements are already made," May said. "Unless someone has an objection." She looked around the room.

Dante glared at Skye. "I should have known you'd manage to get the business for Reid's."

"Uncle Dante, Simon doesn't need our business." Skye paused and then smiled wickedly. "After all, people are just dying to get in."

Vince snickered and the twins tsked.

Dante turned red and sputtered. "You . . . you have no respect —"

"As to the car," May interrupted, "Mom wanted Skye to use it as long as she needed, but when it's sold the money is to be divided among the great-grandchildren."

The twins buzzed.

"Okay," May continued, "now for the personal stuff. Mom wants us to each take what we want and then sell whatever no one claims."

"What if more than one of us wants something?" Ginger asked.

"She's thought of that. We're to draw numbers and keep going around until there's nothing left that we want." May held up a bowl filled with slips of paper. "That's why she requested that the grandchildren not bring their spouses or children."

"So, whoever gets number one gets first choice?" Gillian rose to her knees.

"Right." May mixed the chits up with her right hand.

"Who gets to draw first?" Hugo edged forward on his seat.

"Oldest to youngest. Mom had everything figured out." May brought the dish over to Dante.

She then selected a number herself. After putting it in her pocket, May went over to Minnie. "Your turn."

Minnie shrank back in her seat. "Let the girls go first."

"Sorry, but that's not how Mom wanted

it." May stood firm.

Mona was the last of the children. Hugo was the eldest grandchild, then Vince, then Skye.

"I can never remember. Which twin is older?" May asked.

"I am." Ginger snatched one of the two remaining slips from the bowl.

To Skye Vince whispered, "Bet that's the last time she ever admits it."

May sat back down and glanced around the room. "Who drew number one?"

No one spoke. Everyone rechecked their chit and then looked at one another.

Eventually, Minnie raised her hand. "But I don't know what I want."

Ginger and Gillian began whispering furiously to their mother, who looked more bewildered as they spoke. She finally nodded.

"I want the dining room set." Minnie sank back in her chair like a deflated balloon.

Skye hoped this didn't bring on another of Minnie's spells. In the past, in any kind of stressful situation, Minnie would close herself in her bedroom and read cookbooks for days on end. She'd come out during the wee hours of the morning and raid the kitchen, then retreat back to the bedroom. She wouldn't talk to anyone, and an attack could last from two or three days to a week. No one could break her out of one once it started.

"That includes the buffet and china hutch, right?" Ginger hovered over her mother.

Voices flooded the room. When they quieted, May said, "Yes, anything that is a set goes together. We aren't doing this fork by fork."

Dante stepped toward May. "What gives you the right to say so?"

"If we're going by this letter, Mom asked me to settle any disputes." May looked at Dante without blinking.

He grumbled, but having number two he took the antique sleigh-style bedroom set.

"Three?" May's eyes searched the assembly.

Gillian flashed her paper triumphantly. "I want Grandma's good jewelry."

"There's only a necklace and earrings. And it isn't a set. You'll have to choose one piece." As Gillian opened her mouth to argue, May continued, "If you argue you automatically have to go last."

"Fine, I'll take the emerald earrings." Gillian stuck out her lip.

Ginger shot Skye a malicious glance. "I have number four. But before we go on, I

184

want to bring something up. Since Skye, as the oldest female grandchild, already got the Leofanti emerald ring, wouldn't it be fairer for her to go last now?"

"No." May's look dared anyone to disagree. "So, what do you want, Ginger?"

"I'll take the emerald pendant." Ginger sank back on her heels and whispered to her twin.

"Five?"

"Me, Mom." Skye turned the paper she had been clutching to face the room. "I'd like the oak table by the window. It was Grandma's favorite piece. She talked about it a lot when she was telling me the family history."

Mona was next and she took the silver. Hugo was number seven and wanted the living room set. Vince took the safe, saying he could use it in his shop, and May took the china.

By the conclusion, everyone had four or five things and little was left to be sold.

Besides the table, Skye ended up with an old trunk, an incomplete set of pink crystal wineglasses, and the everyday dishes. No one mentioned Bingo, and she didn't remind them.

As they all got ready to leave, May cleared her throat. "I have one more announcement."

They all looked at her expectantly.

"Chief Boyd found the body of Mrs. Jankowski yesterday in the abandoned well out back. With her, they found a pan of brownies, which they believe were poisoned. They were probably responsible for Mom and the housekeeper's deaths."

The room was filled with voices asking questions.

May shook her head. "That's all I know."

The family broke into clots, hauling away their loot and whispering about May's announcement.

Skye walked out with her parents and Vince. They were the first to go, leaving the others still picking over the last little items.

As Vince loaded Skye's table into the Olds, he asked her, "Why didn't you take one of the more valuable items when it was your turn?"

"Like I said, this was Grandma's favorite piece." Skye paused.

"There's something more," Vince prodded.

Skye reddened. "Well, not that I believed her, but she used to say it was magical."

CHAPTER 11

EARLY TO BED

Skye sat on the closed toilet seat and watched her mother put on makeup at the counter. *Saturday night and nothing to do. Even my parents have plans. My life sucks.*

"Maybe we shouldn't go tonight. Mom only died a few days ago and it feels sort of funny to be going out."

"The Grandma I knew wouldn't want you to sit at home and cry. She'd be the first one to arrive at the party and the last to leave."

Tears ran down May's cheek. "You're probably right, but I sure do miss her. I find myself holding the phone and dialing her number before I remember she's gone."

"Our after-school visits meant a lot to me." Skye handed her mother a tissue. "More than I realized at the time. She was quite a 'high-spirited' young lady, as they used to say. I kind of got the feeling her family married her off to Grandpa to calm her down."

187

May blotted her eyes and blew her nose. "She never would talk about that with me. She wouldn't even tell me how Dad proposed or about their first date."

"Grandma said that the marriage had been arranged after her original fiancé died."

"I never knew that." May wiped away another tear. "Will you write all this down so you don't forget?"

"Oh, don't worry. I taped all our conversations."

"Good." May took a deep breath and turned back to the mirror. After a few seconds, she held out two containers of eyeshadow. "Which do you think would look better with my dress?"

"You're wearing the taupe silk?" Skye studied the palettes. "Go with the shades of wine; I think the brown would wash you out."

Nodding, May began the delicate operation of applying the color to the crease of her eyelid. "You sure you don't want to go to the wedding reception with us?"

"Mom, I wasn't invited, remember?" Skye studied her mother's handiwork.

"They probably forgot you were back in town." May clicked the case shut and reached for her mascara. "You really don't need an invitation. The announcement in the paper said all friends and relatives were welcome. It's not like it's a sit-down dinner."

"No, I barely remember these people. Who are they again?"

"They're your dad's second cousins." May carefully colored her lips. "What will you do while we're gone? I don't like the thought of you moping around here by yourself."

"I am not moping. Maybe I'll take a ride, or visit Vince or Charlie. Simon's got a wake tonight, but we're going out tomorrow for brunch."

"How about Trixie? Now that she's back in town you should try and get together with her sometime." May stood back from the mirror and checked her face.

"It's a Saturday night, and she is married, so I don't think this is the time."

"Married. Seems like everyone's doing that lately." May shot Skye a meaningful look before walking out of the bathroom.

Thirty minutes after her parents left, Skye sat in the La-Z-Boy with Bingo ensconced on her lap. She was flipping through TV channels, but most programs were reruns of things she hadn't wanted to watch the first time around. Six o'clock on a Saturday night offered poor television viewing.

She reached for the phone, careful to leave the cat undisturbed. No answer at Vince's.

Next, she tried Charlie, who was just leaving for a poker game with his buddies.

Skye frowned when she heard this. "But, Uncle Charlie, I thought you weren't going to gamble anymore, after you almost lost everything last fall."

His usual booming voice sounded sheepish. "We play for toothpicks. No money is involved."

"Oh, well, I still don't think it's a good idea. It feeds your addiction." Skye sat up straighter.

Bingo opened one eye and glared.

"Why don't you come with me? It's just Eldon, Homer, and a couple of other old guys. Nothing for you to worry about."

"I can't see me playing poker with the mayor and the high school principal. Thanks anyway, Uncle Charlie. Have a good time."

She sat stroking Bingo for a moment, then got up and grabbed her purse. The cat gave a single sharp meow before settling into the warm spot on the chair Skye had vacated. Skye dumped the bag's contents on the sofa and searched for the piece of paper with Trixie's number on it.

Her wallet, checkbook, sunglasses case, and cosmetic pouch were quickly examined, and thrown back in the tote's gaping maw. Then she made a pile of things for the trash. *This is pathetic. I'm cleaning out my purse for entertainment on a Saturday night.*

Finally, the only things remaining were two crumpled sheets of paper. She smoothed the smallest and found what she had been looking for. Skye scooped up the receiver and punched in Trixie's number.

On the sixth ring, Trixie answered, just as Skye was thinking of hanging up.

Skye could hear other people's voices. "Hi, this is Skye. Is this a bad time?"

Trixie lowered her voice. "Depends on your frame of reference. We have my in-laws over for the weekend."

"Oh, well. I thought you'd probably be busy, but I decided to check just in case you were free. I was thinking we could get together." Skye hoped the disappointment didn't show in her words.

"They're leaving tomorrow. How about lunch on Monday? You are out of school now, right?"

"Yes, thank goodness. Monday would be great. Want to go into Kankakee and do some shopping too?"

"Sounds good to me. Shall I pick you up around ten?" Trixie asked.

"Ten's good, but let me pick you up. I'm not sure where I'll be." After Skye explained about the broken windows, they hung up.

Skye gathered the pile of trash she had accumulated from her purse, and walked out to the waste can in the kitchen. As she tossed in everything, a crinkled paper fell to the floor. She picked it up and flattened it out.

Written in crude printing, all in capital letters, was: "BITCH! KWIT STIKKIN YER NOSE IN OTHER PEEPLES BIZNESS."

Shaken, Skye sat at the counter and stared at the hateful message. In a few minutes she drew a shaky breath, stood, and got a Ziploc from the drawer. Edging the page into the plastic bag with a pencil eraser, she sealed the top, and put it in her purse. She knew she had probably already destroyed any fingerprints, but she wasn't taking any chances. She'd bet money this was the work of Hap Doozier, or maybe Gus Yoder's father.

After Skye had dropped the note off with the dispatcher at the police department, she decided to cruise the downtown area of

Scumble River. As a teenager she had spent many Friday and Saturday evenings riding from one end of town to the other. The kids started at Mayor Clapp's used car lot on the north end of Basin Street, and looped around the McDonald's at the far south extreme. Some called it "shooting the loop"; others labeled it "buzzing the gut."

From the parade of cars crawling slowly by and the honking of horns, it appeared that this tradition had not changed.

Skye rolled down the window and turned up the radio. Pam Tillis was singing about lost love and squandered dreams.

When the song ended, the disc jockey's voice oozed out of the speakers. "This is WCCQ, the Love and Desperation Hour. What can I play for you?"

A low-pitched baritone answered. " 'I'm Having a Bad Day' by The Charlie Stewart Band."

"You got a dedication for that?" the DJ asked.

After a pause the caller answered, "It's to SD."

"Who from?"

Another pause. "Let's just say I'm hoping she can figure that out."

Skye thought, *SD could be me. That voice did sound sort of familiar. Nah.*

She was almost to the south turnaround when she abruptly decided to swing into McDonald's rather than circle it. Skye parked the Buick, then flipped down the visor and used its mirror to straighten her hair. The open window had allowed her curls to be whipped into a beehive. While she was at it, she powdered her nose and added a light coat of lipstick.

Her white shorts and navy striped polo had managed to ride up, exposing her upper thighs and midriff. She smoothed her clothes down as she exited the car. Her Keds squeaked on the cooling asphalt.

The glare blinded her for a moment when she pushed open the door, but she made her way instinctively to the counter. The line wasn't long and she was able to order her ice cream in a few minutes.

The girl behind the counter handed her the clear plastic dish and said, "Here you go, Ms. Denison. You were awesome breaking up that fight last night."

Skye recognized her from the high school, but couldn't remember her name. "Thanks. Did the kids know Gus was going to sneak in?"

The girl's face reddened, and she muttered as she turned to wait on another customer. "Some."

Oh, no, I broke another taboo. I asked one kid to rat on another. There goes my "awesome" reputation. Skye shook her head.

Sweeping her eyes across the room, Skye headed for one in the back corner. She liked to observe without being watched herself. As she neared her favorite table, she noticed it was occupied and started to veer to the next one on the right.

A voice stopped her. "Come sit with me."

When she hesitated, Chief Boyd added, "I'm having a bad day."

Skye slid into his booth and glanced across at him. He appeared haggard. The skin around his eyes was papery looking. "Are you okay?"

He shrugged. "Better now."

Alarms were going off in Skye's head. He was not dressed in his uniform and thus probably off duty. Why would a married man with no children be alone at McDonald's on a Saturday night?

The silence grew awkward and she rushed to fill the gap with words. "Ah, gee, I was just at the police station. I found a threatening note in my purse so I dropped it off."

"What did it say?" Wally sat forward with a look of concern.

She told him, and he shook his head. "Sure seems that someone is not too happy with you. First your tires, then your windows, and now this. What have you been doing to tick people off?"

"My job." Skye made a face. "It's not uncommon for parents to blame others for their children's failings."

"Yeah, some of those kids I get in at the police station, I just want to shake some sense into them. The first thing out of their mouths is: 'It's not my fault.' "

"Oh, it's never their fault. And what amazes me is eighty percent of the time the parents think that way too."

"Yes, and these are the same kids who say to their folks: 'It's my life,' and 'You're not my boss.' It doesn't make sense. If they really believe that it's their life and their parents aren't their boss, then there is no one to blame but themselves."

"Too bad the parents would sue us if we said half of what we're really thinking." Skye snorted inelegantly, then realized what she had done and felt a blush start up her cheeks.

Wally didn't help. He just looked at her with a goofy smile.

Skye glanced around. If anyone overheard their conversation, they would think she and Wally didn't care about the kids they worked with. But in truth they were probably more concerned than the parents who let their children run wild. Like all people in high-stress professions, they needed to vent.

When the silence lengthened, Skye once again searched for a topic of conversation. "So, what's new with my grandmother's case?"

She saw disappointment flash in his eyes before he recovered his usual mild expression. "They've found that her housekeeper was murdered using the same poison."

"Just as we suspected. Now the question becomes, why was my grandmother left in her bed, but Mrs. Jankowski dumped in the well?"

He leaned forward, his forearms on the table. "My guess is that whoever did it thought your grandmother's death would be written off to old age, and no one would bother to find some poor Polish woman with no relatives or friends."

"Or maybe they didn't expect Mrs. Jankowski to die. Maybe she wasn't supposed to get hold of the brownies." Skye, too, leaned forward, lowering her voice. "My aunts were always fighting about what Mrs. J ate. They'd bring a plate of cookies for Grandma, who would eat one or two, and then Mrs. J would polish off the rest."

"If I remember correctly, the contents of both stomachs were similar."

"Did you find anything when you went through the house?"

"Yes. Someone had been violently ill, but the mess had been cleaned up. This supports the physical evidence the doctor found the day she was murdered. He found signs that she had vomited, but had been cleaned up. We found dirty rags, one of your grandmother's dresses, and a set of her underclothing. It was all stuffed down that well."

"That was what Simon was referring to the night of the murder when he said they had found irregularities."

A line formed between Wally's brows. "This is the way I think it went down. The murderer brought over the poisoned brownies. Gave them to your grandma to eat, waited, and when she got sick, cleaned her up. This person changed her into her nightgown and put her to bed."

"Where was Mrs. J while this was going on?" Skye shredded a napkin.

The chief twiddled the straw in his drink. "The murderer must have told her to relax, they would take care of your grandmother. And while she waited, Mrs. J ate a brownie."

"Did the killer clean her up too?"

The chief shook his head. "Nope, just stuffed her down the well, along with her belongings, and the remaining brownies."

"So, the murderer went back inside, straightened up, and then disposed of the rest of the evidence."

Wally shrugged. "That's how it looks."

"Any suspects besides my family?"

"No, it's pretty unlikely that it was an outsider." He took a swallow of his Coke. "It's also damn hard to find the killer when it's a family member. Everyone sticks together, and no one will say anything about the other."

"Whoever did it had to be strong enough to get that well cover on and off. That eliminates the women." Skye ate a spoonful of her melting ice cream.

"Maybe not. We found signs that a chain and a car were used to move the well cover."

"And you said a wagon was used to move Mrs. J's body so I guess that means anyone could have managed it physically."

They were silent as Skye ate her sundae and the chief finished his drink.

Skye scraped the last drizzle of chocolate from the container and wiped her lips with her napkin. "Thanks for telling me all this."

Wally pushed the debris to one side of the

table. "You know I trust you."

She felt her face get hot and half rose from the booth. "Well, I'd better get going."

"Could you stay a little while longer?"

"Sure."

"Did you hear the dedication on CCQ?"

Skye nodded. "The song about having a bad day?"

"Yes." Wally looked down at his clenched hands. "I thought I saw you drive by and hoped you had your radio tuned to WCCQ. I really wanted to talk to you."

Skye sat back down. "Okay."

"Darleen's left me."

"Oh." Skye couldn't think of anything to say. The pain in his eyes made her want to reach out and comfort him, but deep down she knew that wasn't a good idea so she settled for saying, "I'm so sorry."

He buried his face in his hands. "I didn't see it coming, but now that I look back I wonder how dumb I could be. She's never been a happy person."

"No, from the little I know her, I'd say she has a lot of characteristics of someone who is chronically depressed." Skye frowned. She probably should have tried harder to connect with Darleen and gotten her some help.

As if reading her mind, Wally said, "I

made her see a therapist and counselors, but she never cooperated with them."

"You really can't help someone who isn't ready." Skye felt as if she were trying to walk on bubble wrap without popping any of the air pockets. "What happened that made her leave?"

"Well, you know that she's always wanted to have kids and we've never been able to?"

Skye nodded, remembering Darleen's desperation to have a baby. It had almost been Darleen's downfall last autumn during a murder investigation.

"She met a guy in her Bible study group whose wife died in childbirth. He already had two small children and now a newborn . . ."

"So she's in love?" Skye sighed. "The maternal instinct is a tough one to overcome."

"Yes." Wally reached across the table and took Skye's hands. "I feel so helpless."

Looking down at their intertwined hands, Skye searched for the right words. "I don't know what to say. Did you just find out?"

He squeezed her fingers. "Everything was gone when I got home from work today."

"How devastating." Skye felt a weight on her chest as she gazed into his pain-filled eyes.

"She took everything but my clothes — all

the furniture, appliances, kitchen stuff, even the shower curtain. I'll be sleeping on the floor tonight. Why would she be so vicious?" he asked.

"People do strange things in the heat of the moment. Could be she just wanted you to know she was serious about this. Maybe, after things cool down a little, you two can talk and work something out."

They were silent again. Skye hesitated. She never talked about her broken engagement, but she finally said, "I know how much it hurts. The day I got the notice that I had been fired, I got home and found my fiancé had moved out."

"The bastard."

Skye got up. "You do get over it, although there is always a small pain. A reminder."

He followed her. "It'd be a hard thing to forget."

They deposited their trash in the bin and walked outside. Skye unlocked her car door and slid inside.

Wally stood at the window. "Are you sure it gets better?"

She nodded.

"I'm trusting you on this." He stared into her eyes.

Skye caught her breath and struggled to keep her voice even. "I've been there. Call me if you need to talk."

"I might take you up on that." Wally leaned down and gently pressed his lips to hers.

Without waiting for her response, he turned and walked away.

Skye raised fingers to her tingling lips. She felt confused. Wally was all wrong for her. He'd never leave Scumble River. If she were with him, she'd be stuck here forever. Simon was closer to her own age, single, well-off, and more urbane. Everything a woman could ask for. Then why did her heart flutter whenever Wally was around?

Sunday afternoon, one of Skye's favorite times of the week. All the obligations taken care of and still not near Monday morning. She smiled and stretched, snuggling into her chaise lounge, and enjoying the sensation of being back in her own cottage. Everything was perfect. Simon was sitting in the matching chair and the weather was exactly right for being out on the deck. Brunch had been great. He always found the best new restaurants to try. They had gone for a drive through Kankakee State Park, and when they got back they'd found that her windows had all been repaired.

The late afternoon sun had lulled them

both into a dreamlike state. Skye gazed at the lush green trees almost obscuring her vision of the river. She spotted a squirrel dragging an ear of corn that was almost twice its size.

"Shall I put some music on?" Simon asked.

"Something mellow. Do you want a drink?" Skye extracted herself from the deep cushions.

"Sure. A soda sounds good." Simon followed her through the sliding glass doors into the living room.

This was one of the things she liked about Simon. He wasn't much of a drinker. Except for the occasional glass of wine at a fine restaurant, he seemed to prefer soft drinks. Skye poured a can of Diet Coke into two glasses filled with ice. She picked them up and went back outside. Simon was already there, listening to the CD he had selected.

She handed him his drink and said, "Have you identified the poison that killed Grandma and Mrs. Jankowski?"

He put his glass down on the little round table that separated their chairs. "Yes, but I can't tell you what it was."

"I see. You don't trust me." Skye sat on the foot of the lounger rather than stretching out. *The police chief has more faith in me than my own boyfriend. Something to think about.*

"It's not that. I just don't want you to get any more involved in this whole mess than you have to. Finding out who killed her will not bring your grandmother back."

Skye felt a brief flare of anger. "Maybe. Can you at least tell me when you're going to release Mrs. J's body?"

"I called the agency she worked for and asked them to make the arrangements. Didn't they call your family?" Simon looked tired of this subject.

"No, why would they?"

"The woman in charge seemed to feel it was your family's responsibility to bury Mrs. Jankowski. She didn't have any relatives here and no one in Poland has the money for a funeral."

"Uh-oh. I'd better call Mom."

"Sure, go ahead." Simon leaned back in his chaise.

By the time Skye returned to the deck he was asleep.

Chapter 12

Rain, Rain Go Away

Skye watched as the first drop of rain hit Simon squarely in the face. He bolted upright, but quickly regained his composure. She had been reading a new mystery with Bingo stretched down the length of her thigh.

The music had stopped an hour ago, but Skye had been too engrossed in the adventures of the amateur sleuth to put on another CD. Bingo was purring in his sleep, his sides vibrating in time to a rhythm that only he could hear.

Simon wiped the moisture off his face with his handkerchief and looked at his watch. "How long have I been asleep?"

Skye closed the book after marking her place. "A little over an hour."

"Why didn't you wake me?" He stretched and straightened his clothing.

"We didn't have any plans, and I figured you must be tired." Skye swept up the sleeping cat, and put him inside the cottage before he could protest.

Moving to her side, Simon put his arms around her. "You're very understanding. I got called out late last night to pick up a body. I didn't get to bed until after three; then I had to be at church at nine."

"You couldn't have skipped services this one time?" Skye asked.

"No, I was playing the organ for the choir." Simon tucked a stray curl behind her ear.

"I forgot you sometimes play for them." Skye linked her hands behind his neck and leaned back slightly. "Why did you have to go out so late?"

"One of those guys in the survivalist group was cleaning his gun, and it went off." A shadow passed over Simon's features. "He was only twenty-two."

"Oh, how awful." Skye gave Simon a hug. "No question it was an accident?"

"We don't know yet. Witnesses say so." Simon peeked at his watch.

"Do you have an appointment?" she asked.

Shrugging apologetically, Simon said, "Well, I did agree to talk to that boy's parents this evening." Before she could respond, he added, "I have a meeting with your family tomorrow to go over your grandmother's arrangements, and I didn't want them to feel rushed."

"That was very thoughtful of you." Skye pecked him on the cheek and slipped out of his arms. "We were rather surprised that Grandma had made all those prearrangements without our knowledge."

"More and more people are doing that. I feel it's a good idea. One less thing for the family to worry about."

"Why didn't you tell me?" she asked.

"Well, it's a matter of confidentiality."

She arched an eyebrow.

"Your grandmother asked that I not mention it to anybody."

"Surely she didn't mean me." Skye turned and walked into the house.

"She didn't make any exceptions."

"This whole thing has been quite an eye-opener. I never realized how many secrets Grandma kept from us. And I'm learning a lot about my family." Skye paused. "Maybe, in some cases, more than I wanted to know."

They walked toward the front door.

Simon put his hand on her cheek. "It's not that bad, is it?"

"I really miss Grandma. And I knew a lot of my relatives didn't exactly see eye to eye with me, but I think now some of them really hate me."

"You have had a rough time lately. I'm sure all the vandalism hasn't helped either. I was surprised to see the windows fixed so soon."

"Me too. I had called around and all the companies told me two weeks. Then Dad took over, without telling me of course, and voilà, they're all fixed in a few days."

"He fixed your tires too. Jed seems to be a handy man to have around."

"Too handy. At this rate I'll never learn to take care of myself."

Simon leaned down and kissed her. "They're just trying to convince you how nice it is to live close to home, so you won't move halfway across the country again."

"That's what I'm afraid of."

After Simon's departure, the intensity of the rain increased. Skye curled up on the couch and listened to it hit the sliding glass doors. It sounded almost like a spray of bullets. Bingo wedged himself into the bottom shelf of the bookcase, between books by Grant and Isenberg, and yowled forlornly.

Unable to get back into her mystery, Skye turned her thoughts to her grandmother's murder.

Maybe Wally was right. Maybe the murderer was someone in the family. She closed her eyes and shivered. As her grandmother used to say, that would be a bitter pill to swallow. Skye would much prefer it be those survivalists. They certainly had proximity. But would they try to pass off a murder as death by natural causes? Grandma wasn't assaulted, nothing was stolen, and everything was put back to look normal. If a member of that group was the killer, what was the motive?

Grandma's "magic" table caught her eye. She ran her fingertip lightly over the polished wooden surface, straightened the lace runner so that it lay exactly down the center, and adjusted the silver-framed picture of Antonia.

Next, Skye wandered into the kitchen and peered distractedly into the fridge, still puzzling about her grandmother's death.

Why would anyone want to kill Grandma? Maybe Uncle Dante because he really wanted the land. But since it was in trust and he was the trustee, he had control anyway. She needed to look into the details regarding that arrangement as soon as possible.

Minnie was the only other one she could think of who had even a slight reason to want Grandma dead. Even though they had a housekeeper, Aunt Minnie had insisted on cooking every meal for Grandma, which meant running over to the farm three times a day. Maybe she was tired of taking care of her, especially if her own mental health was deteriorating. Her spells had been getting closer together and of longer duration since she started going through menopause. Now instead of one every few months, Minnie was likely to have one every three or four weeks.

Skye closed the refrigerator door without taking anything from its shelves. She opened a cupboard and stared inside. She knew neither her parents nor Vince could have done it. That left Aunt Mona and her cousins. She needed to find out more about them.

Tomorrow she'd go over to Grandma's and take another look around. Maybe she would recognize things that the police had missed. She especially wanted a chance to check out the garage. She was sure someone had been in there Monday, when she found her grandmother's body.

Skye slammed the cupboard door, still empty-handed. What had she been thinking of? She couldn't go during the day unless she wanted everyone and his brother to know what she was doing.

Too many of her relatives lived along that road and routinely passed by the farm several times a day. The house was plainly visible as they drove by. There was nowhere to hide the car. Even if she pulled it into the garage she risked being caught in the act. Skye realized she had to go while it was dark. Tonight would be the perfect time. Fewer people would be out because of the storm.

She changed into black jeans, a long-sleeved black T-shirt, and stuffed her hair underneath a dark baseball cap. The only flashlight she could find was in the glove compartment of the car. She hoped the batteries would hold out.

During the drive to her grandmother's, she tried not to think of what she was about to do. Skye knew it was dangerous, but she had weighed the odds and decided to take the risk. She had briefly considered calling someone to go with her, but her parents' latest assaults on her independence left her reluctant to ask for help from anyone.

It was nearly ten o'clock when she parked the Buick at the farm. Storm clouds covered the moon, blotting out the little natural light available. Skye got out of the car and hurried through the rain toward the garage's side entrance. She clutched the flashlight tighter and forced herself to step inside.

She swept the flashlight's beam around the unfinished walls. Hanging from nails were rusted shovels, broken rakes, and other discarded yard tools that no one had touched since Grandpa had died. Jed took care of the lawn using his own equipment.

Skye felt disappointed and shook her head at her own foolishness. What had she expected to find in a garage?

A car-sized space was empty, but the remaining floor held three boxes, a discarded kitchen table, and a broken rocker. Skye squatted next to the first carton and eased open its flaps. It was filled with old magazines. *Reader's Digest*, *TV Guide*, and *Better Homes and Gardens* shared space with *Country Living*.

Skye pulled up the rocker and positioned the flashlight's beam to fall on the contents of the box. She began going through the periodicals, checking each title and shaking them to make sure nothing was hidden inside.

The second crate held more of the same — *Family Circle*, *Redbook*, and *Outdoor Life*. Skye resumed her inspection.

After an hour all she had to show for her trouble was a mountain of subscription cards, a sore derriere from the cracked seat of the chair, and dirty hands.

Sighing, she pulled over the third container. This one was secured with packing tape and after breaking two nails she decided the only way to open it was with a knife. Not seeing any suitable implement in the garage, she tried picking the carton up.

The medium-sized box was deceptively heavy. She struggled to get it into her arms and walk with it to the car. It was a relief to dump it into the backseat. Thinking of Simon's admonishment the night her tires were slashed, she locked the car doors.

Skye was completely wet by the time she returned to the garage, and could feel her damp hair curling tightly as she put everything back the way she had found it. She was walking out when she heard a fluttering sound overhead. Frightened, she swung the light upward. A bird was perched on a board that ran the length of the building.

These strips of wood had been erected for additional storage. Skye swept the area with her flashlight. It was empty except for a trunk.

No way was she climbing up there to look into a chest that had no doubt been there since her great-great-grandparents came over from Italy. But even as the thought crossed her mind, Skye was dragging an old ladder with several missing rungs to the middle of the floor. Shaking her head at her own stupidity, she stuck the flashlight into her cleavage and climbed. As she went farther toward the ceiling, the heat and dust increased, and she fought to keep from sneezing.

Once she reached the trunk she discovered that it was too heavy to bring down the ladder. But the lid opened easily, and she leaned against the top step and felt inside.

At first, Skye thought the chest was empty, but she finally felt something on the bottom. She inched up one more step and was able to curl her fingers around the object and lever it up enough to grab. It was heavy, and her hand ached by the time she got it back to the ground.

Skye gently eased it onto the table and illuminated it with her light. It was a family Bible. Just as she opened the black leather cover her flashlight flickered and went dead. Swallowing a scream, she clutched the book to her chest. She shook the flashlight and flicked the switch on and off; it still wouldn't work.

She forced herself to wait a few moments for her eyes to adjust to the darkness, then made her way out of the garage. The rain had stopped momentarily, and the moon glowed brightly. She looked at her watch. It was after twelve-thirty and she had to go to the bathroom. Mom was right. You should always go before you leave home.

She fished the key from her pocket, unlocked the Buick, and tucked the Bible next to the box in the backseat. After relocking the vehicle, she headed inside to use the facilities.

The key had been replaced on the window frame's nail and Skye had no trouble gaining entrance to the house. She caught her breath when she entered the kitchen. Almost everything had been removed. The cupboard doors hung open, their shelves nearly bare. All the appliances were gone except for the old stove. Everyone must have stayed after she and her family left and picked the place clean. It looked as if a swarm of locusts had come through and spit out the few things that weren't tasty enough to swallow.

Feeling a twinge of disgust, Skye hurried to the bathroom, hoping no one had decided they wanted the fixtures. In there, both the linen closet and medicine cabinets had been similarly ransacked, with only a few empty prescription bottles left lying on their sides. The toilet gleamed whitely, and she sighed in relief as she attacked the zipper on her jeans.

After she was finished, Skye washed her hands and was then forced to let them air dry, since even the curtains were gone. It was late and she was tired, but this was her chance to take one more look and see if she could spot anything the police had overlooked.

The rest of the rooms were similarly bare. She wondered what they'd do about the house. It was old and needed major renovations. The land it occupied was probably worth more than the building, but she hoped the new owner wouldn't just tear it down.

Her last stop was the living room. She flicked on the overhead light and stood in the entrance, picturing it the way the room had looked the many times she and her grandmother had sat and visited there. Grandma's La-Z-Boy was always to the right of the big window. Next to it was the "magic" table and on the other side was the chair Skye always occupied.

Everything was gone now. The room had been painted only a few months earlier and the cream walls gleamed in unblemished splendor.

Whoa, what is this? Skye moved over to the window and looked at the wall underneath the sash. A small dark mark marred the plaster. It was only an inch and a half long and a half an inch wide, but to Skye it stood out as if it were delineated in neon.

She squatted next to it and looked all around, even checking the underside of the wooden sill. Nothing. Someone must have bumped it when they were moving out furniture yesterday.

A cloud covered the moon and darkness enveloped her as Skye left the house. No one had replaced the broken outside light and suddenly she felt as if she were being watched. She ran to the Buick, unlocked the door, and jumped inside. She hit the lock buttons as quickly as she was able.

On the drive home, Skye constantly checked the rearview mirror, sure she was being followed, but there were no other vehicles on the road. At least none trailing her with their headlights on.

By the time she got to her cottage, Skye had convinced herself that it was all in her imagination. There had been no one watching at her grandmother's and no one had followed her home. She was being silly.

Pushing her fear away, Skye opened the car door. After trying to lift both the Bible and the box, she decided to take one at a time — the heavier load first. The last thing she wanted was to drop the family Bible in the mud.

She heaved the box into her arms and fumbled her way inside. Bingo was waiting for her by the door and wound around her feet as she tried to walk through the foyer. She dropped the carton on the sofa, grabbed a letter opener from her desk, and cut through the packing tape. Prying open one flap, she saw an issue of *Modern Maturity*. All that trouble for another box of old magazines.

Disappointed, Skye started back to the Buick. She was halfway down the front sidewalk when she noticed that someone had the car door open and was reaching into the vehicle's backseat. A sound of protest escaped Skye's throat and the figure straightened, clutching something to its chest.

The intruder stared at Skye through the slits of a ski mask. The eyes glittered with hatred, and for a moment Skye thought they looked familiar, but before she could get a good look the trespasser whirled and raced down the driveway.

Skye ran to her car and looked inside. The Bible was gone. Great, now her relatives had another transgression to blame her for. She had lost the family Bible. She had to get it back. The thief was tall, well muscled, and ran with an athletic grace. Skye knew she'd never catch up on foot.

She jammed her hand in her pocket and came up with the car keys. In seconds she had jumped into the Buick and backed it out of the driveway. Skye headed toward town, the direction the robber had headed. There was no sign of the figure, and when she reached the crossroads she was stumped. The darkness made it impossible to see more than a few feet ahead of her. Which way had the intruder chosen? Probably neither. Most likely the invader had left the road and was long gone. She had blown her one chance to retrieve the Bible.

As Skye pulled back into her driveway, she realized how foolish she had been to pursue the thief. She was alone and vulnerable. This thought made her hurry inside and lock the door. Her father had given her a shotgun after her windows had been broken. She had hidden it in the seat of the hall bench. Heart pounding, she grabbed the weapon, leaned against the foyer wall, and thumbed the gun's release. The barrels and stock separated. Two red shells rested in the barrels. It was loaded and ready to go. All those sessions with Jed and Vince shooting tin cans had taught her all she needed to know about firing a shotgun.

★ ★ ★

Skye woke to Bingo's yowls. He was standing on her chest. She had fallen asleep on the couch after sitting there for hours mentally replaying the night's events and clutching the shotgun. Bingo continued to vocalize until she got up. The fur on his back stood up in a ridge down his spine. His tail twitched and his ears were moving like radar dishes.

She followed him to the foyer. Skye kept her body against the wall and peeked out the small pane in the door. A shadowy figure was trying to open the Buick's trunk.

Gripping the shotgun, Skye flipped on the porch light. The intruder froze and looked toward the house. It was the same figure as before. Skye ducked back inside. For a second she thought the person was going to charge the cottage, but instead it ran into the trees.

Skye sank onto the couch and waited for her heart to regain its normal rhythm. This was an interesting development. The Bible must not have been what the intruder was after. What could the burglar want?

If the robber had followed her, and watched her at her grandmother's, then Skye was probably seen carrying two items to her car. Maybe the intruder didn't even

221

know what it was looking for, but couldn't afford to have Skye stumble across something incriminating by accident. Possibly the person wanted both items, no matter what they were.

Her gaze fell on the box full of magazines. *I'd better look through these right away.* She reached for the carton, pulled it across the coffee table toward her, and tipped it over. At first a few magazines fluttered to the floor, then a lifetime's worth of snapshots spilled out.

Questions raced through her mind. Was it significant that these particular pictures had been saved? Who had saved them — Antonia, May, or maybe one of her siblings? Were they stored and forgotten or were they hidden? Skye had always found it odd that Antonia had so few photos of her children growing up. Had something happened and all snapshots been banished?

Skye knelt down near the heap of slick black-and-white images. They ranged in size from tiny one-by-one squares to a couple of eight-by-ten enlargements. Only a few were in color. Skye carefully separated a photo from the group. It showed Dante as a boy in a cowboy suit holding the reins of a pony. His smile was pure joy. When had he lost that emotion?

It took Skye several hours to sort through and examine the pictures from her grandmother's box. It was nearly eight in the morning before she finished. In one pile she put pictures of people she recognized. In another, pictures with information written on the back. The last group contained photos of people she couldn't identify. None seemed more recent than the early 1970s.

Skye put the unknown ones in a large manila envelope, and set them aside, intending to ask her mother to go through them. The other two batches she studied closely. Again she wondered if the person who had stolen the Bible had in fact been looking for the box of photos. And if so, which of the hundreds of pictures was the thief after?

She stood and stretched. Pins and needles shot up her legs from sitting on the floor.

Skye limped into the kitchen, fed Bingo, and made herself a cup of tea. What was her next move?

She took her mug into the bathroom and turned the shower on as hot as she could stand. After shedding her nightgown, she stepped into the stall.

Skye abruptly stopped lathering her hair with shampoo. A chill ran down her spine and she quickly rinsed out the suds. *Someone is watching me right now. I can feel it.*

Her eyes flew open and she spotted Bingo sitting on the bathmat scrutinizing her. He licked the crumbs of his breakfast off his whiskers and looked smug.

Once her breathing returned to normal, she asked, "If you're so smart, why don't you tell me who killed Grandma?"

Bingo blinked and lifted a paw for a wash.

After dressing, Skye gathered up the pictures and drove to her brother's salon. She quickly told Vince what had happened and watched him lock the photos in his safe. She swore him to silence, promised a longer explanation later, and ran back to her car.

Next she headed to the police station to report the theft of the Bible. She knew she should call her parents, and probably Simon, to let them know what had happened, but there was nothing they could do except worry or tell her to stop trying to find Grandma's killer. She didn't need them to remind her that what she was doing was dangerous. It was her choice and her decision, nobody else's.

CHAPTER 13

SKYE AND TRIXIE WENT TO TOWN,

RIDING IN A MUSTANG

Two pieces of luck shortened her stop at the police station. Her mother wasn't working and Wally was out on a call. Skye was able to convince Thea, the dispatcher, not to summon the chief and to allow Skye to fill out the paperwork herself. At the same time Skye wrote her mom a note and asked her to stop by Vince's and look at the pictures to see if she recognized anyone.

It was a couple minutes before ten when Skye started down Trixie's lane. By Scumble River standards, she was late. To most citizens ten o'clock really meant nine-forty-five. She had almost canceled her date with her friend, but realized she really needed to buy a dress for her grandmother's funeral in two days.

The old farmhouse was in the process of being remodeled. The outside was covered with Tyvek material and huge holes in the front and sides were sealed with plastic.

Skye picked her way carefully up the worn wooden steps. The porch had been stripped and a sander lay in a corner.

Before Skye could ring the bell, Trixie pulled open the unpainted door and tugged her inside. "What fun. I haven't been shopping in ages. Are you looking for anything special? Do you want something to eat or drink before we go?"

Skye gave Trixie a quick hug. "I need an outfit for the funeral. And no thanks to the offer of refreshments. Let's just get going before something else in my life blows up."

"What are you talking about?" Trixie grabbed her purse from the newel post.

"I'll tell you all about it in the car." Skye nudged Trixie out the door.

"Okay, but I'm driving." Trixie led the way to her Mustang convertible. "No offense, but that Buick of yours is pretty sad."

"None taken. I'm just borrowing it till I get the insurance check." Skye got into the passenger's side and put on her seatbelt. As they roared toward Kankakee, she told her story, sometimes competing with the wind to be heard.

When Skye finished, Trixie said, "Wow. Do you think everything that's been happening to you is being done by your grandma's killer? Or maybe it's some of those awful parents you had run-ins with?"

"Got me." Skye shrugged. "Maybe both. I'm beginning to feel like the most hated person in Scumble River."

"Well, then, shopping is just what you need." Trixie flashed an impish grin. "I know maxing out my credit cards always makes me feel better."

"I don't know about that. I can max mine out at the gas station."

"Want to stop at the mall first?" Trixie asked.

"Sounds good to me. Then let's go to K's Merchandise. I have got to get an answering machine."

Shopping for clothing was tricky. Skye needed Plus Sizes while Trixie required Petites. Except for the large department stores, few dress shops carried that combination of merchandise. They finally decided to alternate, one place for Trixie, then one for Skye.

Their first stop was Pretty Petite. Trixie held up a short red dress for Skye's inspection.

"It looks like a long tank top. Isn't it a bit . . . revealing?" Skye asked.

"Yep, it's for our ninth anniversary. He won't tell me where we're going, just says to dress up." Trixie held the garment against her body. It came to mid-thigh. "I've always wanted a sexy red dress."

Skye nodded thoughtfully. "Why don't you try it on? Take this dress, too." She held up another dress with a flared skirt and triple spaghetti straps that crisscrossed in the back.

Trixie's giggle could be heard clearly in the waiting area where Skye sat on an overstuffed chair.

Coming out from behind the oatmeal-colored curtain, Trixie twirled in front of Skye. "What do you think? I know I don't have the cleavage, but can I get away with it?"

The front of the bodice hung loose, but the rest of the dress hugged Trixie's small body.

"It looks okay, except for the bust." Skye tilted her head. "Would you consider one of those Wonderbras to fill out the top a little?"

"Maybe. Let me try on the other dress and see if I have the same problem."

"Go ahead. I'll be right here." Skye resumed reading. She always carried a book in her purse for anytime she had to wait.

The second dress fit without having to resort to unnatural means and Trixie bought it. As they strolled the mall, window shopping and gossiping, Skye began to relax.

They were nearing an escalator when Skye spotted her cousin Hugo's wife, Victoria. Skye knew she had to be in her early thirties but she looked much younger. Smooth blond hair fell straight to the middle of her back and blue eyes shone from a sun-kissed complexion. She wore a short navy-and-white polka-dot slip dress over a slim, toned body.

Skye was filled with instant loathing, a deep mingling of envy, contempt, and self-pity. It wasn't a feeling she enjoyed or was proud of.

She froze. Before she could decide what to do, Victoria looked around, then abruptly turned and walked rapidly in the other direction.

Skye grabbed Trixie and pointed at the retreating figure. "Do you remember my cousin Hugo?"

"Yes, good-looking, but a little too smooth?"

"Right, there goes his wife, Victoria. I wonder what she's up to."

"What do you mean?"

Skye described Victoria's actions. "Maybe my imagination is running overtime, but it was almost as if she didn't want to be seen, or saw someone she wanted to avoid."

"Or maybe she just forgot something," Trixie suggested.

"That's probably it. I'm not too fond of her, so I was doubtlessly thinking the worst of her." Skye sighed. "She's hard to like."

Trixie patted Skye's arm. "I have heard her referred to around town as Mrs. Perfect and Queen Victoria."

Skye nodded. "Yeah. I don't think she has many friends. I should try again, I suppose. She is family."

"Why is she so disliked? Is it just her incredible looks?"

"I'm sure that's part of it, but everything she says has a barb attached. Sometimes it pinches right away. Sometimes it's like a time bomb, waiting for the right moment to detonate."

"And?"

"She's materialistic and a snob and she's raising her son, Prescott, to be just like her." Skye looked in the direction Victoria had headed. "I can't figure out how Hugo supports her in the manner she demands. You wouldn't think selling cars would earn that much income."

Skye sat back in the restaurant's plush red velvet seat and sipped an iced tea. "I forgot to ask. Did you get the job at the high school?"

"Yes, they called this morning." Trixie grinned.

"Great. We'll be working together. Unless, of course, I'm fired by next year." Skye felt her chest tighten as she said the words.

"I'm sure everything will be fine. You'll come up with something that will satisfy the superintendent."

Skye decided to change the subject. "What do you think of the restaurant?"

"Sort of elegant for the Kankakee I remember."

"Don't worry. Kankakee may now have Chez Philippe, but it still has a Farm and Fleet store, too." Skye picked up the huge menu.

"What a relief. We wouldn't want to have to run all the way to Ottawa for a Farm and Fleet fix. How would the citizens of Scumble River survive without it? Where would they get their clothes, candy, and car supplies?"

Skye snickered and added, "Don't forget electronics, hunting equipment, and livestock needs."

Giggling, Trixie added a few more essential items that could be purchased at the discount store.

"But I must admit," Skye said, feeling forced to be honest, "I have found some nice brand-name clothes there and the prices are about thirty percent less than Carson's or Field's."

"Me too," Trixie confessed. "I just don't normally admit where I got them."

Both women were laughing so hard the waiter was forced to raise his voice. "Good afternoon, ladies. Are you ready to order?"

They agreed to share a plate of tomato basil bruschetta. For her main course Trixie ordered a steak sandwich with Gorgonzola butter and fries. Skye decided on the seafood salad.

When the waiter finished the grand production of writing down their order and left, Skye asked, "Have you worked in a school before?"

"No, I just got my certification. I worked in a public library for a while as a clerk."

"Schools are a different situation. I've been trying to figure out what it is that makes things so intense." Skye paused to allow their appetizer to be served. "The special education coordinator at my last school used to blame it on so many women having

PMS at the same time. His other favorite excuse was 'mental pause,' as he so charmingly called the change of life."

"What a jerk. I'll bet you didn't let him get away with crap like that." Trixie scooped up a piece of toasted bread with chopped tomato and basil sprinkled on top.

Skye smiled thinly, but didn't offer that that same man had fired her. "The best explanation I have so far is that no matter what we do it's eighty percent odds that we'll be in trouble with either a parent or an administrator."

"That sounds a little dramatic."

"Not at all. If you call a student for doing something wrong, six out of ten parents will argue about your decision. On the other hand, if you let something pass to give a kid a chance to straighten up, some other child will tell his folks, who then will complain to the superintendent."

"Sounds rough."

"And that doesn't even touch my job. Almost everything I have to say upsets someone. If I don't find a referred student eligible for services, the teacher is mad at me. If I do find a handicapping condition, the parent is upset. And if I can't tell and need additional tests, the administration is irritated."

"Hard to believe anyone wants to be a school psychologist."

"Believe me, they don't tell you this stuff in graduate school, and even in your internship you are rarely made aware of the everyday realities of the job." Skye moved her hands out of the way, allowing the waiter to center her salad in front of her.

The women turned back to their previous topic.

Trixie asked, "Has the staff of the high school been friendly to you?"

"In their own way." Skye speared a shrimp, a piece of lettuce, and a black olive. "The thing with my job is that I only pop in and out of the building, and rarely have a chance to socialize in the lounge. Even when I do, I think I make a lot of them uncomfortable because they think I'm analyzing everything they say and do."

"I suppose you get that a lot as a psychologist."

Skye shrugged. "The other weird thing is that there are still teachers working there who taught us."

Trixie shuddered. "Not Mr. Zullo? His freshman English was the worst class I've ever been in."

"Yep, he's still there. He's only in his fifties."

"Yuck. He always made me feel so uncomfortable. He stood too close, and I know he was trying to look up my skirt or down my blouse."

"Yeah, me too. I observed his class a couple of times."

"Did you see anything?"

"He's not going to make any moves on the girls while I'm watching."

"Did you talk to the principal?"

"Homer?" Skye shook her head. "What's the use? Besides, I have no proof."

Trixie scowled. "You need to be invisible."

Skye opened her mouth, but a commotion at the door drew her attention. Her cousin Hugo, his wife, Victoria, and a familiar looking middle-aged man were standing at the maître d's podium.

Skye's eyebrows shot into her hairline. Could her cousins' dining companion really be who she thought he was? She deliberately dropped her napkin so she could take a good look at the man without anyone noticing.

Victoria's voice could be heard clearly even under the table. "What is the problem? You have our reservation; I can see our name written in your book." She stabbed the ledger with a gleaming fingernail the shape of a dagger.

"But, madame, the booth you requested is still occupied. If you insist on that particular spot you must wait. I could seat you elsewhere immediately." Philippe's French accent thickened.

Victoria crossed her arms and turned to Hugo. "Do something, sugar. I want 'our' table."

Hugo glanced at the man, who was now standing a little apart from them, and patted Victoria's arm. "Sure thing, sweetheart."

Slipping his wallet from his jacket pocket, Hugo selected a bill and approached the restaurant owner. They spoke in whispers for a moment. Philippe finally accepted the money and walked over to a banquette in the back of the room. It was occupied by two women sipping after-dinner coffee and chatting.

He bent low and whispered to one of the women. She listened, consulted with her friend, and nodded. The women got up and moved toward the bar. A busboy appeared instantly and cleared the table, resetting it with fresh linens.

Victoria's scowl turned to a dazzling smile as she was seated between the two men.

As soon as the three disappeared behind huge menus, Skye leaned over to Trixie and whispered, "Do you know who that guy with Hugo and Victoria is?"

Trixie shrugged. "He does look sort of familiar, but I can't put a name to him. Why?"

"Because if he's who I think he is, I now have a plausible suspect in my grandmother's murder."

CHAPTER 14

ASHES TO ASHES,

WE ALL FALL DOWN

The next day the weather took a turn for the worse. It was hot and humid, and afternoon clouds portended a storm could break loose at any moment. Skye stood with her parents and Vince in the mirrored foyer of the Reid Funeral Home, waiting to view her grandmother's body. She tugged at her navy linen suit, which suddenly felt a size too small. Even the strand of pearls around her neck felt as if they had shrunk. The building was supposed to be air conditioned, but too many people crowded in too small a space had defeated even the strongest equipment.

She followed the pull of Vince's hand through the double doors. It was finally their turn to enter. As the eldest, Uncle Dante and his family had been first. Skye could still hear Aunt Mona muttering from the bottom of the stairs about being last. Minnie and her crew were caught in the middle, as usual.

At first the blast of cool air was a welcome relief, but the subtle odor of death beneath that of the flowers made Skye want to turn and run away. Instead, she drew a ragged breath and turned right, walking toward the front of the room. The bronze casket stood beneath a soft pink spotlight. Huge floral displays on wire stands ranged along both sides.

May was on the kneeler, head bent in prayer. Not being Catholic, Jed stood behind her, his hands folded. Vince guided Skye to their mother's side and she knelt.

Skye swallowed hard and looked at the wrinkled face of her grandmother. Antonia's nimbus of white hair was artfully arranged and her features looked peaceful. An emerald-green rosary was entwined in her fingers.

Skye stood, allowing Vince to take her place. She examined the cards on the flowers and plants, and was astonished at the number of arrangements.

Vince and May were finished and Skye rejoined her family as they stood in front of the coffin for a moment of silence. In that instant she vowed, *Grandma, I will find out who did this to you. Even if it's one of us, I know you'd want the guilty person to be punished.*

May joined Dante in the line of cushioned chairs in front of the rows of folding chairs. Jed and Vince moved to the back of the room.

Skye looked for Simon. She wanted to run her theory about Hugo by him before she spoke to Hugo himself. Even though Simon rarely agreed with her, he almost always had a unique way of looking at matters that inevitably came in handy.

"So, when I saw Hugo and Victoria eating lunch with the guy from the Castleview housing development company, I knew who had killed Grandma and why." Skye sat back in her chair.

Simon leaned forward. "Tell me again why Hugo killed your grandmother."

They were in his office in the back of the funeral home. The door was tightly closed, but Skye still checked to make sure no one was listening. "Number one: Hugo lives far beyond his means, and if he cuts back I'm betting he'll lose Victoria, not to mention his son."

"Okay, say we accept that premise even though you don't have proof. After all, Hugo could make a lot more selling cars than you think. Or maybe Victoria doesn't care as much about money as she seems to."

Skye choked on a mouthful of tea. "Right, and Scumble River is the center of culture and elegance."

He looked at her steadily for a moment. "Ready to go on?" She nodded. "Fine. Even agreeing to all the previous assumptions, how can you get from a simple lunch to this Castleview fellow buying your grand-mother's farm for a housing development?"

"Well . . ."

"Besides, didn't you tell me that your Uncle Dante controls the trust? How could Hugo benefit? The money would go to the children, not the grandchildren."

"There are lots of ways around a thing like that. Dante could be in on it, the trust could be a lot less airtight than we think, or . . . Hugo may have figured a way around those problems."

"Maybe. But this is a long way from proof."

"I'm going to talk to Hugo today. See if he makes any slips."

"You'd better be extremely careful. If, and I do mean *if*, Hugo is the killer, it would be very dangerous for him to know you're onto him."

Skye bounced up from the chair and faced Simon. "Gee, thanks, I was going to go straight up to him, and tell him I knew what he was up to and that he was the killer. Your way sounds so much better."

"You've always got a comeback, don't you?" Simon drew her into his arms and whispered against her lips: "So how about an answer to my question?"

Skye gave him a quick kiss, wiggled out of his arms, and slipped out the door without replying.

Back in the visitation parlor, Skye sat down on the folding chair vacated moments earlier by Victoria. She could still smell the other woman's Obsession.

Leaning close to Hugo, she spoke softly, "Hi, how you doing?"

He gave her a startled glance and pulled slightly away. "Fine. Just fine."

"Sure is something about Grandma. I always thought she'd just go in her sleep. Hard to believe someone killed her."

Glancing nervously around, Hugo whispered, "We shouldn't talk about that now. Someone might hear us."

"Oh, but we don't have anything to hide, right?"

"No, no of course not. Don't be ridiculous." He mopped his forehead with a large white handkerchief. "It's just not very respectful."

"You're probably right." Skye forced herself to agree with him. "So, how's the family? Prescott is in third grade now, right?"

Hugo beamed. "Yes, and then there is talk of double promoting him. We're waiting for the results of this last year's achievement test."

"You must be very proud." Skye turned slightly. "He's in the Brooklyn School District, right? You live across the county line."

"Right. But he goes to a private school in Kankakee."

"Wow, that must be expensive. Not to mention a long ride. Do they send a bus?"

"It's costly, but Victoria, I mean, *we* feel it is money well spent. If for no other reason than the connections he can make." Hugo took a lighter from his pocket and began sliding it through his fingers. "There are kids at Saint Elmo's from the best families in a sixty-mile radius. You know, a lot of wealthy people from Chicago have moved out this way to get away from the . . . from the crime."

"Yes, I recall." He was speaking of white flight. Skye frowned, but decided if she wanted to get information from him it would be a mistake to tell him what she thought of his morals and values. "You must be a wonderful salesman. It's hard to keep up with that type of crowd. Financially, I mean."

"I make a good living."

"But Victoria doesn't work, does she?"

"She takes the occasional interior design job. We both agree that Prescott is her main occupation."

"Well, selling cars must be better paying than I ever dreamed. Certainly better than being a school psychologist." Skye laughed self-deprecatingly. "But almost anything pays better than that."

Hugo smiled stiffly. "If you'll excuse me, I'm going to step out and have a cigarette."

He was gone before she could think of anything else to say.

Skye was writing her impressions of her meeting with Hugo in a little notebook when Victoria and Prescott sat down. She slapped the book closed as Victoria inclined her head in its direction.

"What are you writing?" she asked.

"Just my grocery list," Skye lied without blinking. "Hugo went out for a smoke."

"Filthy habit, but the poor dear needs something to help him relax."

"Sounds like he works really hard."

"Yes, he insists on making sure we live in the right style."

"That's a beautiful ring. Is it new?" Skye pointed to a huge ruby set in gold.

Victoria twisted it, catching the light. "Yes, I just got it yesterday. It's three carats."

"I was shopping yesterday too, but all I bought was an answering machine and a dress for the funeral tomorrow." Skye tried to sound friendly.

"It was a gift."

"From Hugo?"

"You could say that. At least indirectly." Victoria suddenly seemed bored. "Excuse me, Prescott needs to leave for his violin lesson."

Antonia had left instructions that the wake would be held for one day only, with visitation from one to four and seven to ten. The family took a break between afternoon and evening hours, gathering at May's to eat some of the food that friends and neighbors had been dropping off for days. Many went to their own homes first to do some personal chores. Skye had stopped off at the cottage and taken care of Bingo's needs.

When she got to her parents' house, she found her father leaning against the dog pen. Chocolate sat near the gate. Jed absently rubbed the lab's ears.

"Hi, Dad." Skye kissed his cheek. "What are you doing out here?"

"Chocolate was barking like crazy, and your mother sent me to quiet him down."

"Was anything wrong?" Skye eyed the dog, who glowed with health.

"Nope, just wanted some attention." Jed patted the dog's chest.

"Bingo was a little squirrelly too. Poor thing. Going from spending every minute of every day with Grandma to catching a few hours with me when I'm home. He must be pretty confused and lonely."

"Yeah, I'm sure no one thinks of the animals when they kill someone." Jed gave Chocolate a final stroke. "Too bad Bingo can't talk. He could probably tell us who the murderer is."

Skye nodded. "He's a pretty good watch cat. Yowled his head off when someone . . ."

"Someone what?"

"Came to the door selling magazine subscriptions." There was no need to tell her parents about the Bible.

"Ah-huh." Jed gave her the same skeptical look he used when she tried to explain getting home late from a date as a teenager. "Well, we'd better be getting inside before your ma's sisters drive her crazy." He paused. "They're good people. They try real hard. Maybe too hard."

Skye was surprised to hear her father make that kind of pronouncement. He wasn't much of a talker and never seemed to have much to say about other people. She wondered if he was trying to tell her something.

They made their way into the house through the kitchen. Jed stopped to wash his hands at the half bath off the utility room.

May was at the kitchen sink with Aunt Minnie and Uncle Dante's wife, Olive. Skye kissed her mother and said hi to her aunts.

May gestured for Skye to follow and led her to the other side of the room. She whispered, "I looked at those pictures in Vince's safe. I wrote the names of anyone I recognized on the back. Why did you want me to see them?"

"I found them at Grandma's and thought they'd be valuable if I ever get around to doing the family history."

"Why do you need to keep them in Vince's safe?"

Skye thought quickly. "In case of fire. I'd hate to lose them before I can make duplicates."

May nodded, but looked puzzled.

Both the peninsula counter and the table were loaded with food. Jell-O molds nudged casserole dishes, while angel and devil's food cakes fought the eternal battle of temptation.

Skye edged past the overflow and went through the arch into the living room. Uncle Dante had claimed her father's favorite lounger, where he sat like Napoléon with one hand scratching his belly and the other aiming the remote. A can of beer sat sweating on the oak end table, a white ring already forming on the wood.

Skye's gaze swept the room. She was stunned. Uncle Emmett was eating a plate of ravioli, tomato sauce dripping on the white brocade of the love seat. Vince sat next to him gesturing with his fork, which held a bite of chocolate cake — crumbs flew in all directions.

She watched as, without noticing, Uncle Neal ground a cookie under his heel, leaving an oily patch on the russet carpet. Mona scooted closer to Neal on the sofa and tried to pick up the ginger snap's remains in a paper napkin.

Food in the living room. Her mother never allowed them to eat there. The world as they knew it truly must be ending.

Skye aimed her question at Dante. It had only been a week and she was still angry about the essay contest, so she didn't want to talk to Mona. She also wasn't interested in joining the conversation about tractors that Emmett and Vince were having. "Where are Hugo and the twins?"

Not turning from the television screen, Dante said, "Ask Olive."

Instead Skye headed for the den, a spare bedroom that her parents had converted by adding a love seat, armchair, and television. On her way she fixed herself a plate of food and grabbed the latest mystery from her purse.

It crossed her mind that this might be a good opportunity to talk to some of her relatives about her grandmother's death, but she was too tired to do a good job. Grief and several nights of just a few hours of sleep had caught up with her. One thing she had learned as a psychologist was that if she didn't feel good physically, she tended to make stupid mistakes mentally.

So, instead of pressing on with her investigation she set up a TV tray by the small sofa, kicked off her shoes, and snuggled into the corner. Selecting a carrot spear from her dish, she settled in to read.

Skye half heard the twins and their families arrive a little while later. By the time Hugo and Victoria made their appearance, it barely registered. Skye was deep into the fictional world of the story when the den door was eased open and Aunt Minnie slipped in.

Skye reluctantly put her book aside. "Hi. What's up?"

"Sorry, I didn't know you were in here. I just wanted to rest a bit before going back to the funeral home. It's already past six."

"Have a seat. Did you get anything to eat? How about a cup of coffee?" Skye pushed her tray away.

Minnie sat gingerly on the chair. "I nibbled while we put things away. I don't eat much anymore."

Skye looked from her aunt's plump figure to her own and wondered about genetics.

"How about some coffee then?" Skye slid her feet back into her navy pumps.

"That would be nice, but I can get it." Minnie tried to get up.

Skye beat her to the door. "Sit down. I want another glass of Diet Coke anyway."

When Skye returned with the drinks, she found her aunt with her eyes closed. She set the cup and glass on the tray between them, and curled back up on the love seat.

"I'm not asleep." Minnie stretched and reached for the coffee.

"This whole thing must be a real strain on you. I know you spent more time taking care of Grandma than anyone else." Skye eased her way into the topic she was interested in pursuing.

"I never begrudged Mom the attention."

"Of course not. Everyone said how devoted you were." Skye swirled the ice cubes in her glass. "Still, it had to be hard."

"A little. Mom didn't like to acknowledge that she needed help."

"It must have been tough having to be there three times a day every day to make her meals."

"The others wanted to let the housekeeper do it all, but I knew she wouldn't eat right if we let that foreign woman fix her food."

"Really? You didn't think Mrs. J did a good job?" Skye leaned forward.

"No. She refused to dust and run the sweeper every day. She would only clean once a week." Minnie's cheeks were pink and her eyes had shed their dull look. "She wanted us to put in a dishwasher."

"Grandma wouldn't have liked that."

"No, but she only complained to me. I'd tell May and Mona, and then Mom would say I had gotten what she said wrong." Minnie sat back and ran a hand over her eyes. "I tried so hard to please her and never could."

"I'm sure that's not true. But it would be hard to think that's the way she felt about you." Skye patted her aunt's hand and silently asked her grandmother's forgiveness for lying about her. "I remember Grandma saying you were the one she could depend on."

"You know, Mona and Dante treated her like a child and she never seemed to resent them. And May treated her so casually and still was her obvious favorite." Minnie sniffed and wiped her nose with the paper napkin from the tray. "I must admit sometimes I resented all the time I spent trying to be a good daughter and not getting anything back."

"That would be hard to take." Skye knew how fragile her aunt's mental health was and was reluctant to push her. Still, she had to find out if Minnie was the one who killed her grandmother. She tried to be as gentle as possible. "It sounds as if you're saying it felt like she was throwing all your love and attention back in your face."

Minnie didn't answer.

Skye took a breath and silently apologized to her aunt. If Minnie was innocent, this was an awful thing to say, but if she was guilty, Skye couldn't let her get away with murder. "It must have been a relief, almost, when Grandma died."

Minnie shot out of her chair and threw the door open, banging it against the wall. Her normally soft voice shrieked over her shoulder. "I don't know what you mean. I loved my mother and she loved me. I didn't want her dead."

People gathered from different parts of the house. The twins surrounded their mother and led her off into one of the bedrooms. May shot Skye a deadly look from the sink, while everyone else tried to pretend that nothing unusual had happened.

Vince went over to Skye. "I shouldn't have pressed her so hard," she admitted, whispering. "This could be the thing that pushes Aunt Minnie around the bend."

He put his arm around her shoulder. "Don't blame yourself. She's had that turn signal on for twenty years."

Chapter 15

Roses Are Red,

Lies Are Yellow

Wednesday, the day after the wake, Skye met her parents and Vince at the Reid Funeral Home and rode with them to the church. Saint Francis Catholic Church had been built back when Scumble River was first established in the 1850s. It towered above the other buildings, with walls clad in crumbling brown brick and faded gray concrete overhangs.

Almost a third of Scumble River's population was Catholic, so parking was always a problem, unless you were among the first fifty cars and secured a space in the small back lot. Later arrivals used the side streets, often angering residents whose driveways they blocked.

In front of the church there was room for three or four vehicles, depending on the size of the car and its owner's skill in parking. During a funeral the hearse and limousine took up those spaces.

Jed parked in back and he, May, Vince, and Skye entered the church through the side door. They found seats in the second pew from the front and waited for Father Burns to begin.

Dante and his family occupied the first row. Minnie and her brood sat in back of the Denisons. Mona and Neal were once again last. Skye could hear Mona's complaints from two rows away.

The priest finally started the Mass and they all rose. Skye found it difficult to concentrate on the words of the service. She squirmed and plucked at her clothes as the heat of many people crowded together added to the already uncomfortable interior temperature. Her eyes were continually drawn to the closed casket. It looked much too large for a person of her grandmother's size.

Eventually Father Burns's words penetrated Skye's thoughts. "I could stand up here and tell you that Antonia Leofanti has gone home to be with our Father and is at peace with Him in His kingdom, because that is true.

"I could stand up here and tell you that Antonia Leofanti lived a long life and left a wonderful legacy of family and love. That too is true.

"But when someone, old or young, is ripped from this mortal coil by violence, the question then becomes: Do we seek an eye for an eye? Or do we turn the other cheek?"

Skye missed the rest of what the priest said. Her mind latched on to his question and refused to let go. Vengeance or forgiveness? It was a tough call, but perhaps simple justice was the answer. She had always believed that the consequences should fit the action.

After the funeral Mass ended, Skye followed her parents numbly down the aisle. May climbed into the limousine with her brother and sisters, and Vince rode with the other pallbearers, which left Skye and her father together for the trip to the cemetery.

As she slid onto the front seat of her parents' white Oldsmobile, and Jed settled into the driver's seat, Skye looked at her father's expressionless face.

The air-conditioned interior was a relief and they drove in silence for a while. Jed switched on the radio, then turned it off almost immediately.

"Dad?"

"Mmm?"

"How mad at me is Mom?"

"Aw, she's not mad. She just doesn't like things to be stirred up."

"I didn't mean for Aunt Minnie to have such a hissy fit."

"Well, she's always been real high strung. She's been having those spells of hers since she was a teenager. She didn't even finish high school because she had some sort of breakdown her senior year."

"I never knew that." Skye turned to look at him. "What happened?"

"If I remember rightly, Antonia and Angelo sent her to visit some relatives somewhere." Jed scratched his head. "Seems to me they had Mona go with her."

"Relatives? See, that's exactly why I was trying to get the family history from Grandma before she died. I didn't know we had relatives anywhere else." Skye straightened in her seat as they entered the cemetery.

The black wrought-iron gates that spelled out Scumble River Cemetery and the narrow, tree-lined road always sent Skye's imagination down dark paths, and her thoughts turned to the idea of mortality.

The graveside service was mercifully short, considering the heat and humidity. Father Burns led them in a prayer and then Simon guided them back to their cars before lowering the casket.

Skye picked her way past the graves, stopping to examine a monument shaped like a regulation-sized La-Z-Boy. Mementos had been glued all around it. A football huddled near a beer can, and golf tees were heaped next to a videocassette. The coup de grâce was an ashtray fastened to the chair's arm, a faux cigarette made to look as if smoke were rising from its tip.

Where else but Scumble River would they make a monument out of a man's bad habits?

May and Vince had both elected to ride with Skye and Jed to the luncheon at the new church hall. They entered a large room with folding tables and chairs and plain white walls. Although not fancy, it was at least air conditioned. They were among the first to arrive.

Skye noticed her mother's pallor and fetched her a glass of cold punch. "Here, Mom, you look as if you could use this."

May downed the liquid in one gulp and handed the empty cup to Skye. "Thanks."

The silent treatment. Skye hated when her mother stopped talking to her. Usually May never quit chattering, so when she spoke in single words, Skye knew she was in hot water.

"Look, Mom, I'm sorry about yesterday."

"This isn't the place to talk about it."

May spotted people beginning to arrive, and moved toward the door. She whispered over her shoulder, "Just stay out of trouble today."

Skye was scanning the crowd for Vince when someone grabbed her arm from behind and yanked. She turned, swallowing a scream, when she saw her Uncle Dante.

He pulled her toward a door leading to the catechism classrooms. "I want to talk to you, young lady."

Her stomach dropped. Short of creating a scene, Skye could see no way to break loose. "Let's talk here. I was just going to get something to eat. We could sit together."

Dante's eyes narrowed, which caused them to all but disappear under his jutting brow. "Not in public."

She had never seen her uncle like this. He dragged her out of the common area, and shoved her into a room decorated with children's drawings of Jesus. Dante pushed her into a child-sized chair and pulled over the teacher's chair for himself. "What do you think you're doing questioning my son?"

"Questioning him? Me? I don't know what you're talking about." She could almost make herself believe her own words, since her conversation with Hugo seemed years ago rather than yesterday afternoon.

"Don't play dumb with me, Missy!" Dante roared. "You talked to both Hugo and Victoria about how much money they had."

"It was just conversation. I hadn't seen them in a long time and commented on how well they seem to be doing." She rounded her eyes. "I had no idea a car salesman could make so much money."

Dante puffed out his chest. "Hugo's the best, and Prescott's going to do even better."

"Yes, that private school is certainly impressive." Skye relaxed a little. She could almost rest her chin on her knees, the chair was so small. "Do you help them with tuition?"

Dante's face turned an alarming shade of reddish-purple and his voice grew louder. "You don't get it, do you? I'm telling you to lay off my family. Quit asking questions."

Skye rose and started edging toward the door. "I'm just surprised you'd agree with Hugo."

"About what?" Dante's bulging brow wrinkled.

"About subdividing Grandma's land instead of farming it." With her hand on the knob she grew brave. "I mean, you were always the one who said if Grandma lived much longer, we'd have to start selling off the land to pay for her care, and it would be such a shame to lose it for farming."

"Subdividing it? What are you talking about?" Dante seemed to notice for the first time that she wasn't sitting any longer, and he started to lever himself off his seat.

"Didn't Hugo tell you about his lunch with that guy from the Castleview housing development company?" Skye eased the door open.

Dante sank back into his chair. His answer was almost inaudible. "No, no he didn't."

That had certainly hit a chord. She'd never seen Dante lose his bluster so fast. As she left the room, Skye said over her shoulder, "I wonder what else he didn't tell you."

Skye saw the twins sitting together at a long empty table. From the debris surrounding them, she surmised that their children and spouses had already been and gone. She quickly took a glass of punch and made her way over to Ginger and Gillian.

"Mind if I join you?" she asked, hoping they weren't too angry at her after the incident with their mother yesterday. She didn't relish being kidnapped again, nor the idea of another five-mile hike home.

Ginger and Gillian paused in their conversation and nodded after a brief hesitation.

"How's your mother? I'm sure sorry about yesterday."

"Did you really accuse her of murdering Grandma?" Gillian asked.

"No! I just commented on how much work it had been for her to serve Grandma three meals a day, and that things would be easier for her now."

Gillian pushed her dish away and sighed. "She's okay. Something happens; then she's fine. At least she didn't have one of her spells."

Her cousins were really being nice about yesterday's incident. Maybe she had misjudged them. "Did her visit to Carle Clinic help with her spells?"

"Could be," Ginger said. "You know Mama, we don't discuss things like that."

Before Skye could reply, two young boys came tearing around the table, chased by two little girls. The boys threw themselves at Ginger, screaming at the top of their lungs.

Skye was astounded when her cousin failed to respond. She neither scolded them for the commotion, nor checked to see if there really was a problem. Instead Ginger sat still while they swarmed over her, grabbing bits of food from various dishes.

The little girls scrambled up on chairs, their short party dresses exposing their thighs and underpants. They too were talking so loudly Skye thought her ears would start bleeding.

Finally, carrying the food they had liberated from their parents' plates, the children ran off, scattering adults as they went.

Skye sat silently, amazed that neither parent had intervened. Ginger took a sip of coffee as if nothing had happened.

"What were we talking about?" Gillian broke off a piece of cookie and popped it into her mouth.

"Ah . . . Ah, your mom's health. Do you know what's wrong with her?"

"Well, part of it is she's going through the change, so she's embarrassed to talk about it." Gillian drew circles on the white paper tablecloth with her damp cup.

"But menopause isn't that big a deal anymore, is it? I thought they had a pretty safe and effective hormone therapy now."

Ginger shrugged. "Mom doesn't want to take drugs, so she's having a rough time."

"You girls can't talk her into it?"

They both shook their heads.

Skye got up. "I'm going to get some water. You all want anything?"

"More coffee would be great. Cream and two sugars. Thanks." Ginger handed Skye her cup.

When Skye returned, her cousins' husbands had joined them. Both looked uncomfortable in their funeral clothes. Flip Allen, Ginger's husband, was a big, hulking guy whose suit appeared to have been borrowed from his little brother. His wrists and ankles showed from their respective cuffs.

He was speaking as Skye slipped into her seat. "Geez, honey, me and the boys have been going fishing up north since before we got married. I can't let them down. They count on my paying my part of the freight."

Irvin Tubb, Gillian's husband, joined in. He was short and round, as his name suggested. "Yah, we been doin' this since high school. What's the fuss this time?"

Gillian lowered her voice. "Money. We could use that money for other things. I need a new washer and dryer, Kristin has outgrown all her clothes, and I'm still waiting for you to pave the driveway."

Ginger nodded. "Yeah, our kids need clothes too, and my van has just about had it. We can't afford for you to go this year."

Flip wrinkled his forehead. "Well, all

right, but I thought you were getting a bunch of money when the old lady died."

Irvin added, "Yeah, you two were always talkin' about the expensive jewelry she had, and how you'd get a good price for it when she finally kicked off."

"Why doncha say it a little louder?" Gillian sneered. "You idiot. Now Miss Smarty Pants over here will think we killed Grandma."

The two men turned a dull shade of red and got up from the table.

Flip mumbled, "What the Christ. We can't never do nothing right. Let's get outta here."

Irvin followed. "Yeah, okeydokey."

Skye sat on a swing in the church playground and dangled her legs. Tears ran down her cheeks. She didn't bother to wipe them off; after all, she had come outside to cry.

Laughter and loud voices could be heard from inside the hall. No one seemed to be mourning her grandmother.

Suddenly she was swept into a bear hug. "Honey, what are you doing out here all by yourself?"

Strong arms held her away so that intense blue eyes could stare into hers. Charlie didn't give her a chance to reply. "I know how close you and Antonia were. But she lived a long life, and she wouldn't want you to cry for her."

"It's not only Grandma's death, it's everything. As usual my life's a mess. I thought as I got older, my life would settle down." Skye sat back down on the swing.

"What's the problem?" Charlie leaned forward, taking the chains in either hand. "If someone is giving you a hard time, why didn't you come to me?"

"Oh, Uncle Charlie, it's not always something you can fix."

"Tell me anyway." Charlie released the links, crossed his arms, and planted his feet firmly in the gravel.

"I don't know where to start." Skye swung back and forth, hoping Charlie would drop the subject.

He gazed at her steadily. "The beginning is always a good place."

"Okay. Overlooking the fact that my grandmother was murdered, and I'm pretty sure a family member did it, I'm also having trouble with my job, my love life, and someone who's playing pranks on me."

"Well, Antonia's murderer will be found and if it's a relative, it's better to know about that person rather than have them in the bosom of your family ready to strike at any time."

"Maybe, but Uncle Dante is in such a state he sort of scares me."

"Why?" Charlie leaned forward, his forehead lined.

After Skye told him about being dragged into the classroom and forced to remain against her will, a stream of obscenities erupted from Charlie. He ended his tirade with, "Don't you worry about Dante. He's just a moron studying to be an idiot."

Skye giggled. "Yeah, and those are pretty much his good points." She felt better, having told Charlie. At least if someone hurt her, Charlie knew that Dante had threatened her.

"Now, what's up with your job?" Charlie moved on to her next dilemma.

She cursed herself. Skye hadn't intended to tell Charlie about that. She didn't want him pulling any more strings on her behalf. "Oh, that's not much of anything. A few angry parents at the end of the school year, that's all. It's taken care of."

"I heard about your tires and windows. Has there been anything else?"

"Someone stole something from my car while it was parked in my own driveway."

"I was talking to Jed and we think you

need an alarm at your house and on your car. You're isolated. It's an invitation for trouble." Charlie took a toothpick from his pocket and stuck it in his mouth. "I talked to a security company, and they're going to come out day after tomorrow."

She didn't bother to remind him that her tires had been slit while she was at her grandmother's, surrounded by people. Instead she said, "I can't afford it and you are not paying for it. Besides, I'd have to check with my landlords before installing something like that on their property."

"But —"

"No buts; case closed." Skye gave him a stern look.

He finally broke eye contact. "Maybe later then. Now, what's wrong with your love life?" Charlie drew himself up to his full height. "If Simon is pressuring you, I can take care of that."

"Thanks, but that won't be necessary." Skye debated whether to confide in Charlie. "The thing is, he's a lot more certain about his feelings than I am about mine. He wants our relationship to be more intimate and committed. I'm just not sure what I want yet."

To her surprise, Charlie didn't yell at her for blowing her chance at an eligible bachelor. Instead he said, "Is there someone else?"

Skye shrugged, her cheeks reddened. "Maybe. No. I don't know."

"Keep seeing Simon as long as he's willing to stick to your terms. When he's not willing anymore, then you'll have to decide."

"Skye, yoo-hoo Skye, over here." A loud, demanding voice rang out when Skye re-entered the parish hall looking for her parents.

Mona was sitting with her husband and Father Burns.

"Yes, Aunt Mona?" Skye presented herself at their table.

"Sit down, dear. Neal and Father want to talk to you." Mona gestured to a chair opposite them.

"You know, I was just looking for my folks. Maybe we could chat later."

"This will only take a few moments." Mona's voice was lined with steel.

Sighing, Skye complied with her aunt's demand. "Yes, Father? Uncle Neal?"

A pained expression crossed the priest's face. "Skye, it really could wait, but I'm afraid your aunt and uncle are quite persuasive."

"Yes, they are."

"It's about you joining the church's Young Advocates group."

"I've never heard of them."

Father Burns' opened his mouth to explain further, but before he could speak a voice screamed, echoing across the dining area. "Help! Help! Mom's dying."

CHAPTER 16

SEE, SAW, MAY'S LAW

Stunned silence filled the church hall. Ginger appeared at the entrance of the banquet room, crying, and Father Burns headed toward her. As Skye ran after the priest, she yelled to Neal, "Call 911."

Mona followed Skye toward the ladies' room, but edged in front of her at the door. Skye stepped over the threshold just in time to see Mona shove Gillian aside and bend over Minnie's body.

Water dripped from the pipe under the sink, making the gray tile floor appear slimy. The smell of ammonia and mold was overpowering. Minnie lay facedown with her arms over her head but bent at the elbow. Her flowered dress had crept up, revealing a white slip and gartered hose. Small blue pills were strewn near her head and hands.

Skye tried to kneel beside her aunt. "I've had first aid training; let me take a look."

Mona thrust her away. "Haven't you

done enough? This is all your fault."

"Huh?" Skye rocked back on her heels, nearly falling. "What are you talking about?"

"If you hadn't been grilling Mona yesterday, she wouldn't have tried to kill herself today."

Gillian shouldered her aunt aside. "What are you saying? Mom didn't try to commit suicide."

Mona put an arm around her niece and pointed with the other hand. "See those pills?"

All three women stared at the tiny blue tablets scattered near Minnie's hand.

Skye parked the Buick outside the police station, but made no move to get out of the vehicle. Pictures of Minnie lying on the bathroom floor played in an endless loop in her head. Even her morning swim hadn't been able to distract her from that memory. Intellectually she knew that no one could cause another person to kill herself. But emotionally, she was having difficulty believing it. And even if she wasn't the cause, she should have been able to see how desperately unhappy her aunt was, and insisted that she get help.

She finally forced herself out of the car

and went into the building. The portable radio on a shelf behind May's head blared out a baseball game. When Skye entered, the sportscaster was announcing the score: "Cubs 2, Brewers 11."

May's shoulders sagged and she turned the volume down.

To her mother's back Skye said, "You know, Mom, rooting for the Cubs is like rooting for Bangladesh in a food fight."

"I told you not to come here." May didn't turn around or react to Skye's joke.

"Don't be mad, Mom. I really need to talk to you." Skye reached to buzz herself past the locked door.

"Stop that." May slapped her hand away from the button. "Go home and quit causing trouble. I'm not mad. I'm hurt that you could think those awful things about my brother and sisters."

"I'm sorry." Skye tried once again to release the door lock.

"Fine, go home and mind your own business." May kept a wary eye on the latch.

"I can't. I can't let the killer get away with it. Is that what you want?"

"Maybe." A tear rolled down May's cheek. "Remember, we are talking about my brother and sisters. Remember how you felt last year when Vince was accused of murder."

"I am sorry, Mom." Skye tried to hug her but the counter between them was too wide.

Wiping away the drop, May said, "Then quit bothering everyone. Let Wally handle the investigation."

"He's happy I'm helping."

"Wally can figure it out without you." May paused to answer a call, then continued. "He seemed real excited when he got the toxicology results this morning."

"Oh?" Skye hoped her mother would elaborate.

"Yeah, seems they figured out what the poison was." May made a note in the log.

"And?" Skye tried to keep her voice even.

"Well, he didn't tell me what it was."

"But you peeked at the report, didn't you?" Skye tried to sound as if she didn't care about the answer.

"I might have noticed something when I was doing some other filing."

"So?"

"Something like 'jack trophy kirk's ass.' I can't pronounce it."

"Why did it take so long to find out the type of poison? The autopsy has been done for days."

"It has something to do with how many kinds of poisons there are to check for, how long the tests themselves take, and how much of a priority our sample is —" May was interrupted once again by the phone.

Skye took the opportunity presented by May's distraction to make a note of the toxin so she could try to look it up at the library later.

May hung up and turned back to Skye. "That was Gillian. The doctors have decided to keep Minnie in the hospital for a while."

"But I thought she was okay after they pumped her stomach last night."

"Minnie refuses to admit she took the pills. She says she did not try to commit suicide. So they're keeping her for psychiatric observation." May uttered the last two words with great difficulty.

The women were silent for a while. The only noise in the station was the static of the radios.

Finally, Skye said, "You know, Mom, it's possible Aunt Minnie killed Grandma, and then couldn't stand the guilt, so she tried to kill herself."

Tears overflowed May's eyes. "I'm afraid that's what everyone is going to think, but I just can't picture Minnie being able to do it."

"I know what you mean. She's usually so indecisive. But if she's emotionally disturbed, who knows what she's capable of doing?" Skye handed her mother a tissue.

"Going through the change has been real rough on her, 'cause she won't take the medicine her doctor gave her. I've been begging her to at least take the capsules to help her sleep, but she refuses to take anything at all." May paused, then added softly, "I guess she took those sleeping pills yesterday though."

"The twins told me she didn't want to take drugs." Skye's face took on a faraway expression.

"What are you thinking?" May asked. "You look as confused as a cow on Astro-Turf."

"If she wouldn't take hormones for her menopausal symptoms, would she take pills to commit suicide?"

May stood up. "No. She's always hated taking medicine. She usually wouldn't even fill the prescriptions."

"Mom, this could mean that Aunt Minnie is telling the truth. Maybe she didn't try to kill herself. Maybe someone tried to kill her."

"Who would want to kill Minnie?" May sat back down.

"The same person who murdered Grandma. The real killer could be trying to throw suspicion on Minnie." Skye was scribbling furiously in her notebook. "Call Wally right now. He's got to get Aunt Minnie some protection, or the next time she might not make it."

Skye and May sat across from the police chief in the combination coffee and interrogation room. Both women had told their stories, and he was now asking questions.

"Let me get this straight. You think Minnie did not attempt suicide? Instead you think someone tried to kill her?"

"Well, either tried to kill her or make her look like Grandma's murderer." Skye flipped open her notebook. "I've tried to put my reasons in order."

Wally made a go-ahead gesture with his hand.

"Okay. First, this is a woman who will not take medicine. She feels that all drugs are bad. Even ones her doctors tell her to take." Wally opened his mouth, but Skye continued. "Also, she says she didn't take them. I've heard of people claiming an attempt was an accident, but not denying any part of it."

"Look, it's just as possible she overcame her dislike of pills and is embarrassed to admit it." Wally looked at each woman in turn. "Isn't it?"

"Anything's possible," Skye answered for both of them. "Did they find the bottle when they searched the church bathroom?"

"No." Wally looked through the file. "No container on the scene or on her person."

"Don't you find that odd?" Skye asked. "What did she do, carry the pills loose in her purse?"

He shrugged.

"Another thing, when they pumped her stomach, could they tell if she had swallowed the pills whole, or were they added to something she ate or drank?" Skye paused and thought. "Too bad all the dishes will have been washed or disposed of since yesterday."

"Okay, I'll check into it, but I can't afford to have someone guard her door until we have more evidence." Wally wrote in his own notebook. "The best I can do is let the hospital know to keep an eye out."

Skye stopped herself from making a sarcastic comment about closing the barn door when it was too late to do any good. "One more thing."

He was already walking down the hall.

"Could you make sure the hospital doesn't let anyone visit her unaccompanied?" Skye yelled.

His voice floated back. "Yeah, fine, okay."

Skye turned to her mom. "Do you still want me to quit bothering everyone with my questions?" When May didn't answer, Skye added, "If the murderer isn't found soon, he may go after Aunt Minnie again."

"Maybe, but I'm worried that if you keep poking your nose in where it doesn't belong, you might be next."

Looking around at the chaos inside her cottage Skye could almost believe it had been vandalized again, except she knew she had done it all herself. Bingo didn't seem to care. He was nestled among the dirty clothes spilling from the overfull hamper.

After changing to old jean shorts and a ragged T-shirt, Skye started in on the mess. First, she stripped the bed and dumped the sheets in the washer. Remaking the bed with fresh linens was a challenge due to Bingo's desire to play hide-and-seek among the covers.

Next, she sorted laundry and cleaned the bathrooms. Bingo followed her every move, appearing to think she was a giant mouse he was stalking.

Since Skye rarely cooked, the kitchen took only a few minutes to wipe down. This left the great room. She was looking for the furniture polish when the doorbell rang.

Bingo beat her to the entry and was pacing impatiently when she arrived. Peeking through the side window, Skye groaned.

She reluctantly opened the door. "Hi, Simon. Sorry. I'm such a mess. I was just cleaning. You look awfully spiffy for a Thursday afternoon."

"Thanks, I've got a funeral at one. I thought maybe you'd be free for lunch now that school's out." Simon walked into the foyer.

"Gee, I'd love to but, as I said, I'm hardly dressed to go out." Skye led the way into the great room.

"Well, I'm sure no one at McDonald's would mind how you're dressed." Simon sat beside her on the couch.

"How about I make us salad and soup right here?"

"I'd really like to take you out, but if that's your best offer, I accept." Simon loosened his tie, took off his suit jacket, and scooted closer to her.

"Ah, good, just let me wash up a little, and I'll get started on lunch." Skye retreated into her bedroom and firmly closed the door.

She reemerged in ten minutes, having washed her face, changed tops, and combed her hair. Simon was in the kitchen, looking into an open cupboard. Bingo was twining around his legs, meowing.

"Looks like it's time for a visit to the Super Value." Simon gestured to the empty shelves.

"Yeah, I've gotten a little behind with my housekeeping chores." She opened the refrigerator and pulled out a bag of salad and a bottle of dressing. "Do you see any soup?"

Simon showed her two cans. "Tomato or chicken noodle?"

"You choose. The saucepans are to the left of the stove on the bottom." Skye grabbed bowls, napkins, and flatware. "I hear the final tox screen came in on Grandma. What was used to poison her?"

"You know I can't tell you that. How did you know about it anyway?"

She mimicked him: "You know I can't tell you that."

"Look, let's have a nice lunch without talking about murder." Simon rummaged among the shelves until he found a tray.

"Fine." Skye watched Simon load the tray with their bowls. She added glasses of soda, then led the way to the patio.

They'd finished eating and were laughing about their latest attempt to teach another couple to play bridge when the doorbell rang.

"Were you expecting anyone?"

She shook her head and made her way through the house to the foyer. The chief of police stood in a halo of sunlight on her front steps. The early afternoon sun glinted on his gold badge.

Skye wondered briefly if he was the angel of death. "Come on in, Wally. Nothing wrong I hope."

"No, just thought I'd drop by and talk to you about our conversation this morning. Maybe over lunch, if you haven't eaten."

Before Skye could respond, Simon walked in off the patio.

"What brings you here, Chief?" He casually draped his arm around Skye's shoulders.

"Following up a lead Skye and I came up with this morning."

"Oh?" Simon narrowed his eyes.

"Yep." Wally smiled slightly.

Both men turned to Skye, who frantically searched her mind for something to say.

"Gee, Wally, Simon and I just had lunch, and he has to get going." She glanced at her watch. "Oh, my, it's already twelve-thirty and I know you like to be there to let the family in early."

Simon glowered as he shrugged into his jacket and straightened his tie. "I'll call you tonight after the services." He kissed her cheek and left.

"He didn't seem happy to see me here," Wally said.

"Probably just in a hurry." With a sense of déjà vu, Skye led the way into the great room and sat down.

Wally joined her couch and opened up his notebook. "The hospital has agreed to limit visitors to your aunt."

"But no guard, right?" When he nodded she continued, "So anyone could still sneak in and kill her."

"It's the best I can do without some proof." Wally's eyes never left Skye's face. "At least the psych ward is a lot more secure than the others."

Skye forced herself not to resort to sarcasm. This wasn't Wally's fault. "Did you find out about her stomach contents?"

"No pill fragments. They were probably crushed into some food or drink."

"And that isn't enough proof for you?" she asked.

"No. If she was as antimedication as you say, it's possible that was the only way she could force herself to take them."

"Or, more likely, the only way someone could slip them to her."

"I did go around and stop the trash from

being removed from the church hall. Since you used mostly paper plates and cups, we might still find something. I sent it all to the lab."

"If I had to guess, I'd pick the foam cups to test first. Aunt Minnie drinks lots of coffee with milk and sugar. That would be a good place to put the crushed pills."

"I'll let them know that." He made a note. "Anything else?"

"Well, since you didn't find a container, would it prove anything to you to test the inside of Aunt Minnie's purse for residue?"

"You mean, would the absence of residue prove she didn't take the pills?"

Skye nodded.

"No, negative evidence isn't considered compelling."

"Oh." Skye turned and sat on one leg so she could face him. "Thanks for telling me all this."

The tips of his ears turned red. "Just because I don't have enough proof doesn't mean your thinking wasn't helpful."

"Thanks." Skye gulped. "What a sweet thing to say. I'm so glad you don't think I'm interfering."

"Not as long as you come to me and don't try to investigate on your own." Wally took her hands. "I don't want you to put yourself in danger."

A shiver went down the back of her neck at his touch. His fingers were warm and slightly calloused. She tried to draw away but he tightened his grip.

When she spoke her voice sounded as if she had just finished jogging. "Would it be possible for me to see my grandmother's reports?"

He chuckled deep in his chest. "That might be arranged."

She tried to find something to say, but her focus shifted to his lips, which were moving toward her. This time when she tried to free her hands he let them go, only to wrap his arms around her a moment later.

He smelled like cinnamon and the last thing she noticed before he closed the slight distance between them were his eyes. Usually a warm milk chocolate, they had darkened until they were almost black.

Wally's mouth settled gently on hers, then increased its pressure. At first she nestled closer, allowing her fingertips to explore his jaw and wander into the thick, blunt texture of his hair.

But as he began to deepen the kiss, a tiny part of her common sense pushed its way forward. She levered herself from the circle of his arms.

Skye could barely get enough breath to speak. "This isn't a good idea."

"Why?" A line appeared between his eyebrows. "Are you saying you don't feel anything for me?"

Skye backed toward the foyer. "No. I mean yes. I mean, I do feel something for you. I always have, but this is way too soon. Darleen could still decide to come back."

Wally opened his mouth, then closed it without speaking. He looked at her with troubled eyes, picked up his notebook and tucked it into his shirt pocket before walking to the door. "This isn't the end of it, you know."

Skye nodded and whispered to his back as he walked toward his squad car, "I know."

She sighed and started in on the remaining chores. She finally understood what the song, "Torn Between Two Lovers" meant. Hustling Simon out so quickly had been a bad idea. But having both men in the same room was far too uncomfortable. She needed to make some decisions pretty darn soon.

The afternoon stretched ahead of her and the cottage felt empty. Skye finished cleaning about three and, after taking a shower, sat down to read. But for once the printed page couldn't hold her attention. Something she had seen or heard was teasing the edge of her unconscious. She knew the only way to lure the bit of information to the surface was to totally ignore it and do something else. It was time to visit the survivalists.

CHAPTER 17

SING FOR YOUR SUPPER

Skye had considered asking Wally to go with her to the survivalist camp, but having the chief of police along did not go with her cover story. She was stopping by to see how Perry Underwood was doing after his problem at school. In fact, if she didn't go alone, her explanation of why she was there wouldn't hold up. She had to be there as Ms. Denison, school psychologist. And Ms. Denison would not have an escort.

If a pickup had not been pulling out as she drove up the road, Skye would have missed the entrance to the camp entirely. A camouflaged gate guarded the entry and there was little evidence on the ground that vehicles regularly went in and out.

She stopped her car and got out. How did the gate open? She put her fingers through the leaf-covered wire mesh and tugged. It slid smoothly to the right on well-oiled tracks. Thank goodness it wasn't locked.

As Skye guided the Buick down the tightly packed dirt lane, she wondered how the heck she was going to locate the Underwoods. Then she realized she could work the circumstances in her favor. She had an excuse to stop and talk to other people as she tried to find them.

Trailers and tents of every description were set up along the hills and lakes. All were heavily screened by dense foliage. This area had been one of the many coal mines, and the unique landscaping was the result.

When the mining companies abandoned Scumble River thirty years ago, the huge holes in the ground and equally large slag heaps next to them were eyesores and dangerous nuisances. After a while, though, some of Scumble River's citizens figured out how to make the mines into money-earning recreational areas. They hauled sand in to line the shallowest of the coal pits and put fish in the deeper holes. While they were getting the beaches and fishing ponds ready, grass and trees were planted everywhere else. Now, people from the city spent their summer weekends paying dearly to swim in an old coal pit.

Skye wondered how the survivalists had been able to afford to buy such a huge tract of recreational-quality land. Either they purchased it before prices rose or someone in their group had a lot of money to throw around.

After what seemed forever, Skye spotted a log cabin to her left. It was bigger and more permanent than any other dwelling she'd seen so far. Perhaps it was the camp's head-quarters. She parked her car between a pickup and a Suburban with a red cross painted on the side, and walked up to the porch.

The memory of Simon's telling her about the shooting out here suddenly popped into her mind. She looked around nervously. Was there a gun pointed at her this very minute? No, she was being silly. He had said it was an accident, hadn't he?

She took a deep breath and knocked on the screen door, smoothing her khaki pants and black polo shirt as she waited. This had been another tough wardrobe decision. What does one wear to infiltrate a survivalist camp? Unfortunately, her camouflage suit was at the cleaners.

Abruptly a huge man filled the doorway and growled, "Yeah, what do you want?"

"I'm Ms. Denison from Scumble River Elementary School. Could you direct me to the Underwoods?" Skye forced her voice not to quaver.

"They went back to Michigan." He turned to go.

"Wait. Ah, as long as I'm here, could I talk to you for a minute?"

"About what? I ain't got no kids."

"But you are the leader out here, right?" She took a wild guess.

He narrowed his eyes. "Why do you say that?"

"Well, it's obvious that you would be the top guy." Skye stole a peek at his face and laid the flattery on thicker. "Your bearing, your aura of authority, your size, they all scream commander."

"Yeah?" He straightened his back and squared his shoulders. "I suppose you're right. The major don't live out here and I'm in charge when he's not in camp." He stuck out a hand bigger than Skye's purse. "I'm Sarge."

Skye swallowed nervously as she watched her hand disappear in his grip, which was surprisingly gentle. "My name's Skye."

"Aw, that's a pretty name." Sarge leaned against the door frame. "So, what you want to know? We ain't got no secrets. We're just getting ready for when civilization fails."

"Well, preparedness is always a smart thing." Skye searched her mind for a good question, figuring this was a limited opportunity. "You may have known my grandmother, Antonia Leofanti. She lived on the farm next to this property."

"Heard of her. Never met the lady." Sarge examined his fingernails. "Saw in the paper she was killed. Shame, not being safe in your own home."

"Ah, no offense, but I know some of your people occasionally forgot where your camp ended and her farm began and went across the line." Skye watched him closely for a reaction. "I was wondering if anyone out here had seen anything."

"We never took anything." Sarge crossed his arms and a stubborn look stole over his features. "But your grandma sure went crazy if we were hunting and took a step on her property. That wasn't too neighborly."

"No, it wasn't. But she was an old woman whose health was already failing. Things bothered her that never used to."

He nodded and leaned back. "Sometimes old folks are hard to live with."

"So, do you think you could ask around and see if anyone noticed anything the day she died?"

"Okay, but I'd've heard if anyone saw anything."

"Let me give you my number, just in case someone remembers something." She fished in her purse and pulled out a small notebook and pen.

While she was writing, a skinny teenager ducked under the older man's arm and ran down the steps. She yelled over his shoulder, "You ain't stickin' me with no needle."

An attractive middle-aged woman wearing an old-fashioned nurse's uniform followed the girl. The nurse was holding a syringe; its metal tip glinted in the sunlight. "This is only a tetanus shot. That barbed wire you cut yourself on was rusty. You need this to prevent you from getting sick."

Without speaking, Sarge stepped off the porch, grabbed the girl in a bear hug, and presented her to the nurse, who administered the injection. The teenager took off as soon as the man released her and the nurse went back inside the cabin.

Skye distractedly thanked Sarge and said good-bye. The nurse had triggered something in the back of Skye's mind. She got into the Buick, waved, and was nearly in Scumble River when it hit her. One of the pictures from her grandmother's box had a similar scene. It showed Mona and Minnie as teens standing on either side of a nurse in an old-fashioned uniform. The Chicago skyline was the backdrop.

Skye abruptly swung the wheel of the car and turned toward her brother's salon. She wanted that picture. Who was the nurse? Why was she with her aunts? And what were they doing in Chicago?

She was sitting on her couch staring at the photo when her telephone rang. Bingo was ensconced on her lap, and she had several coffee-table books featuring Chicago spread around her. She grabbed the receiver just before her new answering machine intervened.

Charlie's rough baritone blared through the handset. "Skye, honey, what you doing tomorrow night?"

"Why?" Charlie had roped her into many unpleasant activities in the past and she was cautious, even though she knew she would end up doing exactly what he wanted her to do.

"The Stanley County Farm Bureau is having a pork chop supper and I got stuck buying two tickets." He did not sound regretful.

"I thought you had to be a farmer to be involved with that organization." Skye eased herself into a kitchen chair.

"Hell, they interpret the rules real loose for this sort of thing. I own a couple of pieces of land that I rent out to farmers, so they bugged me to join. Which means I got to show my face at their goings-on."

"You must belong to every organization in Scumble River."

"I don't like to brag, but it seems real important to people that I be involved."

"That's impressive." She was only half listening as she continued to look at the photo.

"So, you want to go with me, or do you got a hot date with Simon?"

"No. Simon and I don't see each other every night or anything."

"Then you want to go to this supper?" Charlie's voice held a hint of impatience.

"Sure. What time?" Skye reached for a pencil. "What do I wear?"

"I'll pick you up at four. It's over to the county seat, so it will take us forty-five minutes or so to drive it. Wear what you usually wear; it's not fancy or nothing."

"Listen, Uncle Charlie, before you hang up, I've got a picture here that shows Aunt Minnie and Aunt Mona posed with a nurse in Chicago. They look like they're in their teens." Skye examined the images closely. "Do you know anything about that?"

"A nurse, huh? I can't think of anyone. I'll

take a look at it when I come get you to-morrow."

Charlie arrived the next afternoon driving a big black Cadillac DeVille. Skye ran her hand caressingly down the soft leather seats and breathed in the new-car scent. "Wow, Uncle Charlie, when did you get this?"

He tipped back his straw fedora. "I haven't bought it yet. Just trying it out. Do you like it?"

"What's not to like?" Skye smiled. "You look perfect in it." She leaned across the huge expanse of front seat, and kissed him on the cheek. "But what's wrong with your other Cadillac?"

"I bought that used, just to tide me over till I could get around to shopping for a new one."

Before Charlie could bring up her need for a car, or the fact that he'd be pleased to buy her one with his newly inherited wealth, Skye passed him the photo of her aunts. "Do you know who that woman with them is or where this was taken?"

"No, can't say as I recognize her," Charlie said. "But the two girls are definitely Mona and Minnie."

"Darn. That means I'll have to ask Mona, since Minnie is still in the hospital." Skye slumped down and crossed her arms.

"You don't get along too good with Mona, huh?" Charlie smirked.

"Aunt Mona's views and mine don't always agree."

"Of course, not many people's do. Neal pretty much tells her what to think, and he's a self-righteous ass." Charlie paused.

Skye could tell he was getting ready for one of his zingers.

"Neal and Mona are two of them there puritans. And you know the definition of puritanism, doncha? It's the nagging fear that someone, somewhere may be happy."

The pork chop supper was being held at the Stanley County fairgrounds in Laurel. There was one entrance from the main road, a rutted, gravel path that made Skye wince as the beautiful DeVille bounced from furrow to furrow. She could hear rocks pinging off the shiny finish.

Cars were being funneled by men in orange vests to a grassy area beside the tents. Due to the recent rains, there were big patches of mud and bog waiting to trap unsuspecting drivers.

As Charlie edged his Cadillac into the line for parking, Skye examined the crowds and asked, "Who are all these people?"

"Farm families from within fifty miles of here." Charlie kept his eye on the car in front of him. No one was getting ahead of Charlie Patukas.

The line of vehicles had stopped moving and Charlie pounded on his horn. "Christ, this traffic is backed up as bad as my bowels."

Skye screwed up her face. "Gee, thanks for that image, Uncle Charlie."

When they finally parked and joined the hordes of people pushing their way to where the food was being served, Charlie said, "Maybe some of the old-timers around here will recognize that nurse."

"Great. I really don't want to have to ask Aunt Mona." Skye clung to his arm so she wouldn't be pushed away with the crowds.

She was stepping into the meal line when Charlie dragged her away and pulled her behind the structure. For just a second Skye felt afraid. Her fear quickly dispersed as he continued to tug her through the exit.

A woman of about fifty stood near a grill, poking pork chops with a long fork. She wore two red plastic barrettes in her dishwater-blond hair. Stringy bangs covered a sloping, uneven forehead. The indistinct features of her pumpkin-shaped face were red with the heat of the charcoal. Her ragged fingernails had been painted scarlet and matched her Spandex shorts.

Charlie waved the tickets in her face. "Fayanne, give me two plates. I can't wait in that line."

Fayanne Emerick owned the Brown Bag liquor store across from Charlie's Up a Lazy River Motor Court. She kept a ledger in her head, and the accounts had to balance at all times.

"Sure." Fayanne grabbed a couple of plastic plates. "By the way, did you ever talk to that trucker friend of yours about that discount beer he was supposed to look into getting me?"

"He'll deliver on Monday." Charlie grabbed the plates as soon as Fayanne had finished filling them. "Thanks."

When they settled at one of the picnic tables scattered around the grounds, Skye said, "Darn, I should have asked Fayanne about the picture."

"Honey, you got to be careful who you ask and how you ask them." Charlie sawed a piece of meat from his pork chop. "You don't want this getting back to Mona or Minnie."

"So, how should I ask then?" Skye spread butter on a roll.

"Run get me a beer while I figure it out."

Charlie gestured to a group of metal troughs filled with ice, beer, and soda.

Skye made her way to the drinks and spoke to the white denim-clad derriere bent over the bins. "I'd recognize that butt anywhere."

Trixie heaved herself upright from the tubs and waved two cans of Diet Coke triumphantly over her head. "Skye, what are you doing here?"

"Uncle Charlie invited me."

"Owen thought this would be a good way to meet some of the other farm families in the area." Trixie pointed to a serious-looking man engaged in conversation with two guys wearing Caterpillar gimme caps.

"I see he's made some contacts."

"Yeah, I'd invite you over, but you wouldn't thank me for it. All their wives can talk about is canning and baking." Trixie's mobile features made a disgusted face.

"Thanks for the warning. Uncle Charlie will want his beer anyway." Skye started off, but turned back. "You want to go to the beach tomorrow?"

"Sure. Is the afternoon okay?"

"I'll pick you up about one." Skye waved a can and left.

Skye stopped as she neared their picnic

table. Sitting with Charlie were Gillian, wearing a low-cut chartreuse top, her husband, with his beer belly hanging over his jeans, and her daughter, with a scowl on her face. Skye took a deep breath. This was her chance to mend some fences and be nicer to her cousins. They had been very understanding about Skye's involvement with their mother's hospitalization, and it was time to start fresh and try to be friends.

Skye forced herself to smile as she sat down. "Hi. Any news about your mom?"

Gillian shot a meaningful glance at the little girl. "Kristin, can you get Mommy a can of pop?"

After the girl left, Gillian said, "No. I understand we have you to thank for not being able to see her alone."

I should have realized they'd be mad about that and called them to explain. "I'm sorry, I should have talked to you first, but I was so afraid someone would try to hurt her again." Skye popped the top of her Diet Coke.

"So, you don't think Mom tried to kill herself?" Gillian ran her fingers through her hair.

"No, I don't." Skye went over her reasons.

"Well, I don't know if that makes sense or

not, but I knew she didn't attempt suicide."

"Why?"

"Because I have a little psychic gift."

Before she could stop herself, Skye blurted out, "Maybe you could exchange it for a nice sweater." Damn, being nice to her cousins was going to be tougher than she thought.

Conversation deteriorated from that point, and it was a relief when Charlie suggested that they head for the dessert tent.

As they walked away, he took Skye's hand and patted it. "You know that cousin of yours is a few peas short of a casserole."

"Sometimes I'm afraid it's genetic."

Skye put a couple of chocolate chip cookies on her plate. All the sweets had been donated by the officers' wives and were made from scratch.

Charlie picked up a piece of apple pie mounded with ice cream and guided her to another set of tables. Skye broke off a piece of the cookie, which oozed chocolate. She closed her eyes and savored the intense burst of flavor.

"I been thinking about how to show that picture around. How 'bout if you block out Mona and Minnie and just leave the nurse for people to look at?"

"What a great idea." Skye found the photo in her purse. She also managed to find a pad of Post-it notes. After affixing one square to either side of the photograph, she showed it to Charlie. "What do you think?"

He forked the rest of the pie into his mouth, chewed, and swallowed. "Great. Let's get to work."

The old man shrugged and went back to talking about tractors. So far none of the people they had spoken to had recognized the woman in the picture.

Charlie seemed to thrive on the noise and the crowds. He greeted most people by name and easily joined their conversations. Skye found it difficult to keep people straight, and although some faces looked familiar, she could rarely remember who they were. Still, it was interesting to hear their opinions and listen to them talk about a Scumble River that existed before she was born. Maybe she'd ask Charlie about doing an oral history with some of his cronies.

The fairgrounds were bigger than she remembered. People walked on caked dirt and tried to avoid the many spots of mud. Several large pole buildings were interspersed with tents and food stands. These structures were made of huge sheets of metal supported with steel rods.

Representatives from local farm-related businesses handed out brochures and freebies. Skye spotted a cousin from her father's side, Kevin Denison. He was there representing his insurance company, which reminded her that she needed to remind him about her checks. Now the company owed her for both her car and her windows.

Charlie stopped at a group of older women gathered around a picnic table. "Good evening, ladies, do you all know my goddaughter, Skye Denison?"

The women murmured hello and Charlie told Skye their names. At the last one he said, "And this is Hilda Quinn. I believe she went to school with your Aunt Mona and your Aunt Minnie."

"My, yes. I was in Minnie's class and Mona was two years behind us." Hilda's bright blue eyes darted from Charlie to Skye.

"Skye, would you mind waiting here while I take care of some business? I'm sure these ladies will take good care of you." Charlie winked and walked away before she could answer.

With the focus of attention clearly in her direction, Skye smiled and sat down. She wasn't sure how to start, but the others had no qualms.

A woman with meticulously styled hair said, "We're very sorry about your family's troubles."

Skye nodded her appreciation, wondering if she meant her grandmother's death, her aunt's attempted suicide, or the fact that everyone thought one of her relatives was a killer.

The group chatted politely for a few minutes before drifting back into their previous conversations. Skye lowered her voice and directed her question to Hilda. "Did you know my aunts very well when you were at school?"

"Yes, Minnie and I were pretty close until . . ." Hilda's voice trailed off.

It took a moment, but Skye remembered what her father had said on the drive to her grandmother's funeral. Of course, that must be what the nurse in the picture was about. Minnie's breakdown. "Until she left school?"

"Why yes. When she came back she wasn't the same."

"How long was she gone?" Skye studied the other woman intently.

"About a month or so. I remember she left right around Easter and was back before Mother's Day." Hilda took a sip of her coffee.

"But she didn't go back to school, did she?" Skye tried to keep things straight in her head.

"No, Mona did, but not Minnie. It was a real shame too. Not to graduate when you're so close."

"Do you know why they went away?" Skye couldn't think of a way to ask delicately.

"We were told it was for Minnie's health. She had been having spells since she was little. I remember the day she went away, we were walking out of school together after the last bell and your grandfather pulled up in the family car." Hilda's eyes took on a far-away look, as if she was thinking of something she hadn't contemplated in years.

"Wow, you have an impressive memory," Skye said, encouraging her.

Hilda frowned. "Do you remember your grandpa?"

"No, he died when I was three."

"He was an old-fashioned man. Very dignified. He kept himself aloof from most people. It was rare to see him in town without Antonia."

"But he came alone to pick up Minnie and Mona on that day?"

"No, that was another reason why I remember it so well. He had a nurse with him."

To Skye, everything suddenly became

quiet and still. Her hands shook as she extracted the photo from her purse. "Was this the woman?"

Hilda leaned forward and adjusted her glasses. "Yes, that's the nurse. How did you get a picture of her?"

Ignoring Hilda's question, Skye crossed her fingers. "Do you know her name?"

"Well, your grandfather certainly didn't introduce us." Hilda scowled. "He always treated people like he was a king and they were his servants."

"Like Uncle Neal does."

"Right." Hilda nodded. "That lord of the manor attitude."

"So, you didn't get the nurse's name."

"Well, not verbally, but when Mr. Leofanti and that nurse came up to us on the sidewalk, they each took one of the girls by the arm. The nurse was on my side and I could read the nameplate pinned to her uniform."

Skye hardly dared to breathe. "Do you remember it?"

"We'd been reading *The Scarlet Letter* in English class and I thought it was an odd coincidence that the nurse's name was so close to the woman's in the story." Hilda closed her eyes for a second. "Her name was Esther Prynn."

"You have a remarkable memory. I'm amazed." Skye could hardly sit still.

"It helps that I'm an English teacher and my class has read *The Scarlet Letter* every year for the past twenty-five years."

CHAPTER 18

THERE WAS AN OLD WOMAN

The lawyer was late. Skye narrowed her eyes and crossed her legs. She hated being kept waiting when she had an appointment. If she didn't have to ask this jerk for a favor, she would be out of there so fast. But she needed to find out the details of her grandmother's trust and, according to her mother, this bozo was the one who had drawn it up.

Another fifteen minutes passed and Skye could stand it no longer. She put her purse and book on the chair and went up to the desk. "Do you know how much longer Mr. Ginardi will be? I have other appointments this morning."

"I have no idea." The woman didn't look up from her magazine.

"Would it be possible for you to check?" Skye gritted her teeth.

"He doesn't like to be interrupted."

Before Skye could think of anything else to say, a man poked his head out of the doorway behind the woman. When he saw Skye looking at him he flushed. "Ah . . . you must be Miss Denison. Come in."

Skye followed him and sat in the chair he indicated.

He spoke to her without making eye contact. "I'm Bob Ginardi. I'm afraid we'll have to be quick about this. I need to leave in a few minutes."

Skye clenched her teeth. What nerve. First he made her wait over half an hour, and now he was going to rush her in and out. Still she couldn't afford to offend him, yet. "I'll try not to take up too much of your time." Skye got out a notepad and pen. "Since you have only a few minutes for me, let's get down to business. What I need to know is how my grandmother's trust works."

The lawyer frowned. "I really can't talk to you about it since you're not named in the trust."

She reached in her tote and handed him an envelope. "That's from my mother, who is a part of the trust, allowing me to act on her behalf."

"It's not notarized." He slid the paper back to her, a look of relief on his face. "You'll have to make another appointment." Ginardi took out a handkerchief and wiped the sweat from his forehead.

"No." Skye realized this man not only didn't want to talk to her, but was afraid to talk to her. What was he hiding?

The lawyer's features registered surprise.

"I'm not leaving without this information. We are not talking state secrets here. All I need to know is how *my* family's Bypass Trust works. If you feel you can't tell me, I will call my mother and she'll ask the questions." Skye looked at her watch. "But that may take some time."

Ginardi laughed nervously. "You can't hold me hostage."

"Maybe not, but are you willing to call the police to get rid of me?" Before he could answer, Skye continued, "Because if I don't get answers today, the next time I come here will be with my mother, our attorney, and an auditor."

He swallowed. "Okay, no need to get so upset. I have to protect confidentiality." After using his handkerchief again he went on. "I guess I can explain the trust to you, at least in broad terms."

"Fine."

"A simple Bypass Trust means half of the estate goes to the surviving spouse at the time of the other spouse's death. And the other half goes into a family trust with the income

311

from that half going to the surviving spouse, as well."

"So, except for Grandma, no one got a dime while she was living." Skye tried to ease him into being more specific.

"Right." He stared at a point above her head. "In the case of your grandfather's estate, most of the value was in land. The land could not be divided except to pay for Antonia's care, as long as your grandmother lived."

"Was that being considered?" Skye clarified her question. "Selling off some of the land to pay for Grandma's care?"

"We had been deliberating about the sale of some of the land, yes." He looked at the contents of the file. "No decision would have needed to be made until fall. It depended on what kind of year the farm had, and how much the crops were sold for."

"I know my uncles and my father do all the actual farming of the Leofanti land. Do they get any of the profits?"

Ginardi became fascinated with the crease in his pants. "Yes, the business is set up as if they were sharecroppers. They put in the labor, your grandmother put in the land, and the profits were divided, fifty percent to her and fifty percent among your father and uncles."

Skye made a note. "What happens now?"

"The heirs can do what they wish as long as they all agree."

"And if they all don't agree?"

"Then the land will have to be sold and the money divided equally."

Skye took a shot in the dark. "Is that what my Uncle Dante wanted to know when he was in to see you?"

Ginardi squirmed in his seat.

Skye continued to look him in the eye. She had found that pretending to know more than she actually knew could be very enlightening at times.

"Yes."

Skye's next stop was the library. She used the card catalog to locate the Dewey decimal number for poisons and found several books on the subject. She sat down at a table and tried to find a match for the name her mother had mangled.

After she read a few sections she found a likely suspect. Jatropha curcas. The common name was Barbados nut. It was found in southern Florida and Hawaii and the raw seeds had a pleasant taste. There would have been no difficulty getting her grandmother or Mrs. Jankowski to eat them mixed into brownies.

Farther down the page she found the symptoms. Difficulty breathing, sore throat, bloating, dizziness, vomiting, diarrhea, and drowsiness. Wally's guess was right, the murderer must have cleaned Grandma up. She needed to ask the chief if vomit and stool were present when they found Mrs. Jankowski.

The entry ended by saying that the poison, once ingested, took only fifteen to twenty minutes to kill.

When Skye got back to her car she noticed that there were still two hours before she was supposed to pick up Trixie to go swimming. She decided to see if she could take the local doctor to lunch.

Doc Zello was semiretired, working only half-days, but she headed to his office anyway. His was the only car in the lot.

As she walked up the familiar concrete steps and through the waiting area that smelled of antiseptic and cough drops, she felt as if she were ten again. Skye knocked on the closed dutch doors.

Doc Zello's voice bellowed in answer. "I'm not here unless this is an emergency."

She pushed her way in and found him at his desk. "It's an emergency. I'm starving and I'm taking you to lunch."

He looked at her over his glasses. "Looks

like you could stand to skip a few lunches."

"Looks as if you could stand to see a barber."

His wild white hair stood on end. He absentmindedly ran his fingers through it, making it worse. "Okay, so why do you want to take me to lunch?"

"I want to pick your brain."

"You know I can't tell you anything confidential."

"I'll work around it." She took him by the arm and they walked to her car.

After they had driven to the Feedbag, been seated, and had given their order, Skye started her questions. "You've practiced medicine in Scumble River for how long?"

"Over fifty years. I've lived here all my life."

"Do you remember a nurse by the name of Esther Prynn? She was around here in the mid-sixties."

He stroked his beard. "Can't say as I do, right offhand. Why do you ask?"

Skye didn't want to explain, so she ignored the question. "She might have done private duty nursing. Maybe for people who had what they used to call nervous breakdowns."

"That was a long time ago. Are you trying to find her?"

"I don't want to say too much until I'm more sure of my facts, but I think there might be some link between this woman and my grandmother's murder." Unless, of course, Uncle Dante or Hugo did it for the land. Or the twins for the jewelry. Or one of her other relatives for reasons she had yet to discover.

"Your best bet is to check with the nurses' licensing board. They might have an address for her." He held up a hand mottled with age spots. "But if she doesn't practice anymore, then she probably didn't renew her certificate."

"Could you check for me?" Skye turned her head to one side and looked at him through her lashes. "You know, a well-known doctor such as yourself would get a lot better results than a nobody like me."

"Okay." Doc Zello slapped her lightly on the cheek. "But don't think you're fooling me for one minute. I just want whoever killed Antonia to be brought to justice."

"Thanks, Doc."

They sat quietly while the waitress delivered their order and refilled their iced teas.

The meal was almost over when Doc Zello spoke again. "You know, I might have been your grandfather."

"What?"

"I dated your grandmother before she married Angelo. I always regretted not asking her to marry me. She was an amazing woman. You remind me a lot of her. Once she got an idea into her head, she'd never let go until she was satisfied. And she always wanted things to be fair."

"Mom said the same thing right after Grandma died, but I never noticed a similarity between us."

"Antonia saw it. That's why she was telling you the family history." He pushed his plate away.

"It did seem important to her that some kind of permanent record be made." Skye used her napkin and put it aside. "Too bad it'll never be finished now."

"History is never finished."

Trixie was full of conversation and high spirits, halting her chatter only long enough for Skye to show the man at the Scumble River Recreational Club her identification card.

They drove down a narrow gravel road toward the beach. The lane was bordered by grassy areas dotted with trees and picnic tables. Most of them were occupied by young women and small children.

Locker rooms bracketed a crude pavilion

that contained a soda machine and a pay telephone. They changed quickly into their swimsuits; neither wanted to linger in the slimy, mold-filled building.

The beach wasn't crowded. Skye had noted early on that most families seemed to swim in the morning. She and Trixie climbed down the concrete steps and walked along the shore until they found a relatively isolated spot.

After helping Skye to smooth out an old bedspread on the sand, Trixie peeled off the oversized T-shirt she was wearing. Underneath, a cherry-red bikini glowed against her tan skin.

Skye glanced down at her pale limbs. "Trixie, how'd you get tanned already?"

"Tanning booth at your brother's salon. How come you don't use it?"

"No time, I guess."

"Want to take a dip?" Trixie was rocking from foot to foot on the hot sand.

"Sure. Race you to the raft." Skye tossed her cover-up on the blanket, revealing a dark purple one-piece maillot.

Trixie made it to the float a millisecond before Skye and they both flung themselves, panting, on the bleached wood.

"When did you get to be such a fast swimmer?" Trixie asked. "I was on my college swim team, and you nearly beat me just now."

"I swim a lot. Here when the weather is nice and at the high school when it gets cold."

"Oh. Cool. Now that I'll be on staff we can swim together." Trixie rolled to her side and rested her head on her hand. "So, have you found out anything else about your grandmother's murder?"

"Some." Skye was uncomfortable sharing information. She was out of the habit of exchanging casual gossip because most of what she heard at work was confidential.

"Do you suspect Hugo and Victoria?"

"Well, Grandma's farm would be worth a lot of money if it could be subdivided into a housing development. And while Hugo wouldn't get the money directly, I'm sure Uncle Dante would be very generous to his only child."

Trixie shook her head and water flew from her gamin-like haircut. "Yeah, but didn't you say Dante wants to continue to farm?"

"True, but he is sixty already. Maybe Hugo felt he could talk his dad into his way of thinking."

"So, is Dante in the clear?"

Skye squeezed the moisture from her

chestnut curls. "No, I knew Grandma's care was costing a bundle. I mean, do the math. Mrs. J was there twenty-four hours, six days a week. They were only paying her five dollars an hour, but that's still over seven hundred a week. Plus a couple hundred for the woman who stayed on Sundays. So that's over four thousand a month, or nearly fifty thousand a year. Because of that, it turns out they might have had to start selling off pieces of the farm to support her. The lawyer said it would have all depended on how the crops were this year."

"Wow, it's a good thing my mother-in-law didn't need to have someone take care of her for too long." Trixie grimaced. "Oh, that reminds me, how's your Aunt Minnie? Do you think she attempted suicide because she felt guilty about killing your grandmother?"

Skye scooted to the edge of the raft and dangled her feet in the water. "She's still in the hospital. And actually I'm wondering if her so-called suicide attempt wasn't really a murder attempt." Skye told her about Minnie's aversion to pills.

"Why would anyone want to kill her?"

"Maybe she knows something. I've been doing a little asking around and there's a lot more to her past than I ever knew."

Trixie shaded her eyes. "I thought your grandmother was telling you the family history."

"She was, but we didn't get to my aunts' and uncles' generation."

"How about Minnie's daughters?" Trixie eased back into the water.

"They certainly thought there were more jewelry and valuables than there turned out to be." Skye followed Trixie into the water and they headed slowly back to shore. "Their husbands spilled the beans about their misconception at Grandma's funeral lunch."

"Of course you don't suspect your own mother or brother."

"No, thank goodness they have alibis. And I really haven't found a motive for Aunt Mona, besides the fact that she's a mean-spirited, sanctimonious bitch." Skye filled in Trixie about the essay contest at school as they emerged from the water and crossed the hot sand.

"What a horrible thing to do to a child. And to have to sacrifice all your hard work with him. How awful for you too."

Skye settled on the spread and began to apply sunscreen. Trixie joined her and oiled her own limbs.

Skye lay down in the bright sun and was

almost asleep when Trixie's voice woke her. "I know how to check to see who filled Minnie's prescription."

"How?"

"My cousin works at the pharmacy in town. She can check the records for us."

"But isn't that illegal?" Skye asked.

"Only if we get caught."

CHAPTER 19

FIVE, SIX,

MORE NASTY TRICKS

Before Skye dropped her off, Trixie agreed to call her cousin that evening. They parted with promises to stay in close touch.

As Skye went past her parents' place she noticed her dad out in the yard, and on an impulse she pulled the Buick into the gravel drive. She had always found it difficult to talk to her father. His clipped way of speaking, and lack of interest in anything not farm related, made it hard to have a conversation with him.

Won't Dad be surprised? I actually want to talk about agriculture. She grinned as she turned off the motor.

"Mom home?" Skye asked, approaching her father.

"Nope, she's working afternoons. Just left." Jed sat on his haunches looking at a snowblower that he'd turned upside down.

"Is she still mad at me?" Skye warily circled the pile of greasy parts.

He shrugged.

It was the kind of response she had been getting from him all her life. His refusal to communicate at a personal level drove her to say things for their shock value alone.

"Do you think someone in the family killed Grandma?" Skye said abruptly.

He shrugged again. It took a lot more than words to make Jed react.

"Almost every one of them has a motive." Skye stepped back as Jed's tool slipped and oil sprayed outward.

"Any proof?" Jed tightened a bolt and wiped it with a dirty cloth.

"Not really." Skye steered the subject away from her lack of evidence and continued in the same vein. "I was wondering about Uncle Dante. Is he a good farmer?"

Jed was silent, finally wiping his hands on the rag and sticking them in his overall pockets. "Can't really say. Has different ideas than me or Emmett."

"Oh?"

"Emmett and me, we pretty much agree on most things. You know, do 'em the way it worked before." Jed looked at Skye. "Dante likes to try new stuff."

"Is that bad?" Skye's knowledge of farming was surprisingly limited for having grown up in the country.

"Sometimes. Depends if they work or not." Jed flipped over the snowblower.

"And were his new methods successful?"

"Not so's you'd notice."

"Has he bought a lot of new machinery lately?" Skye knew that a simple tractor could cost more than fifty-five thousand dollars.

"Yeah, he likes new equipment. Likes things to be shiny and bright."

Skye pictured her father's machinery. Most of it was decades old, and one would be hard-pressed to tell what color it had started out, but it all ran as if brand-new, thanks to Jed's talent as a mechanic. She knew her father kept Emmett's equipment running too, but she couldn't recall Dante ever asking for help.

"Do you think maybe Uncle Dante was skimming a little off the top of the Leofanti trust?"

Jed took out his pocketknife and started to clean his nails. "You best leave that idea alone."

"Why?" Her tone sharpened.

" 'Cause none of his sisters wants to go down that road."

"Oh, so they know."

"Nah, but they don't want to know

either." Jed finished with his fingernails and replaced the knife in his pocket.

Skye was stumped as to where to go from that point. To buy some time to think she asked a question she had always been curious about. "Why do you farm, Dad?"

At first she didn't think he was going to answer. " 'Cause I like bein' my own boss and doin' what I want when I want." Jed pulled the bill of his International Harvester gimme cap down over his eyes.

She nodded thoughtfully. It was a feeling she could relate to. Jed was gathering his tools and wiping them down. Silences never seemed to bother him. She admired that trait even though she found it difficult to deal with at times.

"Does Uncle Dante make a good living from his land?" Maybe her mother and aunts didn't want to know what Dante was up to, but she still did.

Jed lifted his cap and scratched his head. "Well, now, the last couple of years have been tough for us all. Not enough rain for growing and too much for harvesting."

"Has he had to sell anything off?"

"That would never happen. Selling land is against his religion."

"I'll bet he was upset then when it looked like some of Grandma's land would have to be sold to take care of her." Skye watched as her father coaxed life out of the decrepit snowblower's engine.

"Yeah, he was fit to be tied. Said no way were they selling his heritage."

It was nearly five when Skye parked the Buick in her driveway. She grabbed her tote bag from the backseat and started up the sidewalk toward her cottage.

Blood. There was blood everywhere. Skye had never seen so much blood.

Skye stood transfixed on the sidewalk. Splashes of crimson decorated her door. BITCH was written in four-foot letters across the white siding.

Her eyes frantically searched the surrounding area. *I have got to get a cell phone.*

She backed slowly to the car, and after gaining the safety of the front seat, locked all the doors. Her heart was beating twice its usual pace and sweat poured down her face and puddled under her arms.

Inconsequential thoughts kept crowding into her mind, while the movie projector in her brain insisted on replaying the scene over and over, at different speeds, as she put the Buick in gear and tore out of the driveway.

At the police station her mother took one

look at Skye and ran around the counter. She gathered Skye into her arms. "What happened? You're as pale as milk."

Skye took a deep breath and realized she was going to vomit. Pushing her mother away, she raced for the bathroom. She could hear May and Wally talking outside the door as she washed her face, rinsed out her mouth, and scrubbed at the front of her blouse.

"I'm okay," she reassured them as she made her way out of the ladies' room.

May popped the top on a can of ginger ale before handing it to Skye. "Now, tell us what happened to you."

Wally held a chair and guided Skye into it. "Yes, what in the hell is going on?"

It took her several tries before she was finally able to explain.

The chief's face turned magenta and the pencil he was holding snapped. "This is going to stop right now. I will not have you harassed like this."

May held one of Skye's hands, patting it. "Wally will take care of it. Don't you worry."

Skye smiled weakly. "Thanks, guys." Turning her eyes on the chief, she said, "It has to be either Hap Doozier or Leroy Yoder. The Underwood guy who's with the survivalist group camping behind Grandma Leofanti's land went back to Michigan."

"How do you know that?"

Shit, I promised Wally not to investigate by myself. He's been so cooperative too. Hope he understands my reasoning. She looked into his angry face and said, "Well, you told me you had talked to that group and didn't think they were involved, but I needed to check them out myself. After all, they're right there, cheek by jowl with my grandmother's property."

"So you went out there on your own?" A vein popped out on Wally's forehead.

"I had to go alone. I went as the Scumble River Elementary School psychologist checking on Perry Underwood. They'd know that wasn't true if I had the chief of police with me."

"And did you find out anything I hadn't?" His voice was dangerously quiet.

"No, but Sarge did say he'd ask around for me." Skye smiled. "He was very nice. I wasn't in any danger."

"Sarge, as you call him, has a record a mile long. Much of it for assaults against women and minorities."

"Oh." Skye looked down at her clasped hands. "I guess I made a mistake."

"I'm very disappointed in you. I thought

we had mutual trust and respect. But I see you've been using me."

"No —"

"There's nothing more to say. I told you that betrayal was the one thing I couldn't forgive. First Darleen and now you." He slammed his notepad shut and stood up. "Wait here."

"Where are you going?"

"To do my job."

While she waited, Skye kept an ear cocked for the chief's infrequent radio reports, and started drawing up a chronological list of events. Anything to take her mind off Wally's words. She felt numb now, and knew that later the hurt would be unbearable.

The first time his voice interrupted her thoughts, he related that there was no sign of a break-in at her cottage or any clues to the perpetrator's identity.

Meanwhile, Skye had composed two columns. One for murder-related activities and one for pranks. The slashed tires and broken windows were definitely annoyances. The other events were lined up neatly on the other side. This latest incident had a question mark.

As she wrote, Skye remembered something she wanted to ask May. She poked her head into the dispatch area. May was flipping through a *Family Circle*, obviously still upset.

Skye walked farther into the room and stopped in front of her mother's chair. "I forgot, I have a question for you."

May closed the magazine. "Oh?"

"Yeah, do you remember Minnie dropping out of school her senior year?" Skye hooked a chair with her foot and brought it toward her.

"Yes, it was before you were born and Vince was right around a year old." May looked puzzled.

"Do you recall why she didn't finish?"

"Well, I was really busy back then trying to keep up with Vince and the house and all, but I believe she had sort of a nervous breakdown, and went away somewhere to rest." May frowned. "I think Mona went along to keep her company."

"Did you find anything in that odd? I mean, did Minnie seem to be heading that way to you?"

May chewed her lip. "Now that you mention it, at the time I wondered a little. Minnie seemed okay to me."

"And why take Mona out of school?"

"Mona hated to miss school. She was the

smart one. We all thought she'd go to college for sure, but she seemed different when she got back."

"Different?"

"More serious. Less frivolous."

"Did you say anything to Grandma or Grandpa?"

"Grandma just said that I had been too busy to notice Minnie's condition. Grandpa forbade me to speak of it, and ordered me to forget it." May's eyes widened. "And I did until you mentioned it."

"Wow, Grandpa must have been pretty intimidating."

"Oh, he was, he was." May sat silently, seemingly lost in thoughts of the past, until the phone rang. "Yes, okay, good. I'll tell her." She turned toward Skye. "That was the chief. He said they're pretty sure the blood was from a deer. They found the hide and entrails nearby."

"But no sign of who did it?" Skye got up and fetched her list. She slowly erased the question mark. Another prank.

"No, but he said there didn't seem to be any danger and you can go home."

"Great." Skye sighed. "Any idea how to remove deer blood from concrete and siding?"

"Call the twins. Their husbands hunt all

the time." May went back to her post, the excitement over for now.

Skye considered her mother's advice and decided to go one better. Not only would she consult her cousins for cleaning tips, she would invite them to brunch on Sunday.

The twins might be able to tell her something about Minnie, since she couldn't get in to see her aunt herself, and Victoria might let something slip about Dante or Hugo. Too bad her Aunt Mona didn't have any kids to pump for information.

It was difficult to make herself walk through the bloodied threshold of her cottage. Wally had obviously tried to wipe the worst of it off, but brownish-red streaks remained.

Bingo met her at the door demanding food and attention until a breeze carried in the coppery smell of blood. Suddenly, he danced backward, his fur standing in a ridge down his spine. He streaked out of the foyer and slunk under the bed.

The light was blinking on Skye's answering machine when she got to the kitchen. Before doing anything else, she washed her hands and took a bottle of Ice Mountain from the fridge. After a few swigs of the spring water she sat down at the table and pushed the play button.

"Skye? This is Doc. Pulled in a few favors and got that information you wanted. Esther Prynn is living in Chicago. Here's her address and phone." After relaying that data Doc went on, "Haven't had time to go over my records yet. I'll let you know what I find."

She stopped the machine and made a careful note, then got up to check on Bingo. Only his eyes were visible as they glowed in the darkness.

Creeping forward on her stomach, Skye called, "Here kitty, kitty. Bingo, it's okay, sweetie."

He didn't even blink.

After trying food and his favorite toys to lure him out, Skye said, "Fine, stay there. I never knew you were such a 'fraidy cat."

She returned to the kitchen and played the last message.

"This is Karolyn. I'm calling for Superintendent Wraige. He would like to see you Monday at one to discuss the Clapp matter."

Shit, shit, shit! I still haven't figured out a way to keep my job and my integrity. What am I going to do?

Skye was surprised by her cousins' easy

acceptance of her invitation for brunch. She had always felt a misfit among her family. At parties the conversations centered around children and housekeeping, subjects to which she could contribute little.

The twins had both married before they turned twenty and produced children shortly afterward. Skye was graduating from college while they were changing diapers. She was leaving the Peace Corps when they were sending their firstborns to kindergarten. It was almost worse with Victoria, whose only focus was to be invited to the right parties and belong to the correct country club.

Making an effort to drown out her thoughts, Skye put on a Patsy Cline CD and turned the volume high. At least she had gotten instructions from her cousins for washing up deer blood. And maybe the brunch would give her a chance to get closer to them.

After mixing the cleaning solution as directed, Skye took a brush and set to work.

Skye had a date with Simon the next day. He was picking her up at nine and they were going to spend all of Saturday together. She got up at seven so she'd have time both to get ready and call her mom.

May answered on the first ring. "Are you okay?"

"I'm fine. In fact, I took your advice about asking the twins how to clean deer blood."

"That's great."

"Of course I didn't tell them the real reason I was asking, so make sure you don't tell either."

"Why would I say anything? I'm just glad to see you talking to your cousins."

"Actually, I went a little further."

"Oh?"

"Yeah, well, I, ah, invited them over for brunch tomorrow. Victoria, too."

"That's great. Maybe you'll all get to be closer now that you're home."

"I hope so."

"What are you serving?"

"I'll start with mimosas and Bellinis." The champagne drinks were sure to loosen tongues. "Next, cantaloupe bowls with fresh fruit and quiche. And your famous lemon silk sherbet with dream bars for the perfect ending."

Simon arrived precisely on time, looking cool and elegant in khakis and a short-sleeved denim shirt. Skye wore a denim skort and striped polo shirt.

After Simon gave Bingo the appropriate

number of pets and scratches they got into Simon's Lexus.

Hand on the wheel, Simon asked, "Where to, my lady? Your chauffeur awaits."

"Are you sure you don't have somewhere in mind?"

"Nope, it's up to you." Simon smiled and took her hand.

"Well, last time you let me choose, you didn't like it, but if you're truly a man of your word . . ." Skye trailed off, watching his reaction.

Simon's eyes narrowed as he recalled the instance she referred to. "One qualification: nothing illegal."

"Okay, I can live with that." Under her breath Skye added, "Probably."

"So, what do you want to do?"

"Go visit a little old lady."

Chapter 20

How I Wonder What You Are

One of the reasons Skye needed to talk Simon into going to see the old nurse was because she was afraid to drive in Chicago. She mostly blamed this on her lousy sense of direction, although sometimes she wondered if it wasn't really because May had frightened her when she was a teen with stories of all the awful things that took place in big cities.

Simon's voice broke through her reflections. "What's the address?"

"It's 11502 Avenue D," Skye read off a slip of paper.

He reached into the pouch on the door and withdrew an atlas of the city and surrounding suburbs. After studying it for several minutes, he inserted his business card to keep his page and placed the book between them. "That's on the south side. A changing neighborhood, as they say."

"What does that mean?"

"It means that at one time it was a mostly

working-class Polish area, but about ten years ago poorer minorities started moving in and the whites moved out. The elderly were pretty much left behind." Simon started the car and guided it out of the driveway.

"Why?"

"Most of them hung on too long and when they finally wanted to move, the value of their houses had decreased so much they could no longer afford to go. Because they were on fixed incomes, they had nothing more to add to the pot." He drove steadily, exiting onto Interstate 55.

"I figured Esther is anywhere from sixty to eighty-five. Minnie's friend said Minnie was a senior when she went away, so she must have been about seventeen or eighteen. She's fifty now, so this whole thing took place about thirty-three or four years ago. But if what you say about the neighborhood is true, Esther's probably on the older end of my estimate."

"Let me get this straight. You want to find this woman because she took care of your aunts thirty-three years ago when Minnie had a breakdown. Right?"

"Right. I'd like to know more about what everyone calls a breakdown. There are a lot of mental states that could refer to." Skye watched as he skillfully maneuvered through the thick traffic.

"And you need to know this be-cause . . . ?" Simon trailed off.

"Because I want to know if Minnie has a history of mental illness that would suggest she is capable of harming either herself or others."

"You still question whether she really attempted suicide?"

"Yes, but if she did, she's certainly a prime suspect for having also killed Grandma." Skye was surprised at the lump that gathered in her throat and the sorrow she still felt over her grandmother's death.

They drove in companionable silence, listening to a classical music station that Simon favored. At first Skye knew where she was, but after the third change of highway she became hopelessly lost.

When Simon finally exited onto 103rd Street, it looked as if they had traveled to another country. Signs were in Spanish, Polish, and languages she didn't recognize.

A few turns and Simon stopped the car in front of a detached two-story home. Its siding appeared to be made of gravel and tar paper. The windows and door were heavily barred.

They climbed steep concrete steps,

holding on to the black metal railing. There were two bells. Neither had a name. Skye looked at Simon, who shrugged. Taking a guess, she pressed the bottom bell and hoped for the best.

They waited. They could hear shuffling sounds that seemed to grow nearer. Finally the front door was flung open, leaving the barred storm door between them and the woman on the other side.

Her size and age were hard to determine because she was bent over with a dowager's hump on her back. She leaned on a cane and scowled.

Skye felt herself rushing to find the right words. "Hello, my name is Skye Denison and this is my friend Simon Reid. We're looking for Esther Prynn."

"Yeah."

"Are you Ms. Prynn?"

"I don't go for that Miz crap. I'm Miss Prynn. Have been for the last seventy-five years and will be on my tombstone."

"We're from Scumble River. I understand you did some private duty nursing there back in the sixties." Skye made herself sound more sure of her facts than she was.

"Maybe. Used to help out lots of folks from the country. What's it to you?"

"Would it be possible for us to come in

and discuss this? I'm sure your neighbors don't need to know our business." Skye put her hand on the door handle. This was sort of like a home visit. Not pleasant, but something she was trained to do.

Miss Prynn looked them both up and down, then demanded, "Let me see some identification."

They pressed their driver's licenses against the bars. She squinted between the tiny photos and their faces, finally unlocking the door and permitting them to pass. She carefully turned keys and bolts behind them.

Once inside, they found themselves in a small foyer with scarred wooden steps leading upstairs. To their right was another door.

It was through that portal that their hostess led them to a small living room crowded with dusty overstuffed furniture. There was one hard chair in the room, and Skye, remembering the advice of a social worker during her training, chose to sit there. Miss Prynn settled into what was obviously "her" chair, which left the couch for Simon.

"So, what's so important? I'm missing my TV program." Miss Prynn clutched the remote.

"Do you remember working a case in Scumble River about thirty-three years ago?" Skye sat forward.

Miss Prynn rubbed her temple. "Maybe. I worked lots of cases in that neck of the woods."

"I was told that back in the early to mid-sixties you helped out when one of my aunts had a nervous breakdown. Her name was Minnie Leofanti."

"Mmm, Leofanti. That name does sound familiar. But I'm remembering a different first name." Miss Prynn stared at the blank television screen. "Name was Mona, not Minnie."

Skye, hardly containing her excitement, struggled to keep her voice level. "Well, as I understand it, Minnie's younger sister, Mona, accompanied her when you came for them. Could that be the mix-up?"

Miss Prynn sank back in her chair. "Sure, I remember now. Two girls, both in their teens. Pretty little things. Didn't look at all Eyetalian like their name."

Skye restrained herself from correcting the older woman's pronunciation and explaining about the blonds of northern Italy. "Yes, that would be them. Do you remember where you took them for treatment?"

When Miss Prynn didn't answer, Skye tried another question. "Do you recall what Minnie's diagnosis was?"

Miss Prynn's eyes took on a cunning gleam and she rubbed her hands together. "I might be able to remember. Keep all my records right here for safekeeping and I could go back and look, but you know that information is all confidential."

"I realize that, and I understand your position. I'm a psychologist myself, but this could be a life-and-death situation. I'd be very grateful." Skye tried to connect with her, one professional to another.

"Grateful, huh? Just how grateful would you be?" Miss Prynn's eyes brightened.

Skye frowned. "I'm afraid I —"

Simon cut her off. "How much would it take?"

Miss Prynn smiled. "Ten thousand?"

Simon stood up and took Skye's arm, forcing her to rise, too.

"Five thousand?" The old lady's voice took on a whiny tone.

Taking out his wallet, Simon said, "One hundred, for your inconvenience."

"Five hundred. It could mean my license."

Skye found her voice. "Two-fifty. You don't practice anymore."

Miss Prynn fisted her hands. She looked at the shabby room and small television set. Frustration mixed with anger on her face. "Okay. You know, you're as much of a bitch as your aunt was."

"I don't suppose you'll take a check?" Skye asked, half in jest.

"Cash. Tens and twenties." Miss Prynn stood. "I'll dig out the file tonight. You bring the money Monday morning, first thing."

"Why not tomorrow?" Skye frowned.

"Not on the Sabbath." Miss Prynn locked the door behind them.

It was nearly midnight when Simon dropped Skye at her cottage. They had decided to spend the rest of the day at Lake Geneva and had taken the late dinner cruise.

Simon walked Skye to the door and took her in his arms. "What a great day. I love being near the water."

Skye reached up and smoothed his hair back at the temple. "The company wasn't bad either."

He nuzzled her ear and a shiver ran down her spine. She could feel the sexual magnetism that made him so self-confident. His lips met hers and happiness filled her.

As their kiss deepened, his hand closed over her breast and she pulled away. He was so very good-looking and she reacted so strongly to him; she couldn't let this go any further. Dark memories of her ex-fiancé surfaced. She wasn't ready to completely trust another man.

Simon looked down at her. "What's wrong?"

"We're both tired. Maybe we should talk about this some other time." Skye refused to meet his eyes.

"I've heard that excuse before. I think we need to get this into the open." He waited, daring her to be honest.

Skye sat down on the concrete step. "What more is there to say? I've told you before I wasn't ready for anything but a casual relationship."

Simon joined her on the stair, his mouth spread in a thin-lipped smile. "You told me all right, but that was nine months ago. Most couples move forward, but you're stuck in the past."

She ducked her head. Maybe he was right. She wasn't being very mature or very strong. But the few times she had allowed herself to be totally swept away by love had always turned out disastrously. She was afraid of her own taste in men. "I'm sorry

Simon, but I'm just not ready to go through the humiliation again."

"You think it would be humiliating to love me?" His voice was cold.

"No, that isn't what I mean." Skye looked up at the stars and wished she could be different. "Whenever I become truly, deeply involved with a man I lose my common sense, my good judgment."

Simon's lips twisted into a cynical smile. "You mean you do worse things than breaking and entering or buying confidential medical records?"

Skye narrowed her eyes and looked at him for the first time since they had begun talking. "Comments like that just prove what I'm saying. You don't understand my needs and ambitions, but you expect me to understand yours."

"That's ridiculous." Simon stood up. "How can I understand? You've never told me what happened with your ex-fiancé."

She met his accusing eyes without flinching. "There's nothing much to tell. He was handsome, charming, rich, and held an impressive social position in New Orleans' society. I was awed that he had any interest in me and so unsure of myself that I allowed myself to become his puppet. I agreed with things I felt strongly against. I said things I didn't mean. And I did things I'll regret to my dying day. All to please him."

"You were out of your element, away from home. That wouldn't necessarily happen again." Simon took her hand.

She shook off his touch. "When things went wrong with my job and the threat of a scandal became known, he dumped me and never looked back." Skye stood up and whispered, "He never even said good-bye."

"I'm not like that. Let me prove to you that isn't how all men are."

Skye took a ragged breath. He was slicing open a barely healed wound. "I need more time." Time to forget, to erase the pain. "Can't we just go on the way we've been? Have fun without becoming serious?"

Simon wrapped his hands around her upper arms and forced her to look at him. Rancor sharpened his voice. "No. I want more. And if you aren't prepared to give it to me, then I have to look elsewhere. Time is moving on. I don't want to be sixty when my kids graduate from high school."

He spoke so viciously that she wondered how she could have ever thought him kind. "I'm sorry. I'm just not ready. I lose myself when I'm in love. I'm afraid your opinion will become more important than mine. I'm afraid I'll become so terrified of losing you I'll do anything to keep your love."

"I guess that's it, then." He paused as if challenging her to go through with it. When the silence between them became unbearable, Simon turned on his heel and strode toward his car. Over his shoulder he said, "Don't expect me to call. This time it's over."

Skye watched until the Lexus's taillights were out of sight. What had she just done? Slowly she turned, unlocked the door, and went in. It took a few moments to register, but she finally noticed the light was on in the kitchen. She didn't think she'd left any lights on.

After that scene with Simon, she was in no mood for another intruder or more vandalism. Skye flung up the hinged seat of the hall bench and grabbed the shotgun. She had just about had it. This time she was shooting first and asking questions later.

As she stepped into the kitchen, Skye let the gun slide to her side. The table was covered with food and there was a note in her mother's handwriting: *I was afraid you wouldn't have enough time so I made the food for your brunch. I also cleaned up a little. Hope everything is okay. Love, Mom.*

Skye shook her head. What a sweet thing

to do. It was too late to call and thank her mom, but she'd do that before church tomorrow. Still, she'd have to make it clear to her mother that from now on, Skye would prepare for her own parties or she'd have to take May's key away. It was all too much. Simon, her grandmother's murder, her parents' need to help — Skye curled into the corner of the sofa and buried her head.

Ginger and Gillian arrived together. This was their first visit to Skye's cottage and curiosity shone on their identical faces. Skye guided them through the foyer and into the great room. She had placed a folding table and chairs next to the sliding glass doors, where the view of the river was best.

"Make yourselves at home. Victoria should be here any minute." Skye gestured to the sofa.

"Victoria's coming?" Gillian settled into the corner of the couch.

"She accepted my invitation." Skye raised an eyebrow. "Is there some reason why she wouldn't want to have brunch with us?"

Ginger and Gillian looked at each other. Skye could see the silent communication and was frustrated by her inability to interpret what was being conveyed.

The uneasy silence was broken by the

ringing of the phone.

Skye started toward the kitchen, saying over her shoulder, "Excuse me."

Trixie's voice greeted Skye's hello. "I talked to my cousin. We can see her today at six. That's when the pharmacist goes home for his dinner break."

"I'm surprised the drugstore is even open on Sunday, let alone so late."

"The owner is trying to compete with the new Wal-Mart in Laurel. He can't stay open twenty-four hours, but he is open eight a.m. to eight p.m. seven days a week," Trixie said.

"Great. I'll pick you up about five to. I can't talk now. I'm entertaining my cousins."

"What are you going to do to them? Is this the payback for having kidnapped you?" Trixie asked excitedly.

"Nothing and no. I'm trying to forgive and forget."

"And pry information out of them, I bet," Trixie guessed.

Skye didn't comment. "See you tonight. Bye."

As she rejoined Gillian and Ginger, the doorbell rang. Victoria entered in a miasma of Obsession and a flurry of georgette. Her lilac slip dress and high-heeled white sandals made Skye feel underdressed for her own party.

The twins tugged at their own clothes, making it clear Victoria had the same effect on them.

No one said anything until Skye remembered her manners. "So glad you could make it on such short notice. Please make yourself comfortable. I'll get us some drinks."

Victoria chose a canvas sling chair facing the sofa and sank gracefully onto its seat. "I wouldn't have missed this chance to spend time with my dear cousins."

"I have mimosas and Bellinis. What would you all like?" Skye stood ready to fetch the glasses from the kitchen.

After Skye explained what both drinks contained, the twins opted for mimosas and Victoria asked for a Bellini. Skye filled her own glass with orange juice and 7-UP, adding a little grenadine to disguise the fact that she wasn't drinking any alcohol.

Skye returned to the great room carrying a tray of drinks. She had just served the last goblet when Bingo entered the room. He froze in the doorway and sniffed the air. Walking stiffly, he advanced toward Victoria and launched himself into her lap.

Victoria shrieked and held up her hands

to stop him but Skye heard the chiffon of her dress rip. Skye scooped up the indignant cat, stuffed him into her bedroom, and closed the door.

She turned to Victoria. "Are you all right? I'm so sorry. He's never behaved that way before."

With a stunned expression Victoria examined the tears in the fabric of her dress. "This was brand-new. It cost a hundred and forty-nine dollars plus tax."

"Maybe it could be fixed," Skye offered weakly.

"I don't want it fixed. I want it new!" Victoria's face turned an unattractive shade of red and her voice screeched like fingernails on a chalkboard.

"I'll write you a check." Skye felt a knot in her stomach as she handed over the slip of paper.

After looking it over, Victoria tucked the check into her purse. "I'll let you know how much the tax was." Sitting back in her chair, she said, "I believe I'm ready for that drink now."

Skye sat on the only vacant seat and took a sip from her glass. She searched her mind for a topic of conversation and finally said, "When are Flip and Irv going on that fishing trip?"

"They decided to skip it this year. We're going to spend their vacations camping at the rec club," Gillian answered for them both.

"Oh? I'm surprised. I thought I heard them say they had already made all the arrangements." Skye kept a neutral look on her face.

"Well, with Grandma dying and Momma in the hospital we decided this wasn't a good time." Gillian finished her mimosa.

Skye poured her a refill from the pitcher. "That's too bad. It sounded as if they were really looking forward to it."

Ginger chugged the rest of her drink. "Maybe if we had got Grandma's good jewelry, like she promised us, they could have gone, but no one seems to know anything about that."

Victoria, who had been silent, asked, "Grandma Leofanti had good jewelry?"

"No," Skye answered, "all she had was the emerald ring that she passed to me on my eighteenth birthday as the firstborn granddaughter, a pair of earrings, and a pendant. As it turned out, we each ended up with one piece." Skye filled Ginger's empty goblet.

"What about me?" Victoria pouted.

"Sorry, Hugo chose the living room set."

Skye reappeared from the kitchen with a fresh drink for Victoria. "So, how's Aunt Minnie doing?"

Gillian looked at Ginger before speaking. "Pretty good. They've decided to keep her for a thirty-day observation."

"That's as long as most insurance companies will pay for a psychiatric stay," Skye said.

"That explains it then." Ginger put her empty glass down.

"Can she have visitors?" Skye asked.

"Just Ginger, Daddy, and me." Gillian tossed back her third mimosa.

"Did you ever hear about your mom going away for a rest when she was in high school?" Skye picked her words with care.

The twins shook their heads.

Ginger leaned forward. "A rest? What do you mean?"

"Nothing, really. Someone mentioned they thought they remembered your mom going away for a while when she was in her teens." Skye stood up. "Everyone ready to eat?"

The group moved to the table. Skye had set it with a starched linen cloth and matching napkins. The seafoam-green dishes she had inherited seemed to float on the white expanse. Her everyday flatware had been polished until it looked almost like real silver. The pink crystal goblets she had chosen from her grandmother's estate sparkled in the bright sunlight from the patio doors.

A centerpiece made up of pink roses and ferns from May's cutting garden completed the setting. Skye brought out the cantaloupe bowls with fresh fruit and they began to eat.

"What does Prescott do for fun in the summer?" Skye asked Victoria.

"He's taking golf and tennis lessons at the club." Victoria spooned a melon ball into her mouth.

"Really? When did the rec club start that?"

Victoria laughed. "Not the rec club, the country club in Kankakee."

Ginger frowned. "Wow, that must cost a pretty penny. How long have you and Hugo belonged?"

"Since just after we were married. Not that it's any of your business."

Gillian finished off her fifth mimosa. "Hugo must do pretty well selling cars. Or have you taken a job, Victoria?"

Victoria drained her glass. "As a matter of fact, I have."

As she refilled everyone's drink, Skye

wondered if she would have to drive them all home. "Where are you working, Victoria?"

"That's the wonderful thing about this job and really the only reason I agreed to take it, even though he begged me to."

Skye put steaming pieces of quiche on everyone's plate. "Don't keep us in suspense. Tell us about this wonderful position."

"I'm going to be the hostess for the new Castleview housing development." Victoria stuck out her hand. "Mr. Castleview gave me this ring as a welcome aboard present." She indicated the ruby Skye had noticed at her grandmother's wake.

"The one over by the McDonald's?" Ginger took a bite of her quiche.

"No, the brand new one. The one he's going to build." Victoria dabbed her mouth with her napkin.

"Where's that one going to be?" Skye sat down to eat her own meal.

Victoria giggled. "I'm not allowed to tell."

Skye raised her eyebrows but didn't comment and they each dug into their food. No one spoke until they'd finished.

Finally, her words slurred, Ginger said, "What's the big secret?"

They all looked at Victoria, who gazed

back with a puzzled expression.

Skye rose and cleared the table. She came back with the lemon silk sherbet and dream bars. Conversation was suspended once again while Skye served dessert.

When she finished she took her place next to Victoria and patted her hand. "Victoria, we want to know why you can't tell us the location of Castleview's next housing development."

" 'Cause I'm not supposed to tell."

"Why?"

Her brows drew together and she nibbled on a thumbnail. "I'm not sure, but Hugo and Mr. Castleview said not to, and you can't make me."

CHAPTER 21

SEVEN, EIGHT,

IT'S TOO LATE

It was nearly five o'clock by the time Skye finished driving her tipsy cousins home and helping their husbands fetch the cars in which they had arrived. She couldn't stop wondering just where the new Castleview development was going to be. Hugo had refused to comment, saying that Victoria tended to imagine things.

Skye had released Bingo from his confinement, cleared the great room, and was up to her elbows in soapy water when her phone rang.

After wiping her hands off with the kitchen towel, she grabbed the receiver. "Hello."

"What took you so long to answer?" the voice at the other end demanded.

"Who is this?" Skye asked.

"It's Aunt Mona."

"Oh, hi. Is everything okay?"

Mona's tone changed. "Everything is

fine. I know it's short notice, but Uncle Neal and I were wondering if you could come to dinner tomorrow night. We really haven't had a chance to chat since you've been home."

Dinner with her Aunt Mona and Uncle Neal — there was an appealing scenario. But it was a chance to ask them some questions about Grandma.

"Gee, Aunt Mona, that would be lovely. Can I bring anything?" Skye cradled the handset and went back to washing dishes.

"No, we're just having a simple meal. How's six o'clock for you?"

"Fine. You sure I can't bring anything?"

"No, just yourself. We'll see you at six then. Bye."

There was something odd about the conversation. What was wrong with that picture?

Skye finished up at the sink and dried the counter with the towel. She glanced at the clock, and noticed she had less than fifteen minutes to freshen up and drive to Trixie's.

Settling for a quick brush of her hair and some lipstick, Skye made it to her friend's house with a minute to spare. Trixie was waiting on the front steps, and hopped into the car before it finished gliding to a stop.

Trixie and Skye talked about the brunch

and what Victoria had revealed until they reached the drugstore.

"What's your cousin's name?" Skye asked as she pushed open the glass door.

The sleigh bells that warned the pharmacist of incoming customers almost drowned out Trixie's answer. "Amy."

A young woman in her late teens stood behind the drug counter in the back of the store. She waved at Trixie, who took Skye's arm and guided her down the aisle.

"Good timing. Mr. Bates just left and there's no one in the store." Amy smiled at Trixie.

"This is my friend Skye. Skye, this is my cousin Amy," Trixie said while fingering the products on the counter.

Skye held out her hand. "Nice to meet you, Amy. I really appreciate this."

Amy took three of Skye's fingers for a brief shake. "No problem. Trixie explained everything." Skye hated it when women didn't know how to properly shake hands, but she swallowed the temptation to teach Amy the correct form and instead said, "My aunt's name is Minnie Overby. Can you see if she filled a prescription for any type of tranquilizer or sleeping pill within the last month or so?"

"Easy as pie, now that we're finally using

the computer." Amy tapped a few keys and waited.

Skye held her breath.

"No, no medication of any kind for Minnie Overby within the last six months." Amy patted the machine. "That's as far back as the records go."

"Thanks." That had been a waste. What did it prove? Nothing, except Minnie didn't get her prescription filled in town. Skye's shoulders drooped.

Suddenly she straightened. "Would you mind checking one more name for me?"

"Not at all."

"Try the last name Leofanti and see what you get." Skye wasn't sure what she expected to find.

After a minute or two, Amy looked up from the screen. "I've got lots of Leofantis but only one with a tranq or sleeping pill."

"Who?" Skye tried to see the monitor.

"Just an initial." Amy frowned. "That's unusual. We're not supposed to accept anything but full names. No initials, no nicknames."

"What letter?" Skye tried to keep the impatience from her voice.

"That explains it." Amy went on as if she didn't hear Skye. "This was filled on a day I was out sick, and Mr. Bates's mother helped out."

Trixie broke in. "Amy, honey, we're dying of curiosity. What is the initial?"

"Oh, sorry. It's M."

Skye turned onto her back, trying desperately to fall asleep, but disturbing thoughts kept drifting through her subconscious. Was M. Leofanti the same as Minnie Overby? Where was Castleview building his next development, which was such a secret? What was she going to tell the superintendent?

When her alarm went off, Skye gratefully climbed out of bed and into the shower. She mentally reviewed her wardrobe. What was the appropriate clothing in which to be fired?

She finally threw on a pair of white slacks, striped T-shirt, and a navy blazer. After preparing breakfast for Bingo and herself, she grabbed the atlas and wrote out the directions to Miss Prynn's while she drank her tea. Skye felt a little uneasy to be going there alone, but she could think of no one else who was available. Simon was certainly out of the question. A sense of loss suddenly nipped through her. Fighting that feeling, she forced herself to move from the table and prepare to leave.

The stack of tens and twenties made only

a small bulge in the envelope Skye had tucked them in, but between this money and the check for Victoria's ruined dress, her budget was destroyed for the summer.

It was nearly ten by the time Skye turned onto Avenue D. Narrowing her eyes against the glare, she carefully read the numbers. As she neared Miss Prynn's house, she noticed a police car parked in front.

Skye pulled the Buick a few spaces behind the squad car and hurried up the steps.

Before she could ring the bell, a young police officer thrust open the door. "What's your business here?"

"It's about my aunt," Skye answered without thinking and then could have bitten her tongue.

"You're her niece?"

Skye was confused, but had a feeling if she said no, that would be the end of the conversation. The only reason the police would be answering Miss Prynn's door was if something was terribly wrong. "Yes, her niece."

The officer opened the door wider and gestured Skye inside. "I'm sorry to have to tell you that your aunt passed away sometime between noon yesterday and eight this morning. A friend who dropped her off from church stopped this morning to return a handkerchief that had been left in her car and found Miss Prynn dead. We've been looking for next of kin."

"But Mi . . . Aunt Esther hadn't been ill. Do you know the cause of death?" She could feel her heart accelerating. This whole thing reminded Skye of her grandmother's murder.

"I don't think I'm supposed to discuss that, ma'am. Ah . . . let me ask Officer Spratt." He pulled a walkie-talkie out of his belt. "He's checking with the neighbors."

She looked at the officer a little more closely. There was something odd about his attire. For one thing he didn't seem to have a gun. "Are you a Chicago policeman? Your uniform looks different."

His face reddened. "Well, ah, no. I'm a citizen volunteer. But I'll be going to the academy as soon as I pass the test."

Skye thought fast. If she handled this the right way she could get information the police would never share with her. "How wonderful," she gushed. "That's just what our city needs, more officers like you. Maybe then I'll feel safe walking down the streets again."

His chest puffed out. "No need to worry once I'm on duty, ma'am."

"You're so brave." She forced out a tear. "I'm so upset about my aunt's death. I feel like it must be my fault for not taking better care of her. But I saw her on Saturday and she looked healthy. How did you say she died?" Skye held her breath, wondering if he'd fall for it.

"She was found in the bathroom. She must have had a bad case of the flu." Color crept up from his collar. "You know, lots of older people die that way. There's nothing you could have done, ma'am."

Now I've done it. I can't mention Grandma's murder without admitting I'm not Miss Prynn's niece. Maybe she really did die of natural causes. What did that book say about the symptoms of the poison used on Grandma?

It was obvious the young man was waiting for her to speak. "How terrible." She forced out a few more tears. "Would it be all right if I made a call?"

He frowned and she hurried to explain. "To my grandmother, Aunt Esther's sister."

"Sorry, the phone's not working. It looks like maybe she tripped and yanked the jack from the wall. Would you like to come to the station to make the call?"

"Could I take a quick look around? Aunt Esther was getting some . . . ah . . . family papers together for me and I really need them right away." Skye couldn't believe she was this calm and thinking so clearly.

"Well, I shouldn't . . ."

Skye moved closer and looked at him through her eyelashes. "I understand. You don't really have the authority to make decisions . . . it's just that I need those papers for a scholarship. If I don't turn in my application by tomorrow I'll lose my chance."

"Oh . . . go ahead. As long as I see whatever you want to remove."

I'm really sorry for the trouble he's going to get into for being so nice to me.

She smiled gratefully and headed to the room Miss Prynn had indicated yesterday was where she kept her records. Several rows of filing cabinets lined the wall of what was intended to be a bedroom. A cursory glance told Skye that the system appeared to be alphabetical. She went straight to the L's. The drawers weren't locked and the files were all neatly arranged.

Skye took a tissue from her pocket and used it to rifle past Leanardo, Lemons, and stop at Levins. Where was Leofanti? She quickly checked for a misfile but found nothing. Taking a breath, she looked once again, this time noticing an empty hanging file where Leofanti would go.

Did that mean Miss Prynn had been murdered? But by whom? Simon and Doc Zello were the only ones who knew of Skye's interest in finding her. Did Doc have something to hide? Skye shook her head. No, that was silly. He wouldn't have given out her address. And Simon had no motive at all.

The officer was clearing his throat and Skye swiftly closed the drawer and joined him in the living room. "Guess she didn't have a chance to get what I needed together. I don't suppose I could look around for the papers."

The young man shook his head. "Sorry, we have to go to the station now."

"Thanks anyway."

"Sorry. Do you want to follow me to the station or would you rather ride along with me? I'll make sure you get a lift back to your car."

"I'll follow you." Skye hoped she could slip away without his noticing. "But give me the address just in case we get separated."

He took out his card and jotted the information on the back. "I've got to lock up. I'll meet you by the steps."

Skye waited for the officer to turn away from the front door. She ran to her car, dove inside, and made an illegal U-turn. Taking a right at the next corner, she prayed the young man hadn't noticed the make and license plate of her vehicle.

★ ★ ★

As soon as Skye was sure she wasn't being followed, she stopped at the first working public phone. Using the card the police officer had given her, she placed an anonymous call telling him to look for jatropha curcas poisoning in Miss Prynn's death.

It took her a long time to drive back to Scumble River. She'd gotten thoroughly lost trying to escape from the police. When she glanced at her watch as she pulled into her driveway she was startled to see that it was ten to one. She had five minutes to prepare to meet with the superintendent.

She was back in the car in three minutes, having only grabbed her briefcase and checked her answering machine. There was no message from Simon.

Scumble River High School was deserted for summer vacation. This time of year it was typical for the only people in the building to be administration and custodial.

The outer office was empty when she arrived, so she knocked on the superintendent's door.

When she got no answer, she slipped into the adjoining rest room, glad for the chance to freshen up.

A few minutes later Skye heard the thumping of people knocking into furniture and the loud laughter of the inebriated. She opened the door a crack and peered out.

Dr. Wraige and Karolyn passed by, arms around each other. Their faces were flushed and a wave of alcohol fumes rolled over Skye as they went by the rest room. Wraige whispered into the redhead's ear before kissing her neck. She giggled in response. Skye's mouth dropped open.

The superintendent proceeded into his office and the secretary sat down at her desk.

Great. Now how do I get out of here without Karolyn realizing I witnessed their little love scene? Skye wondered.

Minutes ticked by and Skye was keenly aware that she was now late for her appointment to be fired. She was about to push open the door and test her acting ability when she heard the phone buzz and Mr. Wraige's voice ordering Karolyn into his office.

As soon as the secretary disappeared into the other room, Skye shot out of the bathroom and into the hall. She waited until Karolyn came back to her desk before entering again.

The secretary looked up, then ran her finger down the page of her appointment book. "You're late."

"Sorry, I got tied up and couldn't get away."

"He won't be happy."

Funny, he looked darn right jolly a minute ago. Skye bit back a smile.

After the secretary buzzed her boss, Skye was shown into the inner sanctum and told to sit down. Wraige had tidied up his hair and his complexion was back to its usual gray tone.

"Ms. Denison, thank you for coming in during the summer." He glanced at his watch. "I hope we're not keeping you from anything more important."

"No, not at all."

He paused, obviously waiting for her to apologize for being late. When she didn't speak, he continued. "I hope you had a chance to review that testing we spoke of."

She nodded, but made no move to open the file on her lap.

"And did you find anything you had overlooked before?" Wraige leaned forward, a look of annoyance on his face.

Skye smelled the mouthwash he had used in an attempt to cover the odor of alcohol. "No. As I said before, Cray Clapp is not learning disabled. He has an IQ of one hundred and twenty-nine and his achievement scores are all within the expected limit for that ability level. Furthermore, there are no signs of any processing problems."

"The mayor is going to be very unhappy." Wraige rose from his chair, swaying slightly.

"I'm sorry to hear that, but parents are often unhappy with the outcome of my tests. That doesn't mean I am free to change those results." Skye leaned back and looked into his bloodshot eyes.

"Your lack of team spirit may very well influence our decision whether to keep you on for next year."

"Perhaps you forgot, but if you aren't going to renew my contract you need to notify me in March, according to the union agreement." Skye held his gaze.

"There's always a loophole for incompetence."

"I see."

Wraige smiled cruelly. "And with your past history, ineptitude shouldn't be hard to prove."

"I don't suppose you want to hear the truth about my previous dismissal?"

"I don't really care about the truth."

"Your contract is up for renewal this year too, isn't it?"

"Don't think your Uncle Charlie can save you this time." Wraige sat on the edge of his desk.

"Actually, I was thinking more of the other board members. Especially Mrs. Hopkins." Skye watched his puzzled expression. "Isn't she a close friend of your wife?"

"Yes, Roberta and Patricia are friends. What does that have to do with anything?" His brows met over his nose.

"What if I told you I wasn't late for our meeting? That I was actually early and in the rest room?" Skye waited as he mentally reviewed the afternoon's activities. A series of emotions played across his face.

"So?" His voice cracked.

"Well, if I were called into a board meeting to defend my job performance, I would be forced to tell about this meeting." She noted the way his body sagged against the desk's surface. "And, being the thorough person that I am, I would start my description with you and Karolyn's entrance into the office."

"You have no proof." His face was almost purple with rage.

"Neither do you." Skye rose and gathered her belongings. "Can I count on this being the end of the Clapp matter?"

After a long moment he nodded.

"And the end of talk about firing me?"

An even longer pause, then another nod.

"Fine." Skye turned back before she opened the door. "Just remember, even though psychologists are trained to keep things confidential, we do keep excellent records."

CHAPTER 22

SEE HOW THEY RUN

Skye took a deep breath and leaned back against the headrest. It had worked! She had actually outmaneuvered the superintendent. Surprised to discover she was sweating, she took a tissue from her pocket and wiped her face. Of course, she hadn't gained any friends in the process, and would really have to watch her back in the future.

The first thing Skye did after arriving home was to call the hospital. She confirmed that Minnie had not been released and couldn't have been the one to poison Miss Prynn.

As she hung up the phone, the doorbell rang. Skye looked out the window and saw Junior Doozier on her front step. Junior was the nine-year-old son of Earl and Glenda. He had come to Skye's assistance after the "accident" with her car last fall. For the rest of the year, she had made a point of dropping into his classroom to say hi.

Skye opened the door. "Junior, what a nice surprise. How did you get all the way over here?" He lived on the other side of town.

He thrust an envelope at her. "You need to see this, Miz Denison."

"Okay." Skye stepped aside. "Come on in. I'll get you a soda."

"Read that first." Junior followed her into the kitchen.

She extracted a piece of letterhead stationery and skimmed the contents. It was from the Department of Children and Family Services and said that if Mr. Doozier continued to fail to cooperate with their caseworker, DCFS would take Cletus from him.

"Where did you get this? It's addressed to your Uncle Hap and is very private."

"He had me read it to him. And when I finished he grabbed his rifle and said he was coming over here to kill you." Junior's freckles stood out like specks of blood on his pale face.

"When was this?" Skye asked over her shoulder as she checked the locks on the door and snatched her shotgun from inside the hall bench's seat.

"About an hour ago. I hid in the back of his pickup when he drove off. He stopped at the Brown Bag and I hitched a ride with someone coming this way."

"You sure he said he'd kill me?" Skye dialed the phone as she talked to the boy.

"Yes, ma'am. And he weren't foolin'. He blames you for startin' the whole thing. He thought you'd stop DCFS after he slashed your tires and broke your windows, but you didn't do nothing, so he gave you the last warning. Deer blood on your door."

Why wasn't anyone answering at the police station? "I can't stop DCFS. Once I make a report it's out of my hands. And I didn't understand the warnings."

Finally the dispatcher came on the line. "Scumble River Police Station. Can you hold?"

"No!" Skye shouted into the phone. "Is that you, Thea? It's Skye. Put me through to Wally right now. It's an emergency."

"Sure, honey, just a sec."

A moment later Wally came on the line, his voice expressionless. "Yes?"

Skye explained what Junior had told her.

Wally's tone became immediately forceful. "Stay where you are. Keep the boy with you. We'll pick up Doozier at the bar and then call you."

She hung up and turned toward Junior.

"Chief Boyd will take care of your uncle."

Junior was silent for a while. "I'm sorry I didn't tell you sooner about Uncle Hap. I never thought he'd really hurt you."

"I know. And I appreciate your telling me now. You probably saved my life." Skye patted the boy's shoulder. "Believe me, I know it's hard to figure out what to do when family is involved."

Twenty minutes later, Wally called back to say they had Hap in custody. Skye drove Junior home. He asked her not to talk to his folks, and she respected his choice, but gave him her phone number in case he changed his mind or needed her help.

Skye's mind was preoccupied by the events of the last few hours as she arrived at her Aunt Mona and Uncle Neal's place. They lived in a large house perched on the southern edge of their acreage, surrounded by perfectly maintained farm buildings.

Neal opened the door, his expression unreadable. "Skye, please come in."

Cherry, their twenty-five pound Chihuahua, stood by his side. She looked like a scuba tank with legs.

He led her through the mirrored foyer and into the living room.

"Here," Skye said. "I thought maybe you

and Aunt Mona would enjoy this." She handed him a bottle of wine.

"Thank you. I'll put it away for a special occasion." Neal walked out a door opposite the one they had come through.

Cherry stood and stared at Skye. She ignored the animal, having had her fingers nipped by the dog once before. Instead Skye gazed at the lavish decor. The room was done in brocade and velvet, punctuated with gleaming oak tables, stunning floral arrangements, and a selection of beautifully framed art.

Skye peered inside an imposing curio cabinet in a corner next to the windows. Nestled behind the most immense assembly of crystal and porcelain figurines this side of Marshall Field's, she noticed a bit of black leather.

Skye had her nose pressed to the glass trying to get a better view when Mona and Neal entered.

Her aunt's smile tightened. "Is there something of my collection I could show you, Skye?"

Skye allowed herself to be guided to a seat on the sofa. "No, just admiring the whole effect."

"Thank you. Would you care for something to drink? Dinner will be ready in a few minutes." Mona perched on the edge of a wing chair facing Skye.

"No, thank you."

The ticking of the grandfather clock marked off the seconds as the trio sat looking at each other. Skye searched for something to say.

Mona finally spoke. "We saw you at Mass yesterday. Why didn't you go to communion?"

Skye felt her face turn red and she opened her mouth, but at first no words came out. "You know, Aunt Mona, that's a pretty personal question."

"It is the duty of family to monitor the spiritual well-being of its young," Mona said, as if reciting something she'd memorized.

"I appreciate your concern," Skye managed to say through gritted teeth.

"Father Burns has confession on Tuesdays and Saturdays. Tomorrow it's from nine to ten," Mona said. "You should go."

"Maybe I will. Thank you for the information." Skye wondered how soon she could gracefully leave.

The sound of an oven timer allowed them to retreat to their neutral corners.

Neal looked at Mona and frowned. "Are you going to do something about that?"

Mona jumped up. "Sorry, dear. Dinner is ready."

Conversation around the table did not improve. As Skye's impatience grew, her discretion decreased.

When dessert was served, Skye asked, "Aunt Mona, do you remember going away with Aunt Minnie when you were in high school?"

"No." Mona arched an eyebrow. "What was the occasion?"

"Aunt Minnie wasn't feeling well and needed a rest." Skye looked Mona in the eye. "A nurse from Chicago came and got you and took you somewhere."

"Out of respect for your Aunt Minnie we won't talk about that." A tic was visible under Mona's eye. "I hope you aren't going to drag all of that out."

Neal pushed a little away from the table and crossed his legs. "I don't remember you ever telling me about that trip, darling. Something I should know?"

"It was nothing. Just one of Minnie's spells. My parents panicked." Mona rose from the table.

Skye also got to her feet. "Thank you for dinner." She moved to the foyer. "Sorry to eat and run, but I just remembered. I left the iron on."

When Skye looked back, Neal was shaking his finger at Mona, while the older woman stared at Skye.

It was a relief when the alarm clock rang. Skye had barely dozed all night. Every time she had managed to quit thinking of Simon, Wally's anger popped into her mind. And when she finally forced herself to stop agonizing over the men who weren't in her life anymore she thought of Miss Prynn. She wondered if the police had taken her anonymous call seriously, or if they'd blown it off and marked the nurse's death as arising from natural causes. Or worse, was there an APB out with her description?

After removing Bingo from her stomach, Skye dragged herself into the shower, hoping the water would clear her mind. She pulled on a pair of denim shorts, a white T-shirt, and tennies, then went to feed Bingo. She had heard his yowls through both the closed shower and bathroom doors.

The weather matched her mood. Dark clouds rolled past, releasing sheets of rain. Occasional bangs of thunder and jolts of lightning enlivened the morning.

Skye barely choked down her toast, and could feel a headache starting to form behind her temples. She lay down on the couch.

Now that she knew that Hap Doozier was behind all the pranks, she could clear them from her mind. She was sure she had enough clues to her grandmother's murderer, if only she could put them together in the right way. She closed her eyes and visualized a list of her relatives. Dante was a lousy farmer who liked to spend cash he didn't have, and had been in charge of his mother's money for a long time with no one checking up on him. He would gain little, and actually lose control of the trust, by killing Antonia.

Hugo had met with a housing developer, and his wife claimed she had a job with this same developer. He and his wife spent money like it came free in the mail. But they had no way to get at the Leofanti land except through Dante, who wasn't selling.

Mona? She was a sanctimonious witch, at her husband's beck and call, and so self-centered she would do anything if she thought it was in her own best interest. How would killing Antonia profit Mona?

Minnie was a prime suspect if she had really tried to kill herself. But her motive was pretty weak. If she was tired of caring for her mother, she could have stopped. No one had held a gun to her head. And if Miss Prynn was murdered by the same person, it couldn't be Minnie.

The twins seemed to be short of money and they were disappointed with their inheritance. Nothing there to kill about.

Skye drifted between sleep and wakefulness. The twins might not be happy with what they had inherited, but Skye had gotten the table she wanted. She could still see it under the big window at the farm. Sighing, she turned on her side. Wait a minute. There was something odd under that window last time she was in the house. What was it? A brown mark on the freshly painted wall. What did that mean?

Skye had placed the table in her own cottage a few feet from her sofa. She got up to examine it more closely, kneeling to look underneath it. She ran her hands along the legs and studied the surface. Okay, this table was always under that window. How could it have made that mark on the wall? She remembered when Vince had picked it up to carry it out to her car. He hadn't knocked it against the plaster.

She sat on the floor and rested the back of her neck on the table's edge. Her head slipped farther backward. She straightened and turned around. The top of the table was slightly askew. Pushing the rim with her palm, she was able to nudge the top into a twenty-five degree angle from the base.

A small orifice was revealed. Skye slipped her hand into the hole. At first all she felt was the grain of the wood, but her fingertips soon closed upon something smooth.

As the object came into view she could see that it was an envelope. The stationery was pink and smelled of her grandmother's lavender sachet. Skye slid out a single sheet. Her grandmother's faint handwriting filled the page.

It was addressed to Annamaria Boggio, Antonia's sister, but the stamp had never been canceled.

Dear Annamaria,

Today has been the worst day of my life. Once again I have been weak and allowed Angelo to overrule me. Will my daughter ever forgive me? Her look of panic when we told her she had to go away will remain with me always. She was not comforted by her sister's presence as I had hoped.

The nurse he hired to do the wicked deed and take care of her afterwards seems passable, but she has no warmth and makes it clear she does what she does for money.

I hear Angelo's key in the lock. I will

have to mail this when he is not around as he has forbidden me to write of this matter. Please pray for your niece as her father forces her to get rid of her child.

Your loving sister,
Antonia

Skye's heart pounded. This certainly put a whole new light on things! Since neither of her aunts had appeared pregnant in the photo and they had been gone for only a month, her grandmother must have been referring to an abortion. So who had the abortion, Minnie or Mona? And did the other sister know what was going on?

Skye grabbed the phone and called the hospital. She was in luck. Minnie was allowed to speak on the phone.

After polite chitchat Skye got to the point. "Ah, Aunt Minnie, please stop me if this upsets you, but I was wondering if you remember that time you and Mona stayed with a nurse in Chicago?"

"Sure," Minnie answered readily. "Why would that upset me? Mona needed to have her appendix out. Mom and Dad sent me to keep her company."

"But you were all right?"

"Sure." Minnie's voice reflected her memory of a good time. "It was sort of fun to be in the city. And Mona recovered real fast. It was almost like being on vacation. I even took some pictures . . ." Minnie's voice trailed off. "I wonder what happened to them?"

"I'll see if I can find them," Skye promised. "Thanks, Aunt Minnie; get well soon."

So *Mona* had had the abortion. Did that mean she had killed Antonia? After all these years, why would she kill her mother? If it wasn't to gain something, what else was accomplished by her death?

The family history. Killing her stopped Antonia from talking about the past and thus revealing Mona's abortion. Would her aunt kill to keep that secret?

Skye thought about her aunt and uncle's marriage, about his position in the Knights of Columbus. Mona might kill to protect that.

Skye suddenly leaped from the couch. She reached for the phone and dialed. No one answered at her parents' house.

She swore in frustration. She had to talk this over with someone. What if she was wrong? She tried Charlie and Trixie. No one was home.

Great, I guess I'll have to talk to Wally. Probably should have been my first choice anyway, but he's still so mad at me about going to the survivalist camp. Oh, well, this isn't something I can put off.

Skye reached once again for the phone, but this time there was no dial tone. She looked out the kitchen window, but the storm had worsened and she couldn't see more than a few feet ahead.

Shit, I suppose the electricity will be next. I'd better store some water just in case. Electrical outages in Scumble River had been known to last a long time.

After she filled the bathtub, she'd change and drive in to see Wally. Might as well get the whole thing over with. Damn, he'd be really pissed about the whole incident with the Chicago police.

Skye walked into her bathroom and leaned over the tub. Before she could straighten she felt something poke her in the back. She gasped and whirled around.

A steel barrel stared her in the face. The person holding it said, "Stand up slowly with your hands in the air."

Chapter 23

Nine, Ten,

Round the Bend

"How did you get in here?" Skye asked. "I'm sure I locked all the doors."

"I borrowed the key from your mother's purse," Mona answered. "I'll slip it back in before she notices it's gone."

"What do you want?" Skye stared at the gun Mona held in her right hand.

"You've figured it out, haven't you?" Mona prodded Skye through the bedroom and into the living room.

Skye sat down hard on the sofa. "Figured out what? I don't know what you're talking about."

"Don't pull that innocent act on me. I knew you were closing in ever since you talked to Nurse Prynn. And you made it clear last night at dinner that you suspected me." Mona's mouth was bracketed by wrinkles Skye didn't remember seeing until today.

"I've suspected everybody." Skye's hand

closed over a pen wedged between the couch cushions. It wasn't much of a weapon, but it was the only one available.

"Quit lying." Mona gestured to the patio doors. "I've been watching you through the window, and I saw you jump up and run to the telephone."

"Then you know I've already called the police." Skye looked her aunt in the eye.

"I don't think so. Your first inclination would be to call your mother, and I know she's getting her hair done. Charlie isn't home either. And I cut the wire pretty quickly, so I'll have to take the chance you didn't tell anyone." Mona's voice was firm.

"If I can figure it out, so can someone else." Skye inched to the edge of the seat, palming the pen.

"No. You have knowledge others wouldn't have. With Nurse Prynn gone there really is no one left who remembers."

Skye searched her memory, trying to think of something to say to change her aunt's mind. "Aunt Minnie knows. Isn't that why you tried to kill her with those sleeping pills?"

"I didn't try to kill Minnie. I never intended for her to die. I wanted everyone to think she had attempted suicide so they'd suspect her of killing Mom." Mona rubbed her temple, a faraway look on her face. "She doesn't know anything. She never knew I had an abortion. Minnie has always lived in her own world. She never even knew I was seeing Beau, so she couldn't know I was pregnant by him. She was told I had my appendix out." Mona moved closer to Skye. "Now get up. You need to put a dress on."

"Why do I need a dress?"

Mona ignored Skye's question as she walked her into the bedroom and opened the closet.

"I still don't understand why you're willing to kill rather than have people know that you had an abortion as a teenager." Skye took off her shorts and T-shirt and slipped on the dress Mona handed her. "That is why you killed your own mother, isn't it? Because you were afraid Grandma would tell me about your abortion when she got to that point in the family history."

"You have no idea what I've been through. I begged Mom not to tell anyone, but her memory was getting so bad for the present, and seemed to be getting clearer for the past. I couldn't chance it." Mona stared at Skye. "She just wouldn't cooperate. I asked her for the family Bible. I knew she would have made some note of the baby.

But she said she didn't know where it was. I asked for the pictures Minnie took while we were in Chicago with Nurse Prynn, and Mom claimed they had been thrown out years ago."

Skye opened her mouth to ask a question, but Mona continued with her own train of thought. "There was always someone at the farm so I never got a chance to look for the Bible or pictures when Mom was alive. And I needed to get to Joliet the day I brought her the brownies. She took longer to die than I expected, and the housekeeper's death was an unexpected complication, so I had to go back and search after you all left that night. I was so afraid Neal would wake up and find me gone that I had to rush. You had already made the police suspicious so at least I didn't have to be neat." Mona smiled coldly. "Good thing we live close by. It was easy keeping an eye on who went to the farm after Mom died. I could sit in my living room and watch out the picture window. And when I couldn't be there I set up my video camera."

"So that's how you knew I had the Bible and the pictures. You saw me go by that night, then snuck over to the farm and watched me." Skye visually searched the room for a better weapon than the pen she

392

had slipped into her pocket.

"Right." Mona stared vacantly for a moment. "Let's see, is there anything else we need here?"

Skye glanced at her tennis shoes. Knowing she'd have a better chance of getting away if Mona didn't make her change into heels, she asked another question, hoping to keep her aunt distracted. "But why? Okay, so abortion was illegal. It's not as if anyone could prosecute you now."

"Neal would leave me if he found out. He'd be ruined in the community. How could he go on being the Grand Knight of the KC if this information got out?" Mona scrubbed her eyes with her fist. "Give me your keys. We're going to church."

"Church?"

"You need to go to confession. That way you'll go straight to heaven." Mona's eyes gleamed. "In a way, I'm saving you from years of torment here on earth."

"That's why you knew Grandma and Mrs. Jankowski had gone to confession that day. You arranged it." Skye grabbed her keys from the dish by the door and handed them to her aunt.

Skye preceded Mona outside. The rain had slowed to a drizzle. Mona made Skye get into the car via the driver's side and prodded her over to the passenger seat with the gun.

Using one hand, Mona put the Buick in gear and backed out of the driveway, then continued where she had left off. "Nurse Prynn wasn't Catholic, so she was going to hell anyway."

"How did you find out about me locating Miss Prynn?" Skye asked.

"She called me Saturday, demanding money." Mona kept the gun trained on Skye. "She wouldn't listen when I tried to tell her that Neal would notice if I took a large sum from our checking account. I begged her to let me pay a little bit each week. She said she was too old for the installment plan. So I agreed to bring her the cash on Sunday."

Skye watched the gun barrel as it wavered between her chest and head. "But you didn't bring her money on Sunday, did you? You brought her a plate of your famous double fudge brownies. And instead of pecans you used those nuts you brought home from your Hawaiian vacation. The poison guide said they were very tasty, but extremely toxic."

"I told her I had forgotten the bank was closed on Sunday, and I'd have to bring her the money the next day, but I wanted to give her something to show my good intentions." Mona finished Skye's thought.

"So, when did you steal Miss Prynn's records?"

"I didn't. The old bat wouldn't open the door to me on Sunday. She made me leave the brownies on the step. I didn't know when she'd eat them. And when I came back Monday morning I couldn't get into the house." Mona frowned. "But with you gone the records will be just one among hundreds."

Skye parked the car in back of the church. "Now what?" She didn't mention that Mona's file was missing.

"We go in. You make your confession and we leave. If you make a fuss, I shoot you right here. If you tell the priest, I'll kill him too. Understand?"

"Yes."

The two women entered through the side door of the deserted building. It was over a hundred and forty years old, and the main architectural features had not been changed.

They made their way down the main aisle past rows of plain wooden pews. To the right of the altar were the confessionals. About the size of coat closets, the two outer chambers shared their inner walls with the center booth where the priest sat waiting to hear from his parishioners. There were lights above the doors on the left and right to indicate whether they were occupied. The bulbs were operated by a person's weight upon the kneelers inside. Both lights were off.

Mona sat on the pew nearest the confessional and shoved Skye toward the coffinlike structure. "I'll be right here, so don't try anything. Remember, I can hear what you say in there."

Which was true. The confessionals were far from soundproof, and often those waiting could hear what the penitents in front of them had to confess.

As Skye walked toward the door she put her hand in her pocket and found the pen she had hidden there.

Skye entered slowly, searching for something on which to write. Spotting a discarded Sunday bulletin wedged in the corner, she grabbed it as she knelt on the platform facing the sliding mesh window.

As soon as the screen opened, Skye started the ritual prayer. "Bless me Father for I have sinned." As she spoke, she scribbled furiously.

Sliding the note and the pen to the priest, she held her breath. *Will he believe me? Is there any way he can help me?*

The priest gasped and Skye shut her eyes, afraid her aunt would hear. She was relieved when he began his expected response. The slip of paper came back as she recited her sins.

She squinted to read in the dim light. The note said, "Can you crawl through the window? There's a door leading to the rectory's basement over here."

The priest was removing the screen as he gave Skye her penance. She stood on the wooden kneeler, putting her head and shoulders through the opening. He took hold of her around the waist and yanked. At first it didn't seem as if her hips were going to fit. His prayers took on a note of desperation as he pulled. With a tearing sound, she finally popped through the tight space.

They both froze, waiting to see if Mona had heard the material rip or noticed that the light above the door was now out. When there was no reaction from her, the priest opened a square of wood from the back wall near the floor and nudged Skye down the steps. He then began his prayer of absolution as he joined her on the stairs and replaced the panel. Just before the partition slid into place Skye heard the first gunshot.

Father Burns and Skye locked the secret passage behind them and pushed an old dresser in front of the panel. As they struggled with the heavy piece of furniture they heard more gunshots coming from the church. Skye prayed no one would walk in on Mona's rampage.

"What now?" the priest asked.

Skye noted his heightened color and rapid breathing. "You stay here, and I'll go upstairs and phone the police."

He nodded and sank down into an old chair. "I'll make sure she doesn't get through the passage."

"Good." Skye was halfway up the stairs when the door from the rectory burst open. She yelped and turned to run.

"What are you two doing down here?" the parish housekeeper asked.

Father Burns moved forward and put an arm around Skye. "Skye's aunt is trying to kill her."

"Lord have mercy!" The older woman clutched her chest.

"Stay here with Father. I'll call the police," Skye ordered.

After telephoning Wally, Skye started to check the doors. None were locked. She had just reached the vestibule when the front door burst open.

Mona stood with her gun pointed at Skye. "Did you really think you could get away from me?"

"It's too late. I've called the police. There's nothing left to cover up. Everyone knows." Skye tried to back away.

"Then I have nothing to lose." Mona took aim.

At that moment they heard the first siren.

"Please, Aunt Mona, put the gun down. Don't make the police shoot you," Skye begged.

A look of loathing crossed Mona's features. "This is all your fault and you have to pay." Without warning, she squeezed the trigger.

Nothing happened. Mona squeezed again and again. She was out of bullets. They could hear doors opening and shoe leather slapping the pavement. The police had arrived.

Mona tried to grab Skye, but without a gun she was no match for her niece. Skye stepped into her aunt's grasp, turned sharply, and easily broke Mona's grip. Once again Skye's training in takedowns for uncontrollable kids came in handy.

Enraged, Mona threw the gun at Skye, rushed past and out the kitchen door. Skye hesitated for a moment before running after her. She reached the door just in time to see Mona fling herself into the Buick and squeal out of the parking lot.

A few seconds later Chief Boyd and Officer Quirk ran in. Skye hastily told them what had happened, and Wally sent Quirk in pursuit of Mona. He also radioed for help from the county sheriff, and ordered in all off-duty officers.

May and Charlie arrived at the rectory soon afterward, having heard the dispatches on their police radio scanners.

They were all in the priest's office and everyone was talking. Finally Wally shouted, "Okay, the first person who speaks without being spoken to leaves the room. You shouldn't all be here anyway, but it would take more officers than I have available to make you leave. So sit down and shut up!"

Skye was seated on the sofa between May and Charlie. Father Burns was at his desk. His housekeeper stood behind him as if on guard.

Wally paced between the two groups. Finally he turned to Skye. "Tell me what happened after your aunt showed up at your house."

After Skye ran through the events up to the time she arrived at the church, Wally addressed the priest. "Why did you believe Skye so readily? Your fast thinking probably saved both your lives. When we checked, Mona had emptied six bullets into the confessionals."

Father Burns looked down at the rosary in his hands. "I can't tell you a lot. I'm bound by the seal of the confessional, but let's just say I knew Skye was telling the truth."

Wally narrowed his eyes. "In other words, Mona confessed to you?"

"I really can't say one way or another. Why does it matter?" Father Burns sat motionlessly.

"Then let's move on to the convenient passage between the church and rectory. How long has that been there?" Wally leaned his hands on the desk's edge.

"It's been there as long as the church has been. We were a stop on the Underground Railroad."

"Why didn't I know that?" Wally asked.

"Because we keep it quiet. We don't want to take away from the purpose of the church. We even considered filling in the tunnel the last time we remodeled, but decided at the last minute to keep it open."

"Thank God." Skye sighed.

As a result of Officer Quirk's pursuit,

Mona skidded off the road and wrapped the Buick around a tree on Scumble River Road heading toward Kankakee. The old car didn't have air bags and Mona wasn't wearing her seat belt. She was dead before they reached the hospital.

The family grieved, but among themselves they agreed that it was probably for the best. They would try to remember Mona as she was, before trying to keep her secret had become a burden she could no longer shoulder.

A few days after her aunt's death, Skye received a phone call from someone saying he was Miss Prynn's great-nephew and he had a file that his aunt had asked him to hold for safekeeping. Skye's name and number were on a slip of paper inside the folder, and he wanted to know if she still wanted it.

She said no.

EPILOGUE

It was the second Saturday in September, and school had been back in session for a couple of weeks. As promised, Simon had not called. It had been a sad summer. Skye sat at the counter peeling apples and watching May make applesauce. "Mom, we've never really talked about what happened with Aunt Mona. Would you rather I had left things alone?"

May didn't answer for a while. She finally turned from the stove. "I still miss Mona. She wasn't always like that. She was so smart. We thought for sure she would go to college and have a career."

"Do you know why she didn't?"

"Neal started to court her during her senior year in high school. He was a couple years older and already a successful farmer." May stirred silently for a few seconds. "I think maybe Dad pressured Mona into marrying Neal. I know he always said he wasn't paying for any of us girls to go to college."

"I had no idea. My image of Mona is so different from that." Skye closed her eyes. "I don't remember ever seeing her without her guard up."

"Mona used to be such fun. She loved shopping with me for your baby clothes. She loved taking care of you and dressing you up."

"I don't recall her spending any time with me."

"She stopped when she found out she couldn't have children. After that she changed. Appearances and possessions became everything to her. Everyone had to envy her or she wasn't happy." May wiped away a tear. "And Neal didn't like her to spend much time with her family."

"Why?"

"He didn't think we were good enough."

Skye and May worked in silence for a while. Finally Skye said, "You didn't answer my question. Would you rather I'd left things alone?"

May stopped stirring. "No, I guess some things just can't be swept under the rug. That's what happened with Mona, really. Dad wanted to keep everything hidden."

"Secrets will destroy any family." Skye

concentrated on peeling an apple without breaking the spiral of skin.

"I suppose so." May added sugar to the sliced apples in the pan. "That's why Minnie and I decided to confront Dante."

Skye was halfway through without breaking off the skin. "So you weren't surprised to learn that Uncle Dante and the lawyer were skimming off some of Grandma's money?"

"Not really. I think we all knew he was up to something. He spent so much more money than the rest of us. Even Mom knew. But it was always on farm equipment he used for the estate, so we could tell ourselves it wasn't really stealing. Another family secret no one wanted to face." May sprinkled cinnamon into the mixture.

"Hugo's been very quiet lately about the advantages of selling Grandma's land to a developer," Skye said.

"Your dad and Emmett had a talk with him and that Castleview guy. I think that settled Hugo's hash. They made both of them see we would never sell the land for a housing development." May turned the burner down to let the applesauce simmer.

"Look, I got one off without breaking it." Skye held up the ribbon of bright red skin.

"Good, now drop it on the counter and it

will form the initial of the man you're going to marry." May leaned over to get a better view.

Skye let the peel slide between her fingers. "I can't tell what letter it looks like."

May stepped closer. "It's an R, of course, for Reid." Even though May knew that Skye and Simon had broken up last June, May never gave up on a prospective son-in-law.

Skye tilted her head and looked at the red skin. She could see how her mom thought it looked like an R, but to her it kind of looked like a B for Boyd or maybe even a K. Didn't that new English teacher's name start with a K?

The employees of Thorndike Press hope you have enjoyed this Large Print book. All our Large Print titles are designed for easy reading, and all our books are made to last. Other Thorndike Press Large Print books are available at your library, through selected bookstores, or directly from the publishers.

For more information about titles, please call:

(800) 223-1244
(800) 223-6121

To share your comments, please write:

Publisher
Thorndike Press
295 Kennedy Memorial Drive
Waterville, ME 04901

WITHDRAWN

BY
WILLIAMSBURG REGIONAL LIBRARY